Praise for *Us*

"Matthew McKay's novel is a look at the beautiful and dying songbirds swooping through the mind of a 'manic pixie dreamgirl' such as every reader has seen late at night in one bar or another. It's *Tender Is the Night* as told by a young bouncer who is, in fact, one of the strangest narrators you will ever spend time with. *US* is the story of a woman who is both 'like a piece of shrapnel' and like a dancer from *The Nutcracker*. It's the story of a person who has many voices inside, who is sexy and angry and innocent all at once. In that way, *Us* is the story of all of us.

Reading Matthew McKay's *Us,* I learned a lot about dissociative identity disorder, but more than that, I thought a lot about love itself. Matthew McKay asks hard questions about human relationships. His answers may surprise you."

—CHRIS HUNTINGTON, author of the Fabri Prize–winning novel *Mike Tyson Slept Here*

"Writing with urgency and insight, poet and psychologist Matthew McKay leads us on a journey to the deepest and darkest places in the human heart."

—BARBARA QUICK, author of *Vivaldi's Virgins*

D1527645

Matthew McKay

Boaz
Publishing
Company

This is a work of fiction. Names, characters, places, and incidents are the products of the author's imagination or are used fictitiously. Any resemblance to actual events, locales, or persons, living or dead, is entirely coincidental.

Address all inquiries to:
Boaz Publishing Company
968 Ordway Street
Albany, CA 94706
www.boazpublishing.com
info@boazpublishing.com
(510) 220 6336

Book Design by BookMatters
Manufactured in the United States of America

Library of Congress Cataloging-in-Publication Data
McKay, Matthew.
US / Matthew McKay. — 1st ed.
   p. cm.
ISBN 978-1-893448-12-4
1. Multiple personality—Fiction. I. Title.
PS3613.C545175U8 2012
813'.6—dc23   2012014148

for Jude

The only girl I ever loved
was born with roses in her eyes
but then they buried her alive
one evening 1945
with just her sister at her side

Jeff Mangum
"Holland, 1945"

I

It feels now, looking back, as if I was born to be a witness, a watcher of lives. I seemed weightless, drifting among people who'd throw me a joke, a few offhand words. I watched them beckoning, touching, discarding each other. I watched their hands—gesturing, carving the air. It was a simple, vicarious life, with only the pressure of my longings to give it shape.

Nothing had ever really worked for me. A failed grad student at 26, I was the resident of a single room above a poultry shop and marginally employed at a nightclub called The City Zoo. The Zoo occupied the first two floors of a hotel on Fourth Street. Ground level was a live music hall specializing in power chords and heavy drinking. Upstairs was a *très* trendy place called The Cages, where all the tables were ensconced in vertical rebar, to give the effect of a jail cell.

I walked the short way from my room to The Zoo each night at 7:00. My job was to help the band set up, check their levels, then man the lights and soundboard till closing time. When the last stragglers filed out, I became the night janitor. Which I liked. Because then the place belonged to me; I could stop being whatever was expected. The rooms echoed with the clatter of chairs being turned on tables, the clank of mop head against bucket. Otherwise, silence. The smell of stale beer. A chilly, after-hours peace.

What I'm going to tell you started in The Cages. It was after

2:00 in the morning; I'd just carried my bucket up the back stairs to the kitchen. A streetlamp poured a white, powdery light into the room, reflecting off the tile and stainless steel. I was standing at the sink, getting ready to turn the faucet, when I became aware of a woman's voice coming from the bar. Humming something. I froze long enough to recognize the tune— "Waltz of the Flowers," from the *Nutcracker.* The voice seemed breathy, imprecise, sliding across the notes like a carelessly played trombone.

I gently placed my bucket on the floor. The humming got louder as I stepped toward the double saloon doors that led to the bar. At first, I couldn't see her. The illumination from two small spotlights filtered across the room. They were trained on a pair of elevated cages. When the bar was open, one of them held a string quartet—women in tight black leotards playing Handel and Stravinsky. The other, larger cage was the focus of the club. Each waitress—they were all trained in modern dance—choreographed her own interpretation of a classical piece. Twice an evening each woman performed, taking small, measured steps within the rebar limits of the stage.

I scanned the room. The cages made it difficult to see much of anything, so I crept further in, skirting the edge of the high, stainless steel bar. Finally, in a far corner, I saw her. The girl was wearing black jeans with a dark, checkerboard shirt. She stood motionless, eyes shut. "Waltz of the Flowers" still drifted across the room, the humming like a faint perfume.

There was a sadness tightening the girl's mouth. I was attracted to that. And I liked the way her fingers had begun to stray across her shirt, fretting with the buttons. In the uncertain light she appeared quite young—olive complected, with high cheekbones and generous lips. I found that I liked that too.

The humming grew louder. Then, suddenly, her arms went up, hands curved and open. Ballet form. And she began to turn—one way, then the other. Dropping the lead arm in a kind of bow. Getting faster. Pirouetting and reversing. Arms flung out, then wrapping herself, pausing in a kind of embrace. Now she was doing a high step—throwing her legs way up. Slapping her hands down on her knees as she marched. She went out of view behind a partition. The next time I saw her, she was doing the same step, but viciously slamming her forearms down against her pumping knees. It was a movement so violent that I wondered if she might not break something in her wrist.

Now the tempo of the humming changed and her arms were windmilling, hands brushing her face. The fingers, at first open, soon closed into fists, striking her lovely cheeks. Until I could hear the slapping blows across the room.

With a sudden twist, she turned her back. Her head dipped, arms stretched out like she was dancing *Swan Lake*. Then curling in with a hard shot to her chest. I could see her body rock with the impact. Over and over.

When it was finished, she stood for a long time—eyes closed, face impassive. The humming gave way to a coarse silence.

I thought, growing up, that I understood pain. And silence. But I knew then I understood nothing at all. I cleared my throat.

"Who is it?" Her voice was shrill, frightened. But with a husky undertone.

"The janitor. Are you all right? I saw you . . . "

I didn't finish that because her face had morphed from fear to shame.

"I fell asleep—at the table over there." She pointed vaguely to a dark corner. "No one woke me when you closed, and I just . . . "

"It's OK, I can let you out."

I walked slowly forward, fearing that faster movement might scare her again.

"I . . . tried the door but everything's locked. Dead bolts."

"I know."

"So I thought maybe I was stuck; I'd have to spend the night."

"It's OK now. You got your purse? Leave anything at the table?"

She picked up a leather coat that was lying on the floor, and pulled it on. The front hung open.

I was standing before her now. The girl's brown eyes looked past me, flitting across the back of the bar. She was patting down the buttons on her shirt like they might fly off.

"I'm sorry I scared you."

She shrugged. "It's my fault. I guess I had too much and . . ." The shoulders flicked again.

I wanted to ask once more if she was all right, but one hand began to rake her mane of dark hair. She exuded a compressed energy. All she cared about was getting out of there.

"This way," I said unnecessarily, and led her toward the stairs.

As the girl descended the top step, her hand missed the rail; she made a small whimpering noise as she started to fall. I caught her around the waist, feeling the warmth of her body through the flannel shirt. Her hand brushed my restraining arm. I felt the warmth of that, too. Then I let go. In a higher-pitched voice, the girl said, "Oh." Nothing more. We got to the bottom of the stair, and my key scraped in the lock. She pushed through the door the instant I opened it.

2

When I was a boy, our backyard had a meandering concrete path between the lawn and flowerbeds. And it descended a slight grade, so that if I put my wagon at the top, I could sit in it and slowly coast to the bottom of the hill.

Sometimes I'd go out there on warm evenings. The neighbors' windows were open, and you could hear voices of the newscasters drifting across the lawns. I built a covering for my wagon out of laths and cardboard. I'd get inside and go twisting down the dark path. I could hear my wheels crunching the dirt and leaves. And watched for danger in the inky places beneath lilacs and hydrangeas. I imagined I was leaving home, and at the bottom of the hill I would meet someone. A boy who would talk to me.

I kept arriving at the end where the umbrella tables and plastic lawn chairs bulked in the dark. And then I would pull the wagon up to do it again. Over and over, until the TVs one by one went off, and my mother, rousing finally from her knitting, called me in from the yard.

I suspect this memory comes to mind for a reason. Not as an explanation for anything. But more, perhaps, as a soundtrack that sets the mood, a faint, unnoticed melody behind the action.

The girl stayed with me. I found myself replaying that brief moment when we touched, and listening to the memory of her voice. But also, I saw and heard the slapping. Those blows she rained on herself, hoping perhaps to stop a more grievous pain.

Her name was Margaret, by the way. I still like to say it—in my mind. I say the syllables slowly, like a chant. It's all I can do now—it can't hurt anything.

I next saw Margaret three nights later at The Zoo. Downstairs in the hard rock club where I was doing lights and sound. She was standing by the door in a denim skirt and leather car coat. Arms on hips, eyes working the room.

After a few moments, she turned her attention to the stage, where a bank of amps towered above a beat-up drum kit. "Early Abuse" was lettered on the snare. The band crashed through a cover of "Not Fade Away," then pulled the plugs on their guitars.

House lights came up, revealing the scratched, black walls. And our postage-stamp dance floor fronting the stage. The rest of the room was filled with a mismatched collection of wooden chairs and cocktail tables, glittering with empty bottles. In the lull between sets, waitresses made the rounds.

Margaret remained by the door, fingering the hem of her skirt, then rubbing her thigh. Her lids were at half-mast. At the edge of the dance space, a tall man with a sweat-stained baseball cap rose, did a comic bow to another seated gentleman, and headed toward the restroom. When I looked back at Margaret, she was on the move—toward the just-vacated chair.

She was smiling now, but her lips seemed fixed in a hard line. She was still touching, almost lifting her skirt. Now Margaret stood behind the empty chair, leaning on its back, slightly swaying as if the music were still pouring from the amps. She said something to the guy across the table. She had the same smile, but a shade brighter. The blond back of the man's head started nodding.

Margaret sat down, slouched, and cocked her face to one side. She pointed to Blondie, laughed. She seemed to be talking nonstop; the guy's head bobbed like a woodpecker atop his linebacker's neck. Now the tall man with the baseball cap returned, standing behind her. He looked annoyed. Blondie spread his hands, then gestured in a circle around the room, finally pointing to some chairs along the wall.

The tall guy pulled off his cap, ran a palm over his bald crown, then tried to lift Margaret up by one arm. She yanked away. Blondie half rose, catching the big man's wrist.

"Fuck you." I could hear it all the way at the back of the room. Then the tall guy turned, giving Margaret a blunt shove, and headed for the door.

Margaret and Blondie looked at each other. She shrugged. The smile came back. Blondie signaled the barmaid and ordered something—gesturing to Margaret, nodding. She slouched down again, hooking her arms over the back of the chair. And opened her legs. The man's thick, beefy shoulders seemed to contract as he hunched down, getting shorter. Staring at her underwear.

Margaret didn't seem to notice. She was still talking a blue streak. Big gestures, fixed smile. Blondie wasn't listening. He was making a life's work of studying the white triangle between her legs.

A minute or two later the band shambled back to the stage. They fooled for a while with the mics; the drummer plumped his huge, white man's 'fro. When I looked again at Margaret, she was halfway to the door, arm hooked around Blondie's elbow. They were in a hurry.

I followed them out, as far as the street. Margaret's new friend moved his hand to her hip. She leaned against him, huddling into his bulk. I was surprised to feel . . . resentment. That he could touch her. So easily. While now I could only watch.

But my reaction to Blondie was short-lived. Because there were others like him. Men Margaret found at The Zoo and, I'm certain, other clubs. She stood and swayed before them— between sets—to the music only she heard. And then she sat down . . . exactly the same. Exactly the same.

3

Looking back, I realized that Margaret had been in The Zoo before, probably many times. But she was one of hundreds of patrons who had no importance to me. Until the night I witnessed her dance, the emotional undressing to a pain so raw I felt both afraid and fascinated by it. And, of course, there was the moment I held her, now kept as a remembered sense of her body, the solidity of muscle and bone.

So again and again I thought about Margaret, returning to her like a finger-worn talisman kept to avoid one's fate. I cannot say exactly why, except there are moments in life when the emptiness—something you've always known—becomes intolerable. It may start with a voice coming up from the street, with this tone of affection. Familiar somehow because it is a voice you imagined as a child. But never, until that moment, really heard. Or it might be, on awakening, nothing more than the shape of your dresser and chair.

Whatever the cause, it happens. And you know that the feeling can't be borne. That you must do something. And whom you choose to help you—to help stop it—is almost arbitrary. It is just a person . . . who presents herself at that moment. But this is the thing: once chosen, she becomes what matters.

So I found Margaret. I could say I was drawn to her lovely, full mouth or the sadness in her eyes. And while both are true, the deepest truth is that she was dancing alone in the club that night. That she fell against me on the stairs. And that I could no longer imagine how to keep living my life.

Mooney was the bouncer at The Zoo. I can't remember his given name, but I know he got the appellation because his face resembled—in shape and color—the mottled roundness of a full moon. The man was short with splayed feet that forced him to rock slightly when he walked. He had a slit of a mouth, flattened nose, and expensively marcelled hair. But his worst habit—can you tell I didn't like him?—was dousing himself in stinko aftershave. You could smell him a week after he'd last been in a room.

Mooney lived in a second-floor walk-up across a narrow alley from The Zoo. In fact, his living room looked out on the kitchen window behind The Cages. Rumor had it that the cook, who was a friend of Mooney's, pitched food to him on nights he had off. On this particular night—the memory of which I still find disturbing—Mooney was off. But he was drinking up at The Cages because he didn't have to pay cover, and it was a good place to pick up women.

There was no band downstairs, so they had me tinkering with the sound system for the quartet. Too much hiss, and one of the speakers was dead. Mooney was hunched over at the bar, with his back to the room when I arrived. Within ten minutes Margaret appeared at the head of the stairs.

I had my usual visceral response of excitement and loss. Margaret stood for a moment and surveyed the room. She was wearing black jeans that emphasized her lovely hips, flannel shirt, and her usual leather jacket. Now she started to walk in a careless, sauntering way toward the bar. As she moved, she took off her coat and slung it over her shoulder. Finally she was standing behind Mooney, weight shifting to one leg.

I could see Margaret's head bow. She leaned in, a hand on the man's shoulder. He was staring at her breasts. After a moment, Mooney gestured, indicating a vacant stool on his left. Margaret climbed up, laughing, slapping the bar.

For a while I couldn't see much happening. Their heads were together. Margaret nodding like someone translating a difficult language. Mooney had a shirt with a long, mod-style collar; once or twice Margaret pulled on it playfully. A half hour later they were into some kind of game, stacking shot glasses on the bar. She was swaying to the quartet music—or perhaps her own.

Then they were gone.

Later, as I made my janitorial rounds, I was once again in the kitchen of The Cages. While I filled the bucket in the sink, I looked across the alley—directly into Mooney's window. I would be lying to you if I said I hadn't waited for that moment all evening. But it's also true that I held on till the appropriate time; I didn't rush up there as soon as we closed to spy on the new couple.

As the bucket filled, I noticed Mooney's window was open a crack. A thin light seeped through the living room. I could see vague shapes of a lamp, an armchair. I pushed open the kitchen sash and heard a bass beat pounding from Mooney's place. Now another sound: a male voice. And suddenly moving shadows, a woman backing toward the window. Pale, naked torso. White underpants. She was holding up her hand. Then Mooney came into the frame—batting her hand away, his voice like a razor. "What are you playing? 'Cause I'm not having fun with it."

The woman's dark hair was mashed against the glass, the skin of her back pressed white on the window. I saw now it was Margaret. Immediately I heard a deep, guttural voice—yet clearly female—saying, "Fuck you. Get away."

"No, bitch," he said, "fuck *you*. You're a weird fucking lady. And you can make fun of somebody else. But not me. OK?"

He put his index finger to Margaret's forehead, thumb cocked.

"You've got to think, you've got to ask yourself, 'How weird am I?' 'Cause it isn't regular to come on like fucking Mae West, like a fucking slut . . ." He was getting louder, ". . . and then turn into a little girl at a tea party. And then get all mean and dirty mouthed. What do you think? Is that weird? Do you think that might put somebody off?"

He moved his hand to her crotch.

"Be nice . . . please." Voice high pitched and breathy.

"Be nice." He was mimicking. "Please be nice."

Now Margaret's body pressed upward on the glass, as if he were lifting her.

"Back to being a little girl? Then what? Gonna talk shit again? Gonna get mean? Why don't you get mean now? What did you tell me? I walk like a fucking duck? Tell me more about how I walk; I wanna' hear you tell me now."

"Please."

"No. I want to hear. You thought it was funny, right? I want to hear you say it again."

His voice was a whip—rhythmic, cutting. Pumping higher as he worked himself up. Suddenly I'd witnessed enough. I raced through the saloon doors and down an aisle of cages, then downstairs to the street. It was cold, and mist was settling on my face before I made it across the alley to Mooney's building. I didn't know which bell was his, so I rang all of them. Over and over.

In less than a minute there were voices in the halls. People leaning from windows, shouting, "Who is it?" I could see an old guy, probably the manager, shambling his way in robe and slippers to the front door. I just kept ringing the buzzers.

Finally, the old guy, face mottled with rage, opened the door. "What the . . ."

"There's a woman being raped," I said, "in Mooney's apartment."

"Who?"

But at that moment I saw Margaret behind him, pushing to get around. I shoved the door wider so she could get through. The old man fell back, starting to lose his balance and screaming, "Police."

"Are you OK?" I called to Margaret's back. But she said nothing, already in a dead run and halfway to Market Street.

4

I'd seen violence at school, but never between adults. It was the opposite at my house, where people had a fatal passivity.

My father was a sad man. He had bushy, salt-and-pepper eyebrows that strayed high on his forehead. And ever-pouting lips. His cheeks were fleshy and rouged by alcohol. He was a steady drinker who lived ensconced in his Barcalounger—numb, detached, cynical.

"How you doin', Daddy?"

"Same as yesterday, same as tomorrow."

He had *that* right. TV flickered in the darkened room until he'd fall asleep in a chair. In the early hours I'd hear him finally hit the bathroom and shuffle to bed. Then he got up and went to work and did it all over again.

My mother knitted in the kitchen, listening to classical music. In the dining room, where I often sat with my home-work, the violins intersected with the gunfire and explosions of my father's cop shows.

But none of this means anything; it's just a story. Neither of them hurt me. That's important. My mother, who had long, braided hair pinned up in a bun, used to comb out the auburn strands at the back window. That's important. Because she would sing then, and the sun would touch her thin, porcelain face. She would sing "Danny Boy" and "Kathleen Mavourneen." My mother had a lovely voice and, standing in the back yard, I would imagine that she was happy and in love. With a man who was away. At war, perhaps. And she was waiting for him. Look-ing to that day when they would touch each other again.

So, you see, nothing at home prepared me for what I saw in Mooney's house. But what I *was* prepared for, what I knew best, was fantasy. And the vicarious life. So I set to work at that just as soon as I got home.

I imagined myself where Mooney had been. Standing before Margaret, watching her as she backed toward the window. Her fear didn't interest me; instead I made Margaret coquett-ish, playing a game of sexual tease. I watched the scene again and again, culminating in the first touch of her skin, then the embrace. And as I imagined her body pressed against my own, this ineffable sense of relief would come. As if I had been hold-ing my breath and now, finally, could let go.

5

It was a Friday or Saturday before Margaret returned to The City Zoo. I was outside keeping some kind of order while people waited in line to get in. The night was cold; I could see Margaret's breath illumined by the streetlights as she made her way down Fourth. Above her, a faint array of stars canopied the silhouettes of office buildings.

She made good time, arms pumping, her body straight and rigid. Pushing like a ship's prow through the dark. When she reached the line, she recognized me, giving a thin-lipped smile and a wave. I waved back, but she had already looked away.

Mooney was taking the cover that night, but I didn't see what happened between them when it was Margaret's turn to pay. By the time I got inside and sat down at the soundboard, Margaret was talking to a guy with a sharp, ruddy face and muttonchop sideburns. He had long, simian arms and the first hint of a potbelly. They were standing along the rear wall, far enough away for their words to be lost in the din of surrounding conversations.

Margaret made a lot of quick, slashing gestures while she talked. The guy said almost nothing, but wore a sweet, amused smile. He nervously rubbed the front of his red cardigan, then started plucking at it as if gathering lint.

They stayed for all three sets. As the lights went up again at midnight, Margaret put one hand on the guy's chest, and with the other pulled him down to her. She whispered something. Within thirty seconds they were heading to the door. His face was wide eyed, empty. Margaret carried her smile *fixe*.

After what happened with Mooney, I was afraid for her. I wondered if she might be doing something to invite the abuse. It seemed very possible, considering the beating she'd given herself while she danced. I had some time before the club closed and I needed to clean up. So I followed the couple down Fourth Street. Margaret continued talking. The guy did a good job giving absolute silence.

At Jesse, they turned left. It was a dark, narrow alley, serving warehouses behind the old Emporium. Margaret took the man's arm. A moment later he pointed to a black, beat-up SUV, fitted with a roof rack carrying lengths of pipe. The guy was a plumber.

I was now hiding behind a refuse bin, watching the man fumble with his keys—finally opening the tailgate. The two of them crawled in, pausing to rearrange tools and pipe elbows. Grunting, backsides swaying as they shoved equipment toward the far end of the truck. Finally, the plumber made an awkward turn and pulled the tailgate up.

Then nothing. I stared at the inky windows but couldn't see the faintest shape or movement. After about fifteen minutes, a car rattled down the potholed street. For the briefest moment, the headlights caught Margaret. She was sitting up, astride the plumber I assumed, and looking directly at the approaching car. She had the same thin smile, but the tendons of her neck roped sharply beneath the skin. She seemed scared.

But I must tell you—I didn't think about that. At the moment of the illumination, I could only think of Margaret's breasts, which I saw for the first time, pale and round. And lovely. I realized, as the dark returned and I tried to hold onto the image, that some part of me had followed her for this. To see what was hidden.

I stared into the impenetrable dark of the truck windows. The car that had provided my great moment clattered to the corner of Fifth, and turned north. Now I felt a loss. As if some intimacy had been offered and taken away. The moon, which had been hidden by the bulk of the Emporium, pushed a sliver of light above the roofline. A yearning pulled at me. Something with great mass, with its own gravity, taking me further and further from the familiar moorings of my life.

The truck door opened. A man's legs slid out, pants bunched high up the ankles. He sat for a moment, looking down the street, then stood and helped Margaret crawl across the tailgate. Now they were facing each other, their visible breath mingling in the silence.

The plumber bent awkwardly and kissed Margaret on the cheek. She put a hand to his shoulder. A brushing gesture. Perhaps affection, perhaps pushing him away. Then she turned and headed toward Fifth Street.

I'm not sure why, but I followed. Past the SUV, past the dark warehouses. Glancing back, I could see the plumber standing motionless by the driver's door, staring at Margaret's retreating silhouette.

Margaret turned right at the corner. When I reached Fifth and made the turn myself, she was already halfway to Market Street, walking like she was late for something. But at Market, she stopped. Statue still. I passed her and crossed the street.

Looking back from the far side, I was surprised to see that Margaret's eyes were closed. Her arms stretched out, fingers delicately curved in the ballerina pose. She was taking small, mincing steps—forward and back. A moment later she stepped off the curb, swaying, heeding her private music. In the orange glow of the high streetlamps, Margaret's face was held in a rigid mask. Her feet danced farther into the street. As the signal changed, her hands rose to join above her head. And then the car slammed into her.

It was an old Porsche, the kind that looks like an inverted spoon. Margaret's backside took the impact; her body slid along the hood to the windshield, then got dumped to the pavement. The Porsche squealed to a stop. I couldn't see where Margaret had fallen. And I couldn't get to her because six lanes of traffic were still rushing past.

The driver of the Porsche got out—a short man with close-cropped hair forming a widow's peak. He wore jeans and a corduroy jacket over a thin, fragile-looking body. The guy ran around the far side of his car and disappeared.

When I was finally able to cross the street, a small crowd had formed around Margaret, all pointing and talking. She was sitting up, her short skirt riding above her underpants. Same impenetrable half-smile. The driver was kneeling behind her, hands on her shoulders, kind of holding her up. Margaret's wrist was bleeding, and she waved it vaguely like she was brushing away flies.

People in the crowd shouted out suggestions: "Get an ambulance!" "Cover her."

And when Margaret tried to stand, an old black man put out his hand. "She's in shock. Don't let her up."

But Margaret did stand up. Leaning with both arms on the roof of the Porsche. She announced that she was fine in a breathy, little-girl voice.

The driver stood behind her, hands hovering a few inches from Margaret's coat. Preparing perhaps to catch her if she went down.

"Maybe you'd better wait," he said. "The paramedics will be here and they can check you out. See if you're all right."

"No. I said I'm fine."

"You just been hit by a car, honey," the old black man again. "You don't know what that did to you inside."

"Let me go." Her words suddenly had a harsh, guttural quality. She took a few side steps along the edge of the Porsche, then pushed away from the car and stood up straight.

"Then let me drive you home." It was the guy who had hit her. "If you won't stay to get checked out, let me at least do that."

She turned toward him, constructing the smile. "I shouldn't have . . . stepped off. I was thinking of something and I just stepped off." She was back to the soft, high voice.

Now Margaret started to button her coat, leaving glistening smears on the leather from her bleeding wrist. She pulled down her skirt.

"I should have been watching . . ." Two fingers drifted out in the direction of the hood, touching it, steadying herself. "I'm sorry."

In front of her a line of cars thrummed east toward the bay. The guy who'd hit her took Margaret's arm.

"Get in," he said. "Like it or not, I'm taking you to your door."

6

When I headed home that night, my thoughts held fast to Margaret. I was trying to put together her sexual compulsion with the self-mutilating dance. Had she deliberately stepped in front of that car? Was that part of a pattern of self-harm? Plus, there were the words that Mooney shouted, suggesting that she switched somehow from vamp to frightened child to a cruel "dirty mouth." I went around and around with all that. Making a dozen theories.

But I was doing more than trying to figure Margaret out. I was drawn to her pain. Except for the brief sexual adventures, it kept her alone. Isolated. I understood that. In some way, I felt I lived the same life. Even her compulsions seemed to echo in my endless fantasies—about people I watched but would never be close to. About Margaret herself.

So I imagined scenarios where Margaret and I began talking at The Zoo. About the bands, perhaps. About what happened with Mooney. About what forced her, night after night, into the loveless encounters. I imagined making her laugh. I saw her bending suddenly for a kiss. Then undressing, eyes on me. Grateful. Finally safe.

The fantasy was oddly like one I'd had as a child—a platonic dream of closeness to a boy named Andrew Monet. He was a sweet kid, carrying the mark of the slaughtered lamb. The boys in my grammar school saw that and waited for him daily—in the yard, in the alleys on the way home. They would start by taking the hat his mother made him wear. Throwing it from boy to boy as he ran and reached for it. Until he began to cry. Then they would hit him. Aiming for his testicles and face. The places that would hurt most.

He brought the whole class licorice once, placing the sticks on each desk with a shy little bow. I loved him for that and the sad smile that was part goodness and part resignation. I dreamed of being his friend, of walking home together and helping to protect him. I imagined the things we would talk about. I would visit his house; I would meet his mother. I would sit at their table.

Nothing came of it.

One day I was standing at a urinal in the old boys' bathroom. The one with ten thousand hexagonal tiles and a high frosted window giving on the schoolyard. Monet came rushing in. I had the usual moment of excitement, looking for something to say. But thirty seconds later, four boys sauntered through the double doors. He'd been running from them.

"Hey, Andrew." They surrounded him.

"Don't," he said. "He's the *fag*." Monet pointed at me.

The four boys looked my way.

"He took his zipper down, he told me to touch his thing."

I protested. The boys beat the shit out of me anyway. In his fear, Monet had offered me up.

I didn't see Margaret till late the following week. She was working on a guy with a shaved head and large Adam's apple, who closely resembled a light bulb. He was sitting alone at a table in front of the soundboard when Margaret swooped down on him.

She leaned for a moment on the back of a chair. "Is this seat taken?"

"No."

"Would you like it to be taken?"

Light Bulb was only too happy.

The guy got the fixed smile treatment, the *swaying to unheard music* treatment. And the sudden, too-loud laughter. In a theatrical, Blanche DuBois accent, Margaret talked about circuses. Clowns, I think. Freak shows. She mentioned that she was going to a carnival that Saturday—out at Stonestown.

At some point, Margaret lifted Light Bulb's arm and put it over her shoulder. He worked a hand up beneath her skirt. During the second set, while I was adjusting something on the soundboard, they disappeared.

For the rest of the night I worried about Margaret. But the feeling was marbled with a jealous resentment. That she would choose Light Bulb or Mooney—but never me. Then I began to think about carnivals. The one at Stonestown in particular. And I wondered what might come of it if somehow I ran into her there . . .

7

A Ferris wheel rose as the rickety centerpiece of the traveling carnival. It was doing a slow spin in the back parking lot of Stonestown shopping center. I'd seen Margaret rush like an excited kid through the neon-lit gates, and then watched from a distance as she made the rounds of kewpie doll booths—the duck shoot, the ring toss, darts and balloons.

She was loving it. When Margaret won a thumb-sized stuffie on the camel race, she announced that it was "the best carnival ever" in a thin, little voice.

But the best carnival ever had maybe six rides—seven, counting the walk-through haunted house. Plus the weather was ugly. Gray and arctic. With a stiff wind starting to moan through the rigging of the rides. Margaret didn't seem to notice; her face was flushed and her dark eyes flitted through the crowd.

While eating a hot dog near the ticket booth, I watched

Margaret line up for the Octopus and then the Zipper. The wind had started to gust, snapping the flags, pinning wrappers against the fence. I noticed that the Zipper shivered with each wind burst as it paused to let on passengers.

Now Margaret headed to the wimpy, ten-horse merry-go-round. There was no line and she got right on. For five rides. I could see she was enthralled, leaning out from the saddle, one arm drifting free, fingers tracing wave patterns in the air.

Thirty minutes later she made her way to the Ferris wheel. I watched her lovely hips as she moved, and felt a harsh, familiar yearning. There was a hollowness in my body, a feeling beneath the skin of some vast space.

I had to be closer, to have Margaret within physical reach. She now stood in a line of kids waiting to ride. Her open leather coat billowed; she wrapped her arms around her chest. A minute later I was behind her. Smelling her faint, lilac perfume. Listening to the throaty roar of the diesel that was spinning the great wheel.

She turned and caught a glimpse of me. "Oh . . . you're from The Zoo." Her face tightened.

I made a little wave. "That's funny . . . seeing you here."

"It's awfully windy," Margaret said, glancing away. "I hope it doesn't make us shake too much. You could really feel it on the Zipper. I hate going upside down—I don't know why I got on that one."

I pointed to the sky and said it looked like a serious storm was brewing. Then I asked if she liked carnivals—a stupid question, but I was suddenly full of hope that we might start a conversation.

"Uh huh," she murmured, looking toward the Ferris wheel.

I started to say something, but the operator pointed at Margaret. "You alone?"

"Yes."

He ushered her to a vacant gondola. And me to the next

one. I was excited, playing our little exchange over and over in my head. Not knowing that was it, that we would never speak another word to each other.

Wind keened through the Ferris wheel struts and cables. The whole assembly shook as I neared the top, taking hard gusts coming straight off the sea. I could glimpse the ocean—for the briefest moment—at the apex of the ride. Before descending to the gray asphalt and the waiting line of kids.

On the third or fourth revolution, a cold, sustained blast hit the wheel as I was halfway to the top. We seemed to lean a little. But as the gondola crested, the wind suddenly abated, then hit again—hurricane force—to whipsaw the rig. I heard something crack.

I was looking, that second, out toward the ocean. Watching the lines of white, roiling waves push toward the sand. A simple thought entered my mind. Light, emotionless. The thought that I was about to die. And then a second one—that I had wasted my life.

The left side of the gondola broke free of its bearings. I remember my hands flying up, reaching for something. And the seat starting to tilt, to fall. My weight shifted against the safety bar and it burst open. A cold wind lashed my face. My body hit the axle, snapped backward, ricocheted against the lower struts, and finally crashed with a hollow thud on the passenger ramp. I was dead before I landed.

8

The rain arrived. I was outside my body. I remember watching the drops collect on my face, astonished that I couldn't feel them. My eyes were open. A crimson gash ran across one ear to become a V-shaped canyon in my forehead. There was little bleeding—the face was already growing white. Empty.

The ride operator stopped the wheel. Then stepped gingerly to the edge of the ramp, felt my neck for a pulse.

"Jesus and Mary." A whisper swallowed by the near constant wind.

He rubbed the stubble on his cheek. Then started biting a thumbnail, tearing it. "Better cover the shite up."

The operator ransacked in a supply box and returned with an oily tarp. My eyes were still open. I watched the canvas scrape across my face as he covered me.

At that moment I felt the panic. A sense of being unfettered. Of drifting. The wind blew, but I couldn't feel it. The rain drummed on the tarp above my face. But I was merely a spectator.

Above me now I heard screams and the operator shouting, "I'll get you off. Calm the fook down."

The Ferris wheel again began to turn, stopping to unload the kids from each gondola. They stepped around me on the ramp, faces still locked in fear.

When Margaret finally got off, she stared for a moment at the tarp. Then she used two fingers to wipe the rain from her forehead.

"I was just talking to him," she said to no one in particular. "We were in line, speaking about . . . "

She didn't finish. The rain hit with increasing venom. Drops landed, bouncing upward, and fell again to become a thin lake on the asphalt. Margaret turned, walked with excruciating caution toward the gate. And now came another wave of fear. At the prospect of being alone—without her.

It was then I knew that nothing held me. That I was outside of gravity. Outside of weather. Beyond human connection. The thought occurred, unimaginably frightening, that I could go anywhere.

I screamed. Something foolish like, "Stop" or "Help." But the sound I heard was the memory of my voice. Merely vestigial. The ride operator never turned around. He was shooing a few gawkers, arms making violent pushing gestures.

"Get away, now. Show some respect, you little shites. There's somebody died here."

I shouted again. No reaction. I realized at that moment that I would never again make a sound heard in the living world.

The operator looked up at the great wheel, still shaking in the gusts, and made his way across loose boards and cables to the thrumming diesel. He turned it off. Now there was just the wind. In the distance I could see a stubby-legged boy chasing his hat. A trio of plastic bags tumbled by me toward the gate. I lifted my arm, trying to feel the cold air. There was nothing to lift.

Again panic. I had an impulse to go home but instantly felt the absurdity of drifting through the rooms of my apartment. I couldn't even mix a drink or turn on the TV.

Now I noticed my position changing. I was further from the ground—floating close to the top of the wheel. And rising. Suddenly there was a new fear—that I would be drawn up alone, to some place far above the planet. Away from all familiar shapes and colors, away from the sound of wind, of voices.

I stopped ascending. And then, through some act of will, pulled myself back to the ground. I remained afraid, but at least I had learned something. I could move by mere desire. I could decide where to be and go there.

A corner of the tarp blew off, revealing my forehead and longish, wind-ruffled hair. I felt a sudden great sadness for the man who had died. For his silly, inconsequential vanities. The hair he had so carefully brushed each morning, hoping to be noticed, to be thought attractive, was now dampening in the rain, slowly tangling toward the ground. The sadness had a quiet, meditative quality that seemed stronger now than the fear.

I watched the rain spatter against my forehead. I felt oddly distant from myself. It had been a hollow life. Full of hunger and little plans. And loneliness—desperately covered. Always pretending to be strong or smart or invulnerable.

I drifted back, away from the face. As if to avoid the full impact of my failure. The ride operator was examining the fallen gondola, gently touching the twisted metal. Sirens rose in the distance.

A fork of lightning broke above Twin Peaks. I watched it cut a broken path to Earth. At the same time I could see the operator rubbing beneath his eyes—crying perhaps. And Margaret just arriving at the bus stop on Junipero Serra. I realized then that I could see 360, that I was no longer limited to looking forward, focusing on one thing at a time. The awareness—like everything I was discovering about my life discarnate—unsettled me.

An ambulance leaned hard on the turn into Winston Drive, then snaked left to the Stonestown parking lot. A squad car wailed just behind. Two EMTs got out of the ambulance, one pushing a gurney, and one carrying what resembled a large tool-box. They hurried across the now-empty carnival to bend over my body. As I watched, I found myself drifting away from the Ferris wheel, back to the chain-link fence and beyond. I didn't want to see them open my shirt, probing the crushed ribs, trying to find some signature of a life already gone.

I was moving faster now—across a little verge of ice plant to a sidewalk, and a six-lane boulevard. The cars rushed maybe a foot below me—in a hurry to get home to dinner, to the television. Their headlamps caught the bright, reflecting drops.

On the far side of the street was the bus stop where Margaret waited. I'm not sure why I went to her. Perhaps some vague hope of comfort—to be near someone I'd cared for. Or simply that I was in shock and didn't know where else to go. When I drew near her, she was vainly wiping the water off her leather coat. Big brushing motions. Rivulets ran from her hair down her cheeks and neck. Her corduroy pants were soaked.

Margaret's face held no expression, save a slight tightening around the corners of her mouth. Her eyes seemed to focus in the distance over the roof of the mall. Her breath came in a short, staccato rhythm, with an occasional low sound. Like someone would make as they nod agreement. She stood like that till the 28 bus hissed to a stop in front of us.

Inside, Margaret made her way to the last seat. She dropped into it and immediately began rocking—forward and back, hand rubbing her thigh, hair swaying with each thrust. It was dark out now. Occasional cracks of thunder reached into the bus.

At Santiago Street, Margaret got off. I followed as she quick-stepped two blocks to the corner of 21st. The neighborhood had mostly white, stucco homes, where the shifting television light already played on the walls of living rooms. Margaret climbed a short flight leading to a three-story apartment house. The place had an air of neglect; raw wood showed on the window frames. A concrete-covered yard with a sagging wrought iron fence bordered the sidewalk.

While Margaret fiddled to open her mailbox, I tried to make sense of what I was doing here. Somehow I had made Margaret my link—my lifeline—to the familiar. I felt, without understanding or reason, that I would be safe if I stayed near her. That I could keep at bay the undertone of fear I'd suffered since the accident.

A couple passed me on the street, slinging angry, high-pitched Mandarin. The rain was heavier now, drumming on the asphalt, passing with no resistance through my outstretched hands. Margaret finally, without a single letter in hand, pushed open the front door.

I followed her up dark, thickly carpeted stairs to the third floor. The hall rug had a floral pattern. Roses. Yellowed-paper shades covered a few wall sconces. Margaret's door was mahogany colored, with eight panes of frosted glass. A small brass hook hung on the outside—perhaps for a Christmas wreath.

We went in. Margaret turned on a single floor lamp, which

cast a pale, salmon-colored light into what looked like a study.
Dark, overstuffed chairs bulked against the walls. Rows of
bookshelves flanked two sides of the room. Now she hung her
leather coat on the bathroom door. White tiles. The sound of
dripping. The bedroom chandelier snapped on—three flame-
shaped bulbs and some dangling crystal. On the double bed
was a white coverlet with a pattern of small stars etched in the
nap. A huge stuffed clown—white faced with bulbous nose and
orange fringe of hair—leaned against the headboard.

Margaret peeled off her wet corduroys. Then her black
sweater and jade faux-silk blouse. She stood in her underwear.
For a moment Margaret wrapped her arms around her stomach,
bending slightly, swaying a few times forward and back. Now
she pulled off her underpants, unhooked her bra. She turned to
look in a high mirror, propped above an old mahogany vanity.

The vanity was empty, save for an ornate hand mirror,
brush, and comb—all laid parallel. And a tall porcelain dancer,
posed in mid-pirouette. Margaret reached with a languid, slow
motion toward the statue, pressing a lever on its wooden base.
The "Waltz of the Flowers" tinkled into the room. Then she
stood on half point, leg muscles stretched and defined. The
indentation of her spine grew deep, descending toward her
lovely buttocks. She began a series of small steps, turning. I was
surprised that I had no desire for her.

Just then I felt a piercing grief. Because what had defined
my life—a dark sexual hunger that attached itself to random
females—now seemed entirely lost. I had no idea who I would
be without it.

9

The dance was a short one, concluding as Margaret walked
in half point to the shower. While she was there, the wind

changed direction. Now it was driving rain straight against the windows. Twenty-first Avenue was a river, the white bouncing drops caught in occasional headlights.

Behind me, Margaret's room had a barren look. No clutter, no knickknacks. On the bed table was a tall, wind-up alarm clock. And a hardcover book. Churchill—*The Gathering Storm.* Opposite the bed was a coffee table supporting a boom box and a small-screen TV. That was it—except for the clown and the dancer.

The water shut off. I could see steam drifting from the open bathroom door. Margaret emerged through the mist wrapped in a beach towel. After a glance in the vanity mirror, she opened a door to a deep, walk-in closet. Inside were stacks of out-facing milk crates, each with a jumble of clothes. Socks, T-shirts, shorts, jogging pants were all in particular boxes.

Margaret let her towel drop and pulled on a T-shirt and underpants. She adjusted the waistband and put both hands over her buttocks, moving them slowly toward her hips. One hand then continued to trace the slight convex of her abdomen, her pubis—as if she were verifying the familiar shape of her own body, taking some kind of comfort in the outlines of muscle and bone.

At that moment, I was behind Margaret. And I wanted intensely to reach my arms around her. I wanted to feel our bodies pressing. Not for sex. But trying somehow to join her, to merge.

I started to touch Margaret's shoulder but waited, hesitant. Then I reached again, my hand passing through her flesh.

Instantly I felt the truth. I could move in and out of her body—like wind through the branches of great trees. But nothing of us would join. I could spend forty years in this room; I could watch Margaret grow old. I could whisper in her dreams; I could shout as she dressed up for the clubs. But I would always be alone.

Margaret crossed over to her boom box. She pulled a plastic tray out from beneath the coffee table, selected a CD. A moment later, the first song from Joni Mitchell's *Blue* album cut into the room.

Now Margaret killed the light and crawled into bed. Briefly her hands moved across the coverlet, splayed fingers reading its texture. Then they fell still at her sides. Margaret looked toward the window—at the brilliant drops backlit by streetlights. The music played on.

Now the first chords of "River" made Margaret stir slightly. Her eyes focused on the lit-up dial of the tuner; there was a tightening at the corners of her mouth. Her hands rose and spread—a gesture of indifference. Or surrender.

Now her eyes closed. Hard. Pressing crow's feet into her young skin. She hit herself—a glancing blow on the cheek. The sound of a melon being rapped. Her hand pulled back for another punch. More solid this time. And again it coiled, fist closed.

Now the song came to an end. And there was just the static of rain on the windows. Margaret's arm fell again to her side.

"That's all right," she said in a little girl voice. She took a deep breath and her face relaxed. "That's fine." The word *fine* was drawn out, like she didn't want it to end.

By the time the CD was over, Margaret's breathing was shallow. Her eyes, beneath closed lids, were following something in a dream.

At that moment, I had an acute yearning for the feeling of warmth. The room had no temperature. I could make it cold or hot by mere thought. But there was no pleasure in it. No true sensation. I wanted to feel the air leaving Margaret's parted lips. I wanted to know the warmth beneath the arch of her cheek. Now I slid into the bed, contorting myself to fit the curve of her hips and spine.

I lay there a long time. Listening to her breathing. To the

rain. The blankets had no weight. Her flesh was as permeable as air. I couldn't feel its warmth, its substance. I wanted to wake her. I shouted her name. Rhythmically, like hammer blows. But she slept on. And her body was no comfort. Lying across the bottom of the bed was the stuffed clown. I watched its rubber face, moon white from the street lamp. It stared at the ceiling. Smiling. Impervious.

10

I didn't sleep. And as in life, I found when you don't sleep, you think. I thought about my father delivering lectures to the idiots on his sit-coms. "Don't sit next to her, you fool, she doesn't even like you." "Why don't you just give her your wallet; that's all she wants." "Walk a little slower, honey. He's writing a book about your ass." I thought about my mother, holding her amber necklace to the light, studying some tiny creature trapped in the rock.

I imagined never again feeling cold air flowing across my throat, through my trachea. Never sighing. I remembered my father sighing—a soft, rumbling sound as his eyes searched around the living room. Finding the slight despair in familiar objects.

I realized how empty an hour was. In a dark, dreamless room.

Margaret slept restlessly, her arms wrapped and unwrapped over her chest. For a time her hand pressed against her pubis, like a child needing to use the toilet. While she rolled and turned, I stayed in place. Sometimes our forms overlapped. Sometimes not. The merging happened without feeling. I witnessed it as you would watch a cloud covering the sun, the sudden shifting of shadow and light.

By morning the rain had stopped, but hard gusts still hit the windows, making the casements creak. Church bells rang for the 9:00 mass. Across Margaret's hardwood floor, the sun cast oblongs of lattice light. In the distance a dog barked. And then the rumbling of a streetcar.

At 9:20 the phone rang. Margaret, who'd been lying on her stomach, suddenly arched upward. Then she swung her legs to sit on the edge of the bed. On maybe the fifth ring, she raced, bare feet slapping the floor, to the living room.

"Hello?" High pitched and tentative. Like someone expecting bad news.

"Oh, yes . . . Walker." She listened for a moment. "Thank you for calling, but I'm fine. Except for a bruise or two on my back side." Soft giggle. "So don't worry. I won't sue you." Another laugh, going a bit too long. "I hope I didn't hurt your car, put any dents in it or anything. It's a beauty. A classic. If I did anything to it, I'm sorry. I should have, you know, watched where I was going."

She shrugged, let rip another giggle. "But I'm like that, always kind of somewhere else. Sometimes I arrive, you know, at a place, and I have no idea how I got there. The whole trip is gone, erased."

She was snapping the waistband of her underpants. At the same time both legs were jiggling in a kind of scissors motion.

"Well Walker, I . . ." She started to frown. "That's very nice of you, but it's hardly necessary. Everything's fine. You can forget it happened. I just wasn't watching, you know, where . . . "

There was a long silence. Margaret was pulling the receiver cord, and letting it spring back.

"Well, I suppose. If you really want to, I guess we could go somewhere and have a bite. Or some coffee. Or whatever." She jiggled her way over to an armchair and sat down. "It needs to be someplace close; I don't have a car. There's a place on Tara-val—the Tennessee Grill. The food's greasy but good."

They set a time, and Margaret started to say good-bye. But then, out of the blue, she asked Walker whether girls went for his car. And she did it in this much deeper voice. Sultry, with a Louisiana accent. "Ah mean, you know, when they get in do they kind of run their hand over the dash and get excited? About how cool the car is?"

There was a long silence.

"Ah just wanted to know if it worked for that. You know, for girls. That's all. Ah was just curious." Then she signed off.

Margaret went back to bed and set the big wind-up alarm for 11:30. She drew into a fetal curve and put one hand between her legs, holding herself. Her eyes were on the window. The sunlight was fractured now, caught between thin seams in the clouds. On the floor, once-lucent rectangles had gone dark.

Then Margaret spoke: "Will I see roses or flies?" Voice soft, modulated. "Roses or flies, roses or flies?" She kept repeating it for maybe a minute. Until her breathing changed and I could hear quiet snoring.

I mention this little scene to you for a reason. Not because it's weird, although that was my first reaction. And not because the mantra had any meaning to me at the time. But I mention it because later I would realize it was the first real clue to the architecture of Margaret's core.

When the alarm went off, Margaret jerked awake. Then she dressed in her usual—short denim skirt, flannel shirt, and the leather car coat.

"OK," she said as she headed out the door and into the dim-lit hall. Then she began humming—something I didn't recognize—all the way down 21st and through the door of the Tennessee Grill.

The grill had occupied the same location since the '30s. A counter, with a scattering of diners reading the Sunday paper,

ran along the left side of the restaurant. To the right were
rows of Formica-topped tables, where a few elderly women sat
crumpled in their booths. Several families, fresh from church,
sat near the windows, shoveling burgers and BLTs.

Walker was at a table in the rear. He wore his corduroy
coat with a cobalt-blue woolen shirt. He waved and stood as
Margaret approached. Walker seemed even shorter now than I
remembered him at the accident. Five feet eight at most. And
the face seemed younger—with smooth, slightly ruddy skin and
a good jaw. Faint calipers ran from an aquiline nose to lips that
held a shy smile.

"Hello," he said, and gestured to a chair. "Thank you for joining me."

"'Ah have always depended . . .' and all that." Margaret
smiled as she sat and began fussing with the silverware, lining
everything up exactly parallel.

"How are you feeling?"

"OK. Like I said, my butt's sore. But I'll live." She shrugged.
"And you? How are you feeling?"

"What do you mean?" Walker squinted.

"You must be feeling something." The words seemed rushed,
flint-edged.

"I'm glad to see you. I guess that's what I feel."

"What else?" Margaret looked away—toward a framed
poster on the far wall. Trees in autumn.

"I don't know what else." He rubbed his cheek for a moment.
"I guess I'm nervous."

"OK, that's good, that's something."

"I don't know if it's good. I get nervous sometimes—talking
to people."

"It's good." She was still diddling with the utensils, now using
them to form letters. "At least it isn't bullshit." The voice deepened, Southern accent again. "So what are you doin'? You tryin'
to start somethin'?"

"I'm trying to start a conversation." Walker was rubbing his cheek red. Pushing little running folds in the skin. He looked over toward the counter like there might be some help there.

"Ah mean, you know. 'Cause that probably wouldn't work because . . ." She shrugged.

Silence.

"Because Ah don't usually do that . . . with anybody unless it's just a thing."

"You mean like a one-night thing? Something short?"

She nodded.

"How come?"

Big smile. "It's better . . . so now we know about that." A finger flicked in Walker's direction. "What do you do?"

"I'm a journalist—freelance articles on science, weird phenomena, amazing people. That kind of stuff. What about you?"

"I work for the Ballet." The accent was gone now.

"Dancer?"

"No, no." Margaret blushed. "I used to be, but not now. No, I work in the front office—promotions, group sales, some of the high-end tour companies that give snobby old ladies a shot of culture."

"Do you like it?"

"No. It's a job. There's no relationship between dancing and what I do."

"But you used to dance? Something you did for fun, or more serious?"

"More serious. Since I was five. I spent all my free time taking classes. I was in *The Nutcracker* every year. Worked my way up from a mouse to a snowflake, to finally being Clara—the girl who has the lead."

"Where'd you perform?"

"San Francisco Ballet, of course." There was pride in her voice. "But then I . . . retired."

"So young?"

"I had problems with the director; he pissed me off. I was sixteen and that was the end of it."

"You gave it up?"

"It gave me up. He was Herr Dance Professor. From Berlin. Full of new ideas for the company. I said something. He was turning me for a *plié*, showing everyone how, and I . . . I took his hands off me and said he didn't know shit about dance. That was the end. Nobody could believe I did it. They were like, 'What's wrong with you?' But I was glad. I was done with that shit."

"What shit?" Walker was running his fingers through short-cropped hair, starting at the widow's peak and smoothing all the way back to the collar. He looked alarmed.

"Big man shit. The big man tells you what to do. 'Work harder . . . eat less . . . sweep your arm, don't jerk it . . . reach like you long for him, not like a maid seeking a mop.' The big man owns you—every inch of your muscle and skin—he can do anything he wants with you. 'You are the clay and I am the sculptor,' he says. 'Get your big ass in the back, no one wants to look at it.'"

Margaret spread her hands, a helpless gesture. At that moment the waitress came to take their orders, but only seemed to understand the word "hamburger." They ordered burgers.

"When I was dancing, and the big man would shut his mouth, I felt like I could spin the earth with my body. Like there were lines of force going out from me, giving motion to everything."

"That's lovely. I don't think many people have ever felt that."

Margaret shrugged, flashed a mechanical smile.

"I mean that. I would love to have known a feeling like that."

"Too late. You have to start at five."

The burgers arrived, and the two got busy for a while applying condiments.

"Do you miss it?"

Short, harsh laugh. "Every day."

"Why not dance for another company, where it's not so autocratic?"

"They're all the same. People controlling you. Dancers get used to it—or they don't and leave." Silence. "Do you like the circus?" she suddenly asked.

"Yeah, but I haven't seen one in decades. When I was a kid in Omaha, Barnum and Bailey used to come through once a year. I liked the elephants."

"Circuses are kind of bullshit now. Watered down. They used to have these cool freak shows. Siamese twins, bearded lady, pin-heads, guys with no arms or legs."

"What made that cool?" Walker was wolfing the burger down and seemed like he might be getting ready to leave.

"It made all the people who are freaks *inside* feel better, you know? I mean, there's the two-headed boy making it, looking OK, so maybe you can make it. There's some dwarf who goes on somehow with life, you know, dealing with whatever he wants that he can't have. Long legs, not waddling when he walks—whatever. But he, you know, makes it somehow.

"So I like that. I have a collection of freak photographs—a lot of old circus postcards, Diane Arbus, stuff in that vein. I look at them sometimes and think about what that life means. The loneliness. Eyes sliding all over your body. All the emotional things you want—but it's contemptible because of what you are."

Walker spread his hands several times—as if struggling with a number of false starts before saying something. "That's sad. To be so deprived."

"Yeah. It used to be better for freaks—years ago. They had communities and they, you know, took care of each other. Now they live alone in rented rooms—on SSI." She paused, delicately patting her lips with a paper napkin. "So what else will we talk about? The war?"

"What?"

"I'm kinda fascinated with that." Her voice became slightly professorial and she held up her knife like it was a pointer—locating three spots on an invisible chalkboard. "WWII. I've studied that whole era. What happened to people. Dresden. Stalingrad. Croatia. The French Underground. How people survived. Or didn't. I've studied it so much that sometimes, you know, I think I live more there than here."

"You're young to have an interest like that. It's surprising. How did you get into it?"

"Long story. And you've already finished your burger. We're done, aren't we?"

Walker raised his eyebrows.

"I mean with lunch? There's only the grease left on your plate."

Walker nodded, eyes fixed in the middle distance behind Margaret.

"Hey." She snapped her fingers. "You still here? Wait, I know." Now she leaned forward across the table. And when her voice came again, it was low and Southern. "Maybe you want to examine my bruises." All teeth smile.

Walker pushed back against his chair. "I can't tell what you're . . . are you kidding?"

"OK, you lost your chance." A grunting little laugh. "So what was this? Why did you call me?"

Walker leaned to extract his wallet. "I worried about you. I was curious. And I thought you were . . . pretty."

"Oh God, what a word—pretty. No one's been pretty in forty years."

"I'm sorry. I don't know how to talk to you. I feel like you're leading me on some kind of chase, and just when I start to catch up—bang, you've gone somewhere else."

"People never catch up."

"I bet that's right." He looked at her closely. "What would happen if they caught up?"

Another smile. "They'd be in trouble. And me, too, I guess." She shoved back her chair and stood up.

II

Margaret seemed dangerous, with maybe a touch mean. My father used to say, "The merry-go-round of life has more dogs than horses," and I felt stupid for riding this obsession. I had made her up. From her face and body and a few scraps of odd behavior, I'd invented a person. The real Margaret—this woman who taunted and pulled Walker through a rabbit hole—was like a piece of shrapnel.

That night Margaret headed for a club. I followed her downtown, but I couldn't watch her reprise the usual routine. Instead, I drifted up Market Street, and then across to Leavenworth. High streetlamps cast shadows of the poles and parked cars. Faded, hand-lettered signs marked entrances to the old hotels. I drifted through dark lobbies, where straight-backed chairs faced each other across the empty floor, where the night clerks rustled in their cages.

Not a word. Just traffic roar, and the amorphous, distant shouts of drunks gathered near bar fronts.

Finally I went upstairs, to the men lying in their beds, illuminated by flickering TVs. I saw the cups, the unwashed plates, the newspapers spilling from a chiffonier. I watched them in their robes and undershirts, waiting for sleep. Waiting for coma. My father used to say: "Skin hides well your broken bones."

As I slipped from room to room, it occurred to me that I knew these men. They *were* my father. They were the ones who numbed themselves, who settled into their chairs. They had arrived by natural progression to the place of complete silence, where even the TV, with its gunshots and explosions, was soundless.

The next day Walker called again.

After a few minutes of listening, Margaret said, "I thought we'd had our visit and everything, and we were done. There were a few times down at the Tennessee where it looked like something wasn't agreein' with you." She was starting to drawl. "It might have been the food, but Ah thought it was the conversation."

Silence.

"Walker, you won't find it interestin' for very long. Ah'm an acquired taste that nobody ever acquires." She was shaking her head, then looking around like an animal seeking escape.

"OK, Ah'll be there at 6:00. Ah don't know what you're lookin' for, but Ah don't think this is it."

She snapped the cord for a while. "OK, OK. Ah said Ah'd be there. Don't get a big worry on about it. It's bad for your vessels."

The date, as it turned out, was dinner at Walker's house. His place was an upper flat on Fell Street, overlooking a narrow strip of park called the Panhandle. It was already dark by the time Margaret arrived, but Walker ushered her to a tiny, three-foot balcony hanging off the living room. They climbed through a window to sit on a pair of lawn chairs. Margaret pulled at her skirt, folded her arms across her leather car coat.

"I love it out here, even in the winter. The silhouettes of the trees. The dark lawns. It's such a relief from looking at buildings." Walker shrugged.

A wave of cars, released by a signal, rushed below them. After a minute, their taillights receded up Fell Street, and it was quiet again.

Margaret waved her hand. "Do you love exhaust? You've got plenty of that."

Walker gave a grunting laugh. "You can get high from it."

Abruptly he crawled through the window, and returned in a moment with two glasses of wine. "A nicer way to get high," he said. "Salud."

"I'll have a little, but I get weird when I drink. People tell me."

"That's OK."

"I don't think so. Something tells me you don't cope well with weird." Silence. "So, do you have something cooking, or is it take-out?"

"It's cooking." His face seemed pinched.

"Oh oh. You're already at your limit. I can see it." She touched his knee, smiled. "But I can deal if you can deal. We'll get through this."

He looked for a minute into the branches of a nearby eucalyptus. "So tell me how you got interested in WWII?"

"Well . . ." Margaret paused. The frost from her breath started pumping in shorter bursts. "I was looking—this is years ago when I was maybe sixteen—at some photographs from the Holocaust. It was one of those traveling exhibits, and I just wanted to go. I don't know why. And I found this picture— people on a roof—a man and woman holding hands, the sun's glinting from his spectacles. He has wavy hair and a kind of tired, sweet smile. The woman's hair is flowing, also wavy. She has dark, scared-looking eyes.

"But off by themselves, closer to the roof edge, are two girls. Fourteen or fifteen. Standing arm in arm. They look so much alike, they must be sisters. And this one girl, when I look at her . . . she's familiar. When I look at her, I feel this great love." Margaret touched her chest.

"So I just keep looking at that girl. And the one next to her. And I have this recognition, this feeling of belonging . . . somewhere. Under the picture it says, 'Schloss Family, Holland, 1945. Three days before arrest. Believed to have died in Auschwitz.'"

Margaret stopped talking. The frost from her breath began to slow down; another wave of cars passed.

"Incredible story. Your interest in the war started right then?"

Long silence. "No. Not right then." Her face stiffened. "Of course, I tried to find out about the Schloss family. There's a record of their being transported to Auschwitz. That's all. Nothing before or after. I never even learned the girls' first names."

"But somehow you felt you knew them."

No answer.

"Did that go on—that feeling of connection?"

"Yes."

Margaret got up and threw one leg over the windowsill, then looked back at Walker. "Time to go in."

Walker tried several more times during the dinner preparations to get Margaret to say more. She offered nothing else. Instead she careened back to clowns and freaks, and the differences between American and European circuses.

After dinner—a casserole of some kind, I've forgotten—they settled in the living room. Walker on a Morris chair, Margaret on the red leather sofa. The room had several Maxfield Parrish reproductions, and a Sebastião Salgado poster depicting refugee children climbing on an enormous anthill. The furniture was dark oak, displaying several pieces of Indian pottery, and a small porcelain statue of two children at play.

"So what do we do now? More conversation?"

Margaret poured herself another glass of wine. Her eyes searched around the room. "What's that?" She was pointing to a framed magazine cover.

"*Scientific American.* First place I ever got an article published. A piece on chemicals leeching into the water in Silicon Valley. I got lucky and kind of started at the top."

"Nice. What are you writing now—at this moment?"

"It's about this strange phenomenon I fell into a few years back that I called the *Sunrise Effect*. I did a wry little piece about how certain scientists—who'd labored in obscurity, or were even scorned—would suddenly get recognized. There'd be a stir about them; they'd get awards, major grants. And boom, a few months later they were dead. It was this weird thing, and it happened often enough that you could pretend it was a pattern.

"So, like I say, it was just a throw-away little piece—just entertainment—that appeared in a one-page box in *Psychology Today*. But then . . . "

"Why'd you make something up like that? Why bother to write about a thing that isn't true?" Margaret was leaning forward on the couch, throwing her arms wide open in a gesture of confusion.

Walker examined his fingers, delicately pinching several of the joints. "How can I explain? I'm looking for ideas an editor will buy. Sometimes I come up with something that seems important, sometimes it's merely interesting, sometimes it's clever, but bogus. But that's not the point." He waved his hand. "The point is I started getting a lot of letters about the *Sunrise Effect* article, people telling about friends and relatives who'd experienced exactly the same thing. Sudden validation or achievement, or some dream coming true. And then unexpected death.

"So now I'm doing a book on it, a collection of those stories. They keep pouring in. Somehow people hear about it. And I've come to think there really is something happening, some force at work.

"My very religious aunt called me one day and said I was trying to expose God's plan. Like it was blasphemy or something. But I think of myself as a reporter—trying to show one of the threads running through people's lives."

"People—when they read the book—are gonna get terrified of success." She gave a low chuckle. "They're gonna start refusing awards, stop working on projects. The gross national product will plummet because of you."

Silence. Margaret was running her fingers around the lip of her glass. "Do you like it? Do you like telling the story?"

"Yeah. And I guess I like the attention."

Margaret nodded. Her voice was suddenly harsh. "But the truth is more important. It fucks up the world when you don't tell the truth."

"I think I did discover something true."

Margaret launched a four-star smile. "OK, OK. Good for you. Whatever you look for you can find. But, anyway, I've enjoyed this, I really have. Good food, freezing on the balcony." She laughed. "Some interesting stories."

She pulled at her skirt demurely. "But all the talk is really about one thing. Doing it or not doing it. Don't you think? Don't you think that's what all our talk is about?"

"What are you saying?"

"And if we did it . . ." Margaret rose, ". . . If we did it, except for those few minutes, nothing would change. You know what I mean?"

On the way out the door, she touched him briefly on the chest. "I'm sorry."

The scene with Walker reminded me of something. My mother sometimes visited me in my room above the poultry shop. About a year before my accident, she arrived on one of the few nights I had a girl in there. We weren't undressed, so that was good. But the girl sat slumped and kicking one of her crossed legs, like she was bored out of her mind. There was an open vodka bottle. And her suitcase lay where she'd dumped it on the bed.

I'd met this one at the Zoo—where she'd come direct from the bus station. Her proposition was straightforward, and quite fair. A fuck for a meal and a place to stay. She had ice-blue eyes, and a chronic shrug. As if pretending things didn't matter was a way of life.

My mother asked where she was from, and endured some long story about a family cratered by rage. It was a tale of venial people doing vicious things. The delivery was flat and detached, like badly read dialogue.

"You've had a hard go of it," my mother finally said.

"Yeah, I know. But a couple of nights here with . . ." I think she had forgotten my name. "A couple of nights here and I can put something together. Meet some people. Work my way into something."

My mother looked at the suitcase. "You didn't come here to visit my son?"

"God no, I just met him." She gestured toward the bed. "And he didn't tell me he just had a single. We're gonna be hella cramped in there."

My mother was gone in five minutes. The girl was good to her word, but disappeared two days later. She left a note with an address, but when I went there, it was a crash pad and nobody knew her name.

Oddly, I missed her. I thought about how she had pressed against my body, her offhand, physical generosity. When my mother asked about her, I lied and said we were dating. That she was starting business school to learn computers.

I saw her one more time. Six months later she was dragging her stiletto heels out the side door of a North Beach strip club.

12

It was clear to me—after a few days—that I had taken up residence with Margaret. I wasn't sure I liked her. Or wanted to be there. Each day, without fear of discovery or rejection, I could watch her undress. Something I'd imagined many times. But it meant nothing to me now.

Still I held on. I drifted through her rooms, observing carefully the small events of her life. I often followed on her daily rounds. And when she went somewhere I didn't choose to go, I felt empty. As if I had traveled to a country where I knew only one person—my translator, my connection. And without her, no relationship was possible.

I wondered often if there might be somewhere else to go. Some waiting afterlife, a door that would swing open on a particular heaven or hell. But none appeared. At times I imagined returning to my apartment, yet the loneliness of the place now felt unbearable.

I imagined going somewhere beautiful. Watching glinting diamonds of frost on the upper face of Half Dome. Drifting across the turquoise glacial water of Lake McDonald. Following the snaking Colorado River beneath fire-colored cliffs. But oddly, without Margaret, I sensed that beauty would not touch me.

So I waited, suspended at the border of Margaret's life. No light, no sign. I watched her move through her rooms—an object—neither attractive nor repulsive. Just a slender thread holding me.

In that first week after my demise, I once or twice accompanied Margaret to work. It was, as she described to Walker, a desk job. And not particularly interesting. But I remember an odd little incident that seemed emblematic of Margaret's feelings toward men.

She was in the late morning of a day spent arranging group ticket sales to various corporate and travel entities. A boy came in her office—maybe sixteen or seventeen—with the mail tray. He had center-parted hair framing dark, finely etched features. Long, delicate fingers placed the mail on Margaret's desk. When he spoke, it was in a thick Spanish accent, with *"mi amiga"* thrown in like a grace note nearly every sentence.

"How are you, *mi amiga*?" he bowed slightly.

"My life is a thing of beauty, Manuel." A hint of Louisiana in her suddenly deeper voice. "It's so beautiful, words can't describe it, so I'll just have to leave you to guess."

"But, *mi amiga*, I do not have to guess. Your beauty can be seen." He was smiling broadly.

"Yeah, Manuel. So much beauty, I should have myself bronzed and put in a museum."

He was fooling with the letters now—tapping them, getting them exactly even, putting them down and starting all over again. Margaret was staring at a poster behind Manuel. An Arbus photo of a little group of Mongoloids shot against a gray sky, some watching the camera, some staring insensibly at the ground.

The phone rang. Margaret answered in a singsong voice dripping with cheerfulness. Manuel sat on the edge of the desk; he picked up her letter opener and began scraping his nails. Margaret took it away from him while she was talking, then flapped her fingers in a bye-bye wave.

But as the phone call ended, Manuel remained on the desk, index fingers steepled under his chin.

"Can I help you with something, Manuel? Or are you just gonna sit here and be a paperweight?"

"I'm resting, *mi amiga*. And thinking."

"About what?"

"About you." Big, molten smile. "About whether you have that short skirt on. I can't see under the desk."

"Yes."

"You have that one on? *Si?*"

"Yes."

"And beneath it? Do you have *pantaloncillos*? Some nice ones that . . . " He inscribed a high arch shape with his fingers, ". . . go up on the side?"

"No."

"You don't have *pantaloncillos?*" He sat up slightly.

"I have them. They just don't go up on the side."

"What color are they, *por favor?*"

"Blue."

"Light blue or *obscuro?* Light or dark, *mi amiga?*"

"Light blue."

"But what exact shade? The shade must be a *certeza.*"

"Light blue, Manuel. Just regular light blue."

"*Mi amiga*, perhaps I will have to look. I can't tell the shade from what you say. I really can't."

"Look at this." She gave him the finger. Smiled. "We had one little moment, Manuel. *Un momento poco.* It was over when it began. Thanks for the mail."

He stood up. "They are light blue? *Color de tristeza?* Of sadness? I would like to have seen them." He began to turn for the door.

"Sorry to make you sad, Manuel." She spread her hands.

"No, it is you who are sad, *mi amiga.*"

That afternoon, Margaret took out a red leather journal and wrote the following:

Dear Sister:

I am so tired of it. Of the thing that comes over me. Of putting on this mask that is so tight, so convincing that it seems to be my own face.

But you know my face. This thing was never me. Never me. I am hunger and fear, now. And disgust. How did this happen?

And Walker—what is he planning? I must get rid of him. In the usual way. But I can't seem to do it. Maybe he'll stop calling.

I need to feel you near. Send me another dream. Please, it's lonely. And all my resolutions seem to evaporate. They are born and lost all in the same day. And then I must start over again on the next.

Do you hear me? If you can, tell me something.

Love,
Corine

13

They were on a pedal boat, threshing their way around Stow Lake. Margaret had a loaf of white bread and was throwing crumbs to the ducks. Stow Lake in winter was gray, with ragged, leaning trees along the banks. Patchy lawns sloped to the water. On Strawberry Island, in the middle of the lake, the pump had given out on the man-made waterfall.

Walker had started telling Margaret about a think piece he'd just finished. The title was taken from Nietzsche—"Die at the Right Time."

"What is it, an argument for suicide?" Margaret had stopped pedaling and was stretching her arm full-length, getting a few brave ducks to eat out of her hand.

"No, it's an argument for living. Every day. So when you die, it's always the right time. You haven't put things off. Death doesn't catch you thinking, 'If I'd only done this or that.' You are already living the way you're supposed to."

"Very interesting." Margaret didn't sound very interested. She pulled another slice of bread out of the loaf. "So where do you get the courage, or whatever, for this living right thing? Do people read your article and go, 'Shit, I've been living wrong all my life. Starting right now, I'm gonna do what I'm supposed to.'"

"I think you live differently if you're aware that any moment you can die."

Margaret groaned.

"You obviously don't agree."

"Walker, this is just Sunday sermon shit dressed in a different frock. You know what I mean? If people had the strength or will or whatever to live differently, they would. It's as simple as that."

"Maybe, but I read all these stories—the ones people send me since I wrote that article. The *Sunrise* thing I told you about. A lot of the stories are about how people changed course in life. They started living differently, and then ... "

"Then they died."

"Yes, but they died at the right time."

She threw a piece of bread at him. "You're so fucking earnest."

"I can handle your being a cynic if you can handle the earnest stuff."

She stopped paddling and looked at him closely. "I don't know if I can handle it. Really. And I don't think you can handle my shit either."

An hour later they were at the beach. Which I thought was a bad idea because the fog was rolling across the sand. You couldn't even see the breakers. It looked so cold that for the first time I saw some advantage to being dead.

Anyway, I'm telling you this part because Walker was really pumping Margaret about her fascination with the Schloss family. He wondered why, if Margaret had learned so little about the sisters in the photograph, they continued to be important to her.

"I don't know. It's just something that happened. Like a lot of things there's no explanation for. Why did I love ballet? Why are you losing your hair in front? Things happen."

"Come on, Margaret. You know more than you're saying about this."

"That's right, I do." She pulled up her collar and began vigorously rubbing her fingers together. "I feel like fucking Admiral Byrd out here."

They were walking north, toward the Cliff House, which had been erased by the relentless fog.

"Want to hold hands?" He reached toward her.

"No." But a moment later she took his hand anyway.

"Look, you know, it's just some weird thing. I felt something about that girl because she seemed so familiar. I felt like—in that life—she'd been connected to me."

"You think you were the second girl—her sister?"

Margaret stopped for a moment and watched the fog advancing on them.

"Yes." A small shrug. "I could feel . . . that she had protected me. In the photograph, her arm is around her sister. The younger girl is leaning a little against her. So I knew . . . "

"I'd like to see that photograph."

Margaret didn't say anything, but she dropped his hand. "Don't write about this, OK? I couldn't have this exposed."

"I promise." He was guiding her to some steps in the tide wall. "Do you feel like she's still watching out for you?"

"Yes. I've had dreams about her. They're like messages."

They were walking now on the edge of the Great Highway, up the slope that bends around the craggy outcrop of Sutro Park.

"Where is she now—in heaven? In another life?"

"I don't know."

"What does she tell you? In the dreams."

"That I have to change." A bitter little laugh. "That's why I know your *live right, die right* stuff is crap. I try to change; I can't. I'm like a fucking marionette, a body pulled by strings."

She put two fingers above the bridge of her nose and held them there. Then she walked to the edge of the pavement and leaned against a parked car.

"What's the point of this, Walker? I keep asking you that 'cause it feels like we're in that rye field. You know? The one with the cliff? But nobody's gonna catch us before we fall off."

"I'll catch you."

"I'd fall right through your arms, and break you while I did it. Don't you get it?"

She looked away from him, at the taillights disappearing into the fog.

"Maybe I can't catch you. Maybe you're right." He folded his arms, began a slight twisting motion with his body. "But it's the only way I know."

"Way to what?"

"To be with someone."

"Aw, that's sad shit."

Silence. The twisting was getting worse. Walker looked like he was in some kind of exercise class.

"Look, you asked, I answered. Stop slapping me around. I see something in you. Under the ridicule. Under the anger." He fell silent.

"What?"

"I see where you were cut. Where the pain is." Walker stretched out his hands in a delicate gesture of uncertainty. "And you let me see it because . . . I think you chose me. For reasons you don't know. Or won't admit. You chose me to help you."

"Walker, Walker." She shook her head. "You can't help me. You're lost in your savior script. Let it go."

She wanted to go home then, and he took her.

"Will we see each other again?" Walker asked as he dropped her off.

"Not if we're wise."

Walker handed her his card. "Call me."

14

Dear Mr. Anderson:

The magazine where you published *Sunrise Effect* was kind enough to give me your address. I was struck by the

article. I wanted you to know that the effect isn't just
confined to scientists, entrepreneurs, and the like. I think
it may apply even to people of lowly circumstances, who
would be considered failures by most standards.

I am the only daughter of a great ruin of a man. My
father was a former aircraft salesman who drank himself
out of a job and a family. For the past seven years he lived at
the Sunnyside Hotel, in a tiny, one-room roach trap. Every
hour he was awake was an hour he was in the bottle.

In all the years he lived at the Sunnyside I never saw
him. But that changed eleven months ago. He didn't stop
drinking; he said that wasn't an option. But what he did—
twice a week—was not drink in the morning. He'd dress up
and take the bus out to the school where I teach, and we'd
have lunch.

The first occasion I saw him—after all that time—was a
moment I'd waited for, but given up hope of having. When
he embraced me, his coat smelled of mothballs, and his
arms were thin. But I had my father again. We talked about
everything. My childhood, my goals, the man I loved but
was afraid to marry.

Over the next ten months, he comforted me, he told
me I was beautiful, he encouraged me to be creative in
my teaching, he made little things for me, he gave me his
favorite books, he advised me. He was always—for those
few hours—sober. Always loving.

He helped me, I think, to trust, to believe I was worth
something. I felt that I was healing. The fact that he came
faithfully, prepared to listen, believing in me—it is the
greatest single gift I've been given.

Next week I'm getting married. My father won't be
there. He was killed a month ago in a mugging. I believe
he's one of those people you were talking about.

The letter was xeroxed. Margaret refolded it and put it back
in the envelope. Now she picked up a smaller sheet with a note
written in neat script.

I thought you might be interested in the kind of letters I
get—about the sunrise thing. There are dozens telling the
same story—a late arriving redemption followed (usually)
by a sudden death. I realize now they're not just scientists,
or people with big ambitions, but many were very ordinary.
Some were very broken.

Anyway, you seemed doubtful about the whole thing. So
I wanted you to see an example of the letters. Remember,
you have my number.

Margaret shook her head and dropped the note to her coffee
table. Then she took off her pants and went to bed. It was 3:00
in the afternoon.

15

While Margaret slept, she had a dream. I could see her eyes
moving beneath the lids. I had recently learned to sense what
she was dreaming—through the simple technique of putting
myself inside her. The pictures often seemed vague or partially
formed, the sounds like something spoken under water. But I
was getting better at it.

In this dream I had the impression of a woman, lying down.
Perhaps wearing an apron. And angling away from her the body
of a man. A girl, I think, with long black hair was bending,
reaching toward the woman's face.

It was then I realized the woman's eyes were fixed and vacant.
I could feel Margaret's shock. The girl was placing something
on the eyes. White. Petals or flowers.

The dream went on—now down narrow streets with dark
windows. Margaret's heart was thundering in her chest. I tried,
with all my will, to change the scene. To give her comfort by
adding light or voices. The dream went on impervious to my
interventions.

When Margaret awoke ten minutes later, she was flushed. She pulled off her shirt, sweat glistening beneath her breasts. Then she wiped her cheeks as if she felt tears. But there were none.

That night, after dinner at the Tennessee Grill, Margaret wrote a letter in her leather journal.

Dear Sister:

Why did you show that to me again? You know I have seen it. Was it to remind me of your kindness, how you lay roses on the eyes of the dead?

I know your kindness. I felt it every day. I want to be like you. Believe me. But I am too afraid.

Why must I live in this lonely place? For a while I can stand it; then I do things that are wrong.

I got a letter from Walker. He wants to show himself, be with me in the white room. If he were there, if he could see me, he would run.

I keep thinking every night—I won't get dressed, I won't go out. Sometimes I manage to stay. But the next night I give in, I slip out the door. Excited and despising myself.

Please—come to me, or let me go to you.

Love,
Corine

16

Margaret had done it this time. She met the guy in a little fern bar on Clement Street. The man had an electric blue tie that he kept patting and smoothing like it needed affection. When he wasn't working on the tie, he was squeezing the creases of his slacks or brushing invisible dust from a blazer. His face was narrow and horsy, with a thin nose and sallow, concave cheeks. The man was tall and carried himself with a fake aristocratic air.

They talked about the usual—freaks and circuses.

"If you were going to be born a freak—it was like ordained—what kind of freak would you be?" Margaret gave him her frozen smile.

"I don't know." He was cleaning something on his glass with a napkin. "A kind that wouldn't be obvious."

"But if it was . . . obvious."

He thought a while. "Oh, something that would make money then. If you're going to be a freak, might as well be a rich one."

They went to his place—a condo in Pacific Heights.

"Like it?" he said, as he adjusted the mood lighting with a dimmer.

The place had glass shelves along one wall—all full of figurines from *The Wizard of Oz*, *Cinderella*, and other classics.

"These yours?" Margaret asked, swaying along and looking at the shelves.

He didn't answer.

Margaret stopped by a big vase with phony, magenta-colored sunflowers. "You a sunflower kind of guy?"

"I like to do it in the rear," the man said, getting into an orgy of tie patting.

Margaret turned to look at him. "I think you like it in *your* rear. Sorry, Sweetie, don't have the equipment."

"I do not. I have everything set up in the bathroom so you can get . . . clean."

"Sweetie." It was the southern accent. "Ah don't do that kind of thing. If you want me, you'll have to get it up for the regular place." She peeked into a room that looked like an office. "What's this?"

There were bath towels spread out over the carpet.

"It's for us. It protects the rug."

"What's wrong with the bed?"

Silence.

"Come on, let's take a look at the bed."

The guy didn't move.

"You some kind of clean freak? I got news for you, the poop hole ain't all that clean." Margaret's voice was getting deeper, slightly ragged.

The guy walked slowly over to Margaret and lifted her skirt. He ran the back of his fingers along her underpants.

"OK, you've seen mine, let's see your bed," voice deep and harsh.

"No." The guy pulled out the waistband of her panties and looked in.

"When'd your wife leave? This morning? Time to look for some action, someone for the poop hole thing she won't do?"

Margaret touched the guy's crotch, exploring for a second. "You won't get anywhere with that. I don't think you're even gonna make it through the door. You know what I mean?"

"Get undressed."

Margaret looked at him for a moment. "I think not. I don't fuck on towels, I don't fuck up the rear. And I don't fuck little dicks who make some kind of deal with themselves that anything's OK, long as it's not in the wife's bed."

He slapped her. So hard she went down. Sprawling, then pulling her legs up tight. The guy started taking off his tie.

"Please don't." High, little girl voice.

"You can get undressed here or the bathroom. Everything's set up for you there."

He unbuttoned his shirt, then pulled off his tee. The man had thick, sand-colored hair on his chest. He spent a moment patting it.

Margaret spoke in her tiny voice. "I'm going to tell if you hurt me. I'm going to tell your wife."

"You can call me Bill," the man said.

Silence.

"Say, 'Yes, Bill.'" He gave her a soft kick in the stomach.

"Yes, Bill."

"You know why you won't tell anybody? . . . Say, 'Why, Bill?'"

"Why, Bill?"

"Because then you'd be . . . you know." He picked Margaret's purse off the floor and fished around in it till he found her ID. "Now I know where you live—understand me?"

He kicked her again. "What do you say?"

"I understand."

"Good. Now get into the bathroom and clean yourself out. Come out with everything off."

Margaret got up cautiously and began edging away from Bill toward the bathroom. Bill moved to keep himself between Margaret and the front door.

In the bathroom, Margaret locked the door. The room was decorated with pink, frilly curtains and matching hand towels. A plump enema bag hung over the toilet. Margaret lay down—fetal position—on an oval rug. It was edged with a magnolia pattern. With one finger she traced the petals, repeating "Please" in a high, soft voice.

Bill knocked on the door. "You should be done now; time to come out."

"No."

"Come out now. Otherwise I'll break the door and get you. And I won't be nice as I was before."

"You won't break shit." Margaret's voice had switched to low and angry. "How you gonna explain a smashed up door to your wife? You're not breaking in and I'm not coming out."

It was a standoff. For more than an hour. She was insisting the police be called to escort her out. He wanted her to believe he'd let her go if she opened up. Finally, Margaret offered a compromise. "You can call my friend. He'll come and get me. I'll be safe and you won't have to deal with the police." She described how to find Walker's card in her purse.

When Walker showed up, he was wearing his usual corduroy jacket. But his hands kept pumping into fists, and he looked uneasy. Bill answered the door with an urbane, "Good evening. Mr. Anderson, I presume."

He had the electric tie on again. It fell forward as he bowed and ushered Walker into the living room.

"Your friend is—how should we say—unstable. It was just an ordinary evening between consenting adults, but she grew . . . frightened. Started talking in strange voices. She locked herself in there." A slight waving gesture toward the bathroom.

Margaret, who had heard Walker's voice, emerged from the john at that moment. To my surprise, she rushed at Walker and hugged him.

17

As Margaret and Walker made their way down a geranium-bordered path to the street, I felt oppressed by what I'd seen. The events seemed less important than what they concealed. Margaret's headlong run to escape her emptiness was part of it. But then there was Bill's self-hate, congealed behind his sadism.

Most disturbing was the way Bill reminded me of myself. I remember when I was 19, meeting a girl at a punk show—Neurosis, I think—and taking her home. And the whole night acting like I didn't care, ridiculing her mall-bought clothes. The poser tears she made in her jeans. Her trite, punk vernacular.

All the while, of course, I was consumed with a picture of myself as awkward, stupid. When we had sex, I thrust into her like she was a discardable doll. And I didn't look at her because she was a dangerous object. In her eyes I might see mirrored my true self.

When Margaret climbed in the Porsche, she slumped back and closed her eyes.

"Thank you," she said in the small voice.

She'd been crying. Now she rubbed her face with both hands, smearing the tears across her high cheeks.

Walker wanted to know what happened.

"He was mean . . . he wanted to hurt me. I don't know why." Margaret pressed herself deeper in the bucket seat.

"What did he try to do?"

"Things." The word lilted up at the end, suggesting it was a mystery that couldn't be explained.

Walker glanced to his right, studying Margaret's profile. She was crying harder now.

"It's OK." He touched her hand. Which was resting palm up on her thigh.

"No." Her face contorted. She was letting the tears flow. Across her jaw and down her neck. "No," she repeated. "It isn't . . . not in a long time."

"Why?"

"I don't know." Her voice was returning to normal. "Because I'm fucked up. Because that guy is fucked up. Whatever."

Margaret said nothing for the rest of the ride home.

"You gonna be all right tonight?" Walker asked as he parked on Santiago, just above the peeling facade of the apartment.

Margaret shrugged.

"You want me to come in?"

"For what?"

"Just to help you—I don't know—feel safe."

She thought about that. Margaret was turning her hand over, front to back, slightly slapping her thigh.

"OK. I'll make you tea. Do you like tea?" She looked suddenly anxious.

"Sure. Tea would be lovely."

He followed her down 21st to the steps of the apartment. Inside her place, Margaret snapped on the lights and quickly put the kettle on.

"I never have men here. I always go where they live."

"I'm honored."

"It's not every day somebody rescues me." She gave a mirth-less laugh.

Walker sat on an overstuffed chair in the living room. Salmon-colored light from the floor lamp washed against the rows of bookshelves. Now he rose and ran his fingers along the titles, as if reading Braille.

"Lots of histories, biographies." He called to her in the kitchen.

"Yeah, I told you. I go for that. I read it all the time."

Margaret brought the tea in. Two steaming mugs with a sampling of tea bags crumpled in one hand.

"Choose your poison." She threw the bags down on the cof-fee table.

"How are you feeling now—that you're home and settling in?"

She sipped her tea and let the steam rise into her face. After a silence, she stared across the rim of the cup at Walker.

"I feel like I always do. A little worse, maybe." She shrugged. "I do things . . . to try to feel better. And then they sicken me."

"Like tonight?"

She nodded. Tears began to glisten in her eyes, but she rubbed them away before they fell.

"Every night I sit there." She pointed to Walker's chair. "I pick something to read. Maybe later I go down to the Grill. Then I come home. Maybe I listen to music." She looked at the floor and fell quiet.

"What happens then?"

"I don't know. It's like the room fills up with water." Marga-ret's face tightened, her lips opening in a rictus. Teeth bare. "I can't do this anymore."

She put the tea down and bent, pushing her face into her arms.

"Can I hold your hand?"

"No."

Ten minutes. She cried soundlessly, shoulders convulsing. When she lifted up, the lines framing her mouth cut deep.

"I'm afraid I'll drown in it—every night. I run out of things . . . to do. Sometimes I dance, I exhaust myself. And I manage to stay home. But a lot of times the room fills up and I can't breathe."

Silence. She was trying unsuccessfully to curl her legs up in the chair.

"So I go out."

"Like tonight?"

Margaret nodded. She started to reach for the tea again but fell back in the chair. Now she was running her fingers along her trachea. Pressing hard into the flesh.

"What about friends? Do they help?"

"No."

"Why?"

"I don't have friends." Her hand dropped to her lap. "I frighten people. After a while they can't wait to get away. So I keep it like . . . tonight. I meet a guy. Just to feel something besides . . . "

"I know."

The tears were back. She was making small, strangling sounds.

"Can I hold your hand now?" Walker reached toward her.

Margaret shrugged, let him take her hand. They sat for a while like that. Then Margaret stood up.

"I'm tired. If you want me, you can have me." She pulled the zipper on her skirt and let it drop. Then walked into the bathroom. With a slight echo from the tiles, she continued talking, slipping now into her southern accent.

"Ah don't know why you keep coming around. But after tonight Ah owe you something."

She emerged wearing just her underpants.

"No, you don't." Walker's lips were pursed in alarm. "You don't have to . . . "

"Ah'm ready." She leaned on the back of her chair, swaying slightly. "So it's up to you."

"Isn't this what you're talking about? Isn't this exactly the same thing?"

She took his hand. "C'mon, sweetie. You know what you want. Let's get it over with, OK?"

"Because what happens then?"

She pulled Walker up. "'Cause then it's over. Where do you want to put your hand, sweetie? Up here, or down here?"

She kissed him. "Ah'll help you." She put Walker's hand on her breast. "See how that works—it's easy."

She kissed him again. "Please have a good time because you-all been very nice to me."

"Look," he was whispering, "I don't want this to be another thing that hurts you."

"Shhhh. I know."

She led him into the bedroom, quickly transferring the giant clown from bed to chair. Margaret efficiently unbuttoned Walker's shirt, then raised his arms so she could pull his tee off. She bent to untie his shoes and finally unbuckled his pants, letting them fall.

Light from a street lamp cast slanting frost-colored lines across the floor. Voices raised in an argument drifted up from downstairs.

Margaret touched Walker between the legs. She kissed him again. Sweetly.

"Ah would appreciate if you'd take my panties off 'cause a girl shouldn't do all the work." Margaret let fly a coquettish giggle.

Walker bent to pull them down. A moment later, Margaret took his hand and drew him into the bed.

"You're very beautiful," Walker said softly.

"Ah know, sweetie. And it's for you. Let me have your hand . . . what do you want to touch? I'll take you there."

The seduction continued. But when Walker got on top to

mount Margaret, a strange thing happened. That harsh, angry voice I'd heard before erupted.

"Do her, fucker. Do her. Just fuck. That's what you're for. That's what you're here for. Do her. Get it over with. Come on, fucker. Put it in and get it over with. Just cum in her, that's what you're here for."

Walker stopped moving.

"C'mon, c'mon. Do her." The raspy chant continued.

Walker pulled off and rolled to his side.

"What's the matter with you?"

The chanting ceased. Margaret's eyes, for a while reduced to narrow slits, opened.

"Please." In the high, little girl voice. "Please, I'm sorry. I'll be nice. I don't know why he says those things."

"Who says those things?" Walker was rubbing his forehead like he was doing a spit shine.

"I don't know. Please don't leave. Everybody leaves." Margaret rose up to whisper in Walker's ear. "I'll tell you a secret. She can't stand it."

"What?"

"That they leave."

Walker examined Margaret's face. Her lips were pulled into a pale little smile. For a long time nothing happened.

"I'll stay with you," he finally said.

"That would be good." Almost inaudible.

"Who are you; who am I talking to?"

"I don't know, but I have to sleep now. Would you hold me? Not my breasts, I don't like that."

Walker didn't move.

"Around my tummy, OK? And be like spoons."

Now he reached around Margaret's stomach.

"That's good. She says if you wake up and want to—you know, just do it. Just open her legs. Not now, though. I don't like it."

They went to sleep like that.

18

In the night I hovered above them, watching them breathe. Waiting for the moment when their breaths would start together, then listening as they fell out of phase. And finally synchronous again, the pattern repeating endlessly.

I felt displaced, stinging from a new and deeper cut of my familiar loneliness. Every night since my death I had put myself next to Margaret in the bed, wanting her for myself, though I had nothing to give.

Now the world was empty. At intervals a streetcar rumbled distantly on Taraval. And from the next apartment, the tinny voices from a late-night broadcast scratched the silence. It occurred to me that someone more generous would be happy for Margaret, would welcome this chance for her to be loved. But I was my usual self. Full of hunger.

At the first touch of dawn, I drifted outside. A pink corona lay above Mt. Davidson, and a thin light made its way westward—street by street—until I could finally see the trees swaying over McCoppin Square.

Now I wanted to feel the cold. Because all I could do was look through Margaret's windows—at the shadowy chairs and books, at the pale glint of the mirror. At the sleeping bodies in her bed.

In the morning, Walker woke up to a muted thudding sound. Coming from the bathroom. In the doorway, he watched while Margaret extended her fists as far from her body as she could reach, then punched hard into her chest. There was a hollow sound as her fists struck the sternum.

Margaret didn't see Walker as he came at her from the doorway. In a moment he grabbed her wrists, wrapping his arms around her, and was holding her securely from the back.

Walker looked at her in the mirror. "Never, never do that again. Do you understand?"

"Why?" It was a voice I'd heard only once or twice. Melodious, calm.

"Because I won't let you." He tightened his grip on her wrists. "You're never to hurt yourself like this. Margaret, promise me. Tell me you won't do this again."

She relaxed into him, letting him hold her. After a moment, her head dropped.

"OK." Spoken in her usual voice. "But what will I do . . . if I need this?"

"I don't know." He turned her and guided her back to the bedroom. "Good thing it's Saturday. We can spend the whole day figuring it out."

19

Walker treated Margaret to breakfast at the Tennessee Grill. They were sitting under a framed photograph of Bryce Canyon. A patina of grease coated the glass. The coffee arrived, and they sipped for a while in silence.

"So now what?" Margaret was absently scratching the back of her hand and looking away from the table.

"How 'bout you tell me what happened last night."

"What part?"

"Us."

"I just . . . say things. When I fuck."

"Sorry, Margaret, that won't work. It's more than that."

"It's just moods I get into."

"Bullshit. I felt like I was with different people. Some weird belle who's all about sex, some scared little girl, this angry . . . person. Talking shit at me." Now Walker was looking away, too. Their eyes roamed around the Grill. "It scared me."

"I know. That's what happens."

"Why the voices? What are you doing?"

"I just feel like talking like that."

"OK, fine. What if you don't feel like it?"

"I always feel like it."

"So you're saying . . ." He turned back to look at her.

". . . that you can't control it."

Margaret shrugged.

"OK, look. The little girl voice—whatever it is—is referring to other people. You said, 'I don't know why *he* says those things.' And '*She* can't stand it.' Who are those . . . people?"

The food came, and Margaret started to eat in silence. She was cutting her sausage very slowly, delicately.

"'If you want to do it, just open *her* legs.' That's what you said. What *is* that, Margaret?"

"It's me."

"Does it happen every time you have sex?"

Margaret put down the fork and worked on her lips for a while with a napkin. Then she folded her hands on the edge of the table.

"Yes, usually. And other times, too. I don't know . . . it's just me. But—I told you—people don't like it. So I . . ." She picked up her fork and began shoving the pieces of sausage back together. ". . . so I don't see them again."

Walker looked for inspiration toward the grease-mottled Bryce Canyon.

"Now what?" Her voice was suddenly low and hard. "After you found all this out, now what? You want to hear that shit when you're fucking?"

"No."

Margaret's eyes closed. "So there it is."

Walker leaned toward her. "Open your eyes. Look at me. I said I didn't *want* to hear it. But I didn't say I wouldn't be *willing* to hear it. You understand me? There's a difference."

Back at the apartment, Walker asked Margaret if she was serious about her promise not to hit herself.

"No."

"Why?"

"Because you won't be here after today."

Margaret was sitting in a high-backed chair with upholstered arms that scrolled out delicately. Walker stood looking at her books.

"You don't know me." His voice was angry. "You don't know what I'm going to do. I'll tell you something: if I care about somebody, I don't leave them."

"Good for you. You get the higher station in heaven." Margaret had her legs crossed and was rhythmically kicking with the free one.

"Why are you making it a fucking joke? I'm trying to tell you something."

"It *is* a joke. You rescued me from some pervy asshole and tried to have sex. We've had a total of three meals together. If you think that adds up to a life commitment, you're more fucked up than I am."

"It adds up to *something* for me. No matter what happens, I still want to see you."

"Get smart, Walker. This is all really about wanting to get laid. But that didn't work, remember?"

Walker dropped into a chair and turned to look out the window—at the white siding of the flat across the yard.

"My mother was depressed. Lie-in-bed, look-at-the-ceiling depressed. While she was in the hospital one time . . . my father left." Walker was now looking at his hands, tracing the outer edge of one fingernail.

"I stayed with her. I drove her to the shrinks, I doled out the pills when she didn't want to take them. It was a see-saw—better, worse, better, worse." He looked up at Margaret.

"What happened to your mom?"

"She got tired of it."

Margaret nodded and they sat quietly for a while. Eventually, she rose and opened a window.

"You can smell the garbage cans up here. But . . . you still need air."

Then she came back to him and sat on the arm of his chair.

"You've put in your time. You can leave now. It's OK."

Walker reached for Margaret's waist and pulled her till she fell sideways into his lap. Then he kissed her.

"I want to try again. Do whatever you do; say whatever you say. I would like to make love and . . . let that be what it is." He kissed her again, running his hand up under her shirt to caress her stomach.

"That feel OK?"

"Yes."

"How 'bout this?"

He gently held her breast. Margaret took a shuddering breath.

Walker wrapped his arm around Margaret's back, lifting her slightly. He took his time kissing her cheeks and neck, and finally her lips again.

"Ah think it's time to get undressed." The belle was back.

When they were in bed and his fingers for the first time pressed between Margaret's legs, the breathy voice announced, "I don't like that, it's not a good place. I think we should wait a while."

Walker took his hand away and rolled Margaret so he could caress her buttocks.

"I'm going to sleep now," the little voice said.

Margaret's eyes closed, and then she began to speak again. "Ah hope so. We're doin' something here that children shouldn't be stayin' up for."

When Walker's body was between Margaret's legs, and he

was preparing to enter her, he heard again the angry voice. "Do her, just fuck, get it over with."

"Margaret," he said, "are you scared?"

The chant continued.

"Margaret, look at me. Do you want me inside you?" He waited until there was silence. Finally, Margaret nodded. As Walker made his first thrust, the voice returned to its harangue.

He kissed Margaret and put his lips near her ear. "It's good, it's good. Let go. Let it take you. Feel how good it is when our skin touches. Feel where I am inside you."

The two colliding voices rose to a cacophony. Then Walker fell silent, his face tight and disturbed. The movement of his body slowed. Finally, with what seemed like an effort, he lifted up to hold Margaret's eyes.

"Say whatever you need to say. But just look at me. Just look. It's OK. Say anything, but just look at me."

Margaret kept her eyes on Walker.

When they were finished, he rolled on his back and pulled her body on top of him. The little girl voice said, "That's done. Let's go somewhere."

"Like where?" Walker asked.

"The beach," she said breathlessly. "I think the beach would be nice."

20

As Walker and Margaret lay together, I felt a surging emptiness. Like the whispering of mourners that shreds to a high, discordant keening. I could feel that Margaret had been touched, had begun to open to him. And this momentary unction, this easing of her pain, now seemed to make my aloneness worse.

But I had nowhere to go. I was the audience for this play,

destined perhaps never to leave the theater. Forced to watch, as I had done in life, the story unfold without the slightest chance that mine would be woven into it. For the first time since the day of my death, I found myself wanting to shout, to pound my ephemeral fists against the solidness of wood. Or flesh.

I raged. I whirled through Margaret's rooms, demanding that God release me. Margaret continued to lie on Walker's chest, legs straddling, buttocks open. I could see the bud of her anus, the storm of dark hair around her vulva. The most private place. Where lovers join—and know each other.

I left, flinging myself through the walls and into the street. And then beneath the pavement, to the dark, compressed earth. Full of bricks and broken granite. Inert and silent. Then back to the light, sweeping to the little concrete yard, the garbage cans, entering the rot, bathing in the juice, the bones, the shards of glass. And feeling none of it.

When I returned to Margaret's rooms, her position was unchanged, but she was sleeping. Her body lay heavy, trusting. Walker studied the ceiling—staying still, letting her sleep. As I watched, her eyes began to slide beneath the lids. A dream was starting.

I drew close, suddenly very focused. The moment of the dream was my one great chance—to experience Margaret in a way even Walker could not. To feel the gossamer images of her unconscious. To drift among them. And perhaps—in time—to learn to change what scared and saddened her. A kind of love. A kind of protection.

I entered Margaret's body, aware of the sudden density. The images cascaded—men and women standing, swaying, Margaret crushed between them. Bands of light and dark, the smell of feces, the dreamer urinating down her legs.

She was frightened—I could feel her staccato breath. Now I heard the click-clack of the rails, the sound of coughing. Through open slats, I saw the shadow of coal smoke.

Margaret turned to look outside. She longed for something. She had an image—from some other time. A storm, I think.

I knew then what she wanted, and tried to fuse the images: clean, wind-blown air—now coming through the open slats of the cattle car. The dreamer took a deep breath. I could feel her muscles relax. And I knew I had done something important— for the first time I'd touched Margaret in her sleep. Given her something.

The next night, Margaret danced on half point for Walker. In T-shirt and underpants. And her ballet slippers. The music box tinkled "Waltz of the Flowers" while she did *pliés* and turns. At the end she bowed formally, prima ballerina style, touching Walker's foot with the extended fingers of one hand. Her eyes briefly closed.

"Did you like it?" she asked while Walker clapped. "Because Ah haven't danced in front of anyone in years. Ah hardly know what Ah'm doin' anymore."

"You were lovely. I've never seen anyone with such grace."

"Ah remember when mah mama used to pick me up at lessons. When Ah was little. She'd watch me at the bar and say Ah was born for it, that Ah moved like a willow in the wind."

Margaret sat cross-legged on the hardwood floor and leaned back on her hands. "When she moved to the valley and couldn't come anymore, Ah missed those little things she'd say."

"Who'd you live with if your mother was gone? Your father?"

"Oh, mah father was a back-door man, a man who made the rounds. Ah saw him once in a car—waitin' on a stop light. Mah mama's face got all dark and stormy, and she pointed, said who it was. He didn't look right or left, just hit the gas when the signal changed. That's the only time Ah laid eyes on him."

She was closing and opening her crossed legs like butterfly wings. "When she left, Ah lived with my teacher. He told

Mama Ah had promise, and no one was gonna teach me shit about ballet in Merced. So she gave me over to him."

"Was that good, living with him?"

"He was the big man. He tried to make me . . . into somethin'."

Margaret lay all the way back on the floor. Her legs were still working up and down, but more slowly. "Ah don't care about that. Not now. Ah'm just—right now—Ah'm just wondering . . . "

"What?"

"If you're gonna stay starin' at my underwayer, or if you are gonna take them off."

The invitation, as it turned out, was a mistake for Walker to accept. As soon as he knelt to join her on the hardwood, Margaret closed her eyes and the belle voice disappeared. Instead, she began chuckling, looking away from him.

"Come on then." The guttural, deep voice. "Do it. Put it in. That's what you're here for."

Walker had just pulled down his pants.

"Do it. Then you can leave. You're a big nothing. You're here to do it and leave. She doesn't like your thing. She thinks you take too long to get a hard-on."

"Margaret, look at me."

"No. You're here to do it. On the floor. Scraping your knobby knees. Put it in. When you're done, take your phony nice guy for a walk."

"Margaret, should I stop? Look at me. Tell me what you need."

"Get in or get off."

"Look at me."

"No." She had her head turned toward the window.

Walker pushed up to sit on his haunches. Then he slid backward on his knees until he was looking down the length of Margaret.

"She thinks you smell moldy. She thinks you can't do it."

Walker gently gripped Margaret's ankles, pulling her legs together. Then he reached for her underpants, placing each foot through the leg openings. She lay like a rag doll. He was forced to lift her as he drew the underpants over her thighs and buttocks.

"That wasn't very nice, was it?" The little girl. "Do you still like her?"

"I'm getting beat up here." Walker was pulling his own clothes on now. "Why wouldn't you look at me?"

"He gets scared when he looks at people. Then he can't talk."

"Who's *he*?"

"My pants are wet. I should change them."

"Who's *he*? C'mon, Margaret."

"I could draw him."

Thirty minutes later, on the Formica and stainless steel kitchen table, Margaret finished a pencil sketch. It was a crude rendering of what looked like an adolescent boy. Crew cut, huge biceps and chest. Some kind of tattoo on one arm. Yet for all the bulk in the upper body, the figure's legs were short and pipe-stemmed.

"Do you know this boy? Is he someone important to you?"

Margaret shrugged, said nothing. She was tearing strips off the bottom of the drawing and rolling them into little balls. Walker got up and opened the refrigerator. The shelves were empty except for salad components and some frozen raviolis in the freezer. Walker's mouth widened in distaste, and he shut the door.

"Are you leaving now?"

"No, I was just seeing if there was anything to eat."

"We could go to the Grill." The little voice sounded hopeful.

Walker shuddered. "I'll take you somewhere else. There's a good Italian place up on 18th."

During the meal, Margaret returned to her normal voice—

the usual digs and bantering. But she seemed nervous. Like some mounting pressure was threatening to break—psychologically—her stays and fastenings.

They talked briefly about Margaret's mother and her move to Merced. The woman had served as a legal assistant for a well-known law firm in San Francisco. In the course of working on a water rights suit, she'd met an orchard owner whose land was just beyond the Merced city limits. Margaret's mother had a brief, long-distance romance, then married the man on her thirtieth birthday. Margaret was nine.

"How did it feel to basically lose your mother at nine?" Walker cleared his throat, as if preparing for a longer speech.

Margaret hesitated. One hand touched her face, inscribing delicate circles below her cheek. Then she shot him a blistering smile.

"How did it feel to lose *your* mother?"

Walker laid his fork and knife parallel on the plate, pushing it away. When he spoke, his voice was thin.

"When I was a teenager, I read in a science magazine how some people suffer depression because they don't get enough sunlight. So I made my mother walk. Around and around the block, because she wouldn't go far. I remember one day, after about the fourth or fifth time we passed this bus stop bench, she wanted to sit down. The backrest had an advertisement for a funeral parlor. She kind of rubbed the sign, like she was cleaning it off. Then she said, 'This looks like a nice place, have them take me there when I go.'

"I was destroyed. My eyes started to burn. And I told her to forget it; I don't want to hear that shit. But she said she was sick of dragging herself around, and some day she wasn't gonna be able to. I got mad and told her to stop talking like that.

"So we sat quietly. Finally, she just pointed to the ad and said, 'I want to go there.' That's when I knew I would lose her. And that all the fish oil and vitamins, all the drugs and health food I made her take were destined to fail."

"She was basically done."

Walker rolled one hand over, palm up, studying the lines. Nodding. "So I . . . started to prepare. To practice . . . imagining her being gone. When we got home that day, I went to my room and pretended the house was empty. That I was alone there." Long silence. "I buried her . . . from that parlor."

He was taking a chance telling her all that. I could feel Walker's nervousness. And I knew if it had been me, that I would never have done it.

21

Margaret was reading another of Walker's *Sunrise Effect* letters—one she'd found in his car. She held it pinched between finger and thumb, as if the paper might be contaminated. Walker was standing by a bookshelf, leafing backward through *Roosevelt and Hopkins.*

"My mother was stubborn," Margaret read aloud from the letter. "She spent eleven years trying to prove my brother innocent of the crime of rape. She put her savings into lawyers, then P.I.s. When the money ran out, she interviewed witnesses herself. She hung out at the bar where the victim said my brother picked her up. I never liked the vic, but I thought she was telling the truth. Mainly because women are walking T&A to my brother.

"When DNA testing came out, my mother demanded it. But the police couldn't find the evidence. She went to the papers. Surprise—they found the sample, but the district attorney refused to run the test.

"My mother had to wait for the election to get political leverage. She went back to the papers. The D.A. backed down and ran the test; it wasn't a match. The vic finally admitted she'd passed out and didn't really know what happened."

Margaret read silently for a minute.

"Here it is." Triumphantly. "She hit a tree on the way home from the reunion. After her asshole son got out of jail. I love this shit."

"But these are real people. This stuff happened."

"Sure it happened. Those are the folks who write to you. Most of the time it doesn't—and you never hear from those people."

Walker dropped the book on the coffee table. With a loud bang.

"Is it time to go?" Margaret said, suddenly anxious.

"Why do you brush the thing aside—like it's stupid? I'm try- ing to write a book about this. It's important to me." His voice was petulant.

"I think the stories are nice"—the little girl. "Would you like me to draw Louisa May? She likes to wear short dresses."

"I don't think I'm in the mood for drawings."

"Oh." She sounded hurt. "People like her because she's pretty. She makes a lot of friends."

"Does she have an accent?" Walker suddenly leaned down, arms resting on either side of Margaret's chair.

"What?" Voice high, alarmed.

"A southern accent. Does she have one?"

"Yes." Margaret's eyes closed. "I'm going now. I liked dinner tonight. That was nice—where you took us."

"Do I know Louisa May? Have I met her?"

No answer. Margaret looked at Walker's hands.

"Have I met her?" He pulled Margaret's chin up. "If I ask to talk to Louisa May, would she start talking to me?"

Margaret swept Walker's arm out of the way and stood up. Her body collided with his as she shoved past him, heading toward the bathroom. When the door closed and the lock clicked, Walker put his hands in his pockets. Then he took a few tentative steps toward the window.

The first drops of a new rainstorm were beginning to run down the glass. Arrhythmic pulses of wind made the casements creak, and the drops, lit by a street lamp, start to shiver.

"Don't hurt yourself in there. Remember, you promised."

Silence.

"Margaret?"

"I can't do this." Muffled through the door.

"Come out here and stop fucking around. I'm not leaving, so you have to come out here and face me sooner or later."

"No."

"So who you gonna call for a rescue this time? The game's not working; you didn't get rid of me. What are you gonna do?"

"Ah'm gonna take a little bath." There was a click, probably the door being unlocked. "Ah'm taking mah clothes off and pretty soon Ah'm not going to have anything on . . . there, Ah'm testin' the water. Oh my, it's hot." She drew out the word "hot" like dialogue from a porno flick.

"Sometahms a girl likes company."

"Finish your bath. I'm not going in there for that. When you come out, leave Louisa May, or whoever the fuck the belle is, behind."

Margaret stayed in the tub for a good three hours. Now and then I could hear the water come on, presumably to warm things up. When she finally emerged, wrapped in a striped beach towel, Margaret minced over toward her closet.

"Don't look." Tiny voice. "OK?"

"I've got my eyes closed."

Margaret dressed in a tee and flower-patterned shorts.

"You can open your eyes now. These are daisies." She pointed to the shorts.

Walker was standing on the other side of the bed—idly lifting the clown, then letting it fall back on the coverlet.

"Are you still scared?" he asked.

"Yes. You're big."

"That's not why you're afraid. You've done everything you could to drive me away, and it didn't work. You wanted me gone before I got close enough to hurt you."

Silence.

"Are you going to say anything?"

"She wants to read now."

"Is that it? Is that the end of the discussion?" He flipped the clown up to the head of the bed, arms and legs akimbo. "Fine, take refuge in a book."

Margaret practically ran to the living room and picked up a hardcover volume. She was still into Churchill—but now it was *Triumph and Tragedy*.

Walker fell into a high-backed chair; watched the wind-driven rain slash at the window. Television from a neighboring apartment brought gunfire into the room. In the pale light, lines on his face deepened and blurred.

After a long time, Margaret pointed at Walker. "Churchill's a good writer. You should read him. I've got them all here—every book he wrote."

Walker's attention remained on the window. The rain, lighter and driven west now, streaked diagonally across the glass. Silence.

"You're not going to save me either," Margaret finally said in a matter-of-fact voice. "You're just repeating . . ." She made a slight shrug.

Walker turned toward her, oddly lifting his hand. As if warding off a blow.

"Repeating history? Maybe. I don't know."

"I know." Margaret rose suddenly and headed toward the bedroom, carrying Churchill with her.

Walker followed her. "A part of you wants me around, did you know that? The part that let me in here. To your sanctuary."

"I'm tired." Margaret dropped her shorts and crawled into bed.

"OK, this is your moment to get rid of me. Do you want me in the bed with you? No sex—just holding and sleeping. I have to hear it from you—yes or no."

Margaret had opened her book; her eyes moved across the page.

"Say it—yes or no. 'No,' and I'm out the door."

"OK . . . yes." Very softly, still reading.

Walker put the clown on the floor.

"That's not nice; sit him in the chair."

With the clown now leaning drunkenly in an armchair, Walker pulled back the coverlet and got in bed. Margaret rolled to her side, away from him.

"I still want to read . . . OK?"

"Can I hold you?"

A slight shrug.

"No. You need to say what you want. Out loud. Do you want me to hold you?"

She shrugged again. "Yes." Then Margaret inched backward until her body was against him. Walker arranged himself so one arm fell over her stomach, and the other circled under her neck and around her shoulders.

"I've got you now; you're safe."

"She thinks you don't know shit." The angry voice. "You can't keep her safe."

"It's OK, Margaret. You can let go. I've got your back."

"You don't know shit."

"Yeah, probably. Go ahead and talk. But you're in my arms; you can let go." He rubbed her stomach. "Just relax everything."

"You don't know."

"Right. I don't know. But I've got you. Nothing can happen to you in my arms."

"She thinks your arms are too hairy."

"That's fine. My arms are too hairy."

Margaret closed the book and let it drop on the bed.

"Ready to sleep?"

She took a deep breath. His hand rose and fell on her stomach.

"You're safe," Walker said in a whisper.

"No."

But a moment later Margaret's breathing had steadied, slowed. The shade on her lamp sent a faint pink light into the room. Again the wind shifted; rain drummed at the window.

It killed me how he took all her jabs. And just held her. Because I couldn't have. Yet I felt I'd watched something important, something I needed to remember.

22

Margaret sat reading in the living room, her night disturbed by a foul dream. It was two dreams, actually. The first was of a prison camp—rows of gray barracks fringed by a no-man's land and high barbed wire. Above it was a turquoise sky. Here and there along the fence, bodies hung in grotesque poses. A woman, her dress pulled high on the barbs, had died with one arm reaching through the wire.

Margaret was fascinated. No effort at diversion could stop her slow approach to the body. There was a wind that I turned into voices calling her. She didn't respond. I blurred the image of the guard tower to become a swirling dust funnel. Margaret kept moving toward the hanging woman.

The face was indistinct. I could sense Margaret trying to

focus, trying to see the features. Then, in an instant, the image became clear. She was young, eyes open and fixed. A track of dry blood descended from one nostril. Flies, circling in lazy, unnatural patterns landed on the eyes, the lips. I noticed how very white the teeth were.

The dream ended there. Margaret's heart thundered, and yet, oddly, I could sense relief. As if something worse had been feared. A recognition perhaps, I wasn't sure. After a minute or two, Margaret's breath slowed, her sleep deepened.

The second dream came at dawn. The same place. But now I could see four high stacks. The wind was blowing parallel flumes of smoke at an angle across the sky. Somewhere a baby was crying, and the sound disturbed Margaret. She turned in every direction, trying to locate the child. The crying got louder, and she began to move toward the stacks, searching. I could do nothing to help her with the sound—it was too compelling. Instead I got rid of the smoke, replacing it with the turquoise sky of the last dream.

Still Margaret searched. It was fear that roiled her now, and she began to run between the barracks. Suddenly the crying stopped, like a tape that had been shut off. Margaret stood still. A grief began to well, pressing outward against her ribs. She woke up.

In her chair beneath the floor lamp, Margaret read slowly, finger-brushing the words below each line. The storm was over, and a thin, porcelain light pressed halfway into the room. Margaret looked up; her lips pursed as if considering something.

"Walker?"

He mumbled from the bedroom.

"Walker, Ah wonder what's with you, boya?"

"What do you mean?"

"Whah a young, healthy man like yourself . . ." she coughed delicately. "You know."

"What do I know?"

Margaret pushed out of the chair, and minced her way to the bedroom like she was stepping on sharp rocks.

"Whah nothin' happened last night."

"I held you, that was something. Doesn't that count?"

Margaret sat on the bed; Walker lay facing away from her. "Ah mean, there Ah was, like a flower heavy with nectar. And you didn't even—you know . . ."

"Give up on the belle, Margaret. It's bullshit. It doesn't work."

"Ah just wondered whah . . ."

"Because I'm *afraid*." Walker rolled over. His eyes were narrowed, angry.

Margaret opened her hands. A small gesture of surrender. Then she rose to prop the clown into a more upright position. "He can't look around and enjoy himself if he's all bent over."

Silence.

"Do you really want to talk about this? 'Cause if you want to play with the clown, I can go back to sleep."

Margaret shrugged.

"No. You have to tell me. Do you want to talk about this?"

"I know why you're afraid." Margaret's normal voice. "Because I say fucked-up things."

"No. Not it." Walker was calming down; he touched the bed next to him. "Come."

Margaret turned away from the clown. But moved no closer.

"Lie down. I want to hold you while I talk."

Margaret knelt on the bed. She hesitated and then toppled, letting her body fall parallel to Walker. He pulled her, arms surrounding her shoulders and hips.

"I'm afraid of hurting you. I think all that shit you say is because something feels dangerous when we have sex. You expect . . . damage."

"This is nice." The little girl voice. "She doesn't want to talk, though."

"Then listen. We need to wait until you feel safe, until you trust me." He caressed Margaret's face. "OK? See what I'm saying?"

Margaret pressed into Walker's chest. "Your skin smells like beach sand," she said.

"Yeah, I'm a sandy motherfucker."

There was something in Walker's restraint, his commitment not to hurt Margaret, that touched me. He seemed to be looking past himself, his own desires, to see what was needed. And it gave his voice a certainty when he spoke—as if he had observed Margaret so carefully that it left no doubt as to what she required.

Margaret's next attempt at conversation reminded me of something my father used to say: "If you can't be normal, be weird. Go all the way."

"I got pregnant when I was thirteen." Margaret rolled back a bit so she could look at Walker. "I wanted the baby and they wouldn't let me have it."

"How did it happen?"

Silence.

"Margaret, who was having sex with you at thirteen?"

Margaret rubbed under one eye. After a moment, she worked on the other.

"It started before that. My mother was gone; I belonged to the big man."

"Your dance teacher?"

"I wanted the baby. My mother came back from Merced— she tried to find out who. But I was afraid . . . "

"Of what?"

"I said it was a boy in school. Someone a little older. I knew that I'd have to leave the company, that I'd never dance again, if I told the truth."

"So you covered up for a man . . . who was abusing you?"

Margaret closed her eyes. "They took me to a doctor. He was

a nice man—bushy mustache, rimless glasses. He sucked it out while they . . . talked in the waiting room. About my career, my mother said."

She brushed each cheek vigorously while giving off a soft giggle.

"I dreamed last night about a baby crying. I was trying to find out where it was; looking and looking. I think . . . it was mine."

23

One of the saddest things about being dead is that you can't dream. The closest I ever came was joining Margaret as she slipped into the Holocaust. For a brief moment, I could be in her body—a woman's body—with all its sweet unknowns. And I could reclaim the feelings of heat and cold, the lost texture of skin, the shuddering beat of an anxious heart.

I would give anything to have my own dreams. Even the bad ones. Because I would know myself in them, I could again drift in the familiar emotions. I remember a recurring dream that I hated. There was classical music—like my mother listened to—playing in the background. And somewhere, in some street or doorway, I would see a girl I knew from high school. She was the first girl I ever touched. Awkwardly, against the rough wood of a ball-field grandstand. In the dream I was excited to find her, but she didn't know me. She was cold, and sliding away. Eyes darting. I was shouting, "Don't you remember? We kissed. We touched. Look at me! You can't have forgotten."

But in every dream I had, after a moment she'd duck into a door or waiting car. Sometimes she would flee, and with the leaden feet of nightmares, I would chase her. Losing ground until she turned a corner. Or disappeared into a crowd.

I would love to have that dream again.

24

Dear Sister:

I saw the camp again last night, and I looked for you among the dead. I keep going back to that place. To be with you. To think I had you in my womb; to think I could have taken care of you, as you cared for me . . .

I still wonder if there was something I should have done. That doctor took you out of me—as if it were a favor. As if you weren't mine, weren't wanted.

I'd like to return to that day. To stop them. I despise Maurice for being afraid of what he'd done, for conspiring with my mother to kill you.

I am so alone. Too strange a specimen. I scream behind my calm face. The men have never helped. I hate the flesh that makes them want to touch me.

Walker won't leave. He says I must trust him. (Maurice's words too.) To make me shut my eyes. So I won't see what's waiting.

Love,
Corine

25

It was Monday, but Margaret took the morning off. Walker had gone home already, kissing her very sweetly good-bye, and setting a Tuesday time for his next visit. Margaret smiled, opened her arms for the embrace, and when it was over quickly turned away.

Around 11:00 o'clock, she emerged from her apartment house carrying *The Diary of Anne Frank*. Margaret headed down the steep grade on 21st, then west on Taraval. The sky was clear, with crisscrossed jet vapors out toward the sea. At the Parkside

Library, an angular, '50s era brick building, Margaret hesitated. She started to go up the steps, then turned, her brown eyes scanning the street.

A sudden wind disturbed the eucalyptus above the library; leaves twisted, flickering in the midday light. Margaret made up her mind then, continuing west down Taraval where it borders the lawns of McCoppin Square. She left the street to climb into the park. Past the tennis courts, and up the path toward a skimpy playground. She sat on a low retaining wall near the slide—feet splayed, knees together, the posture of a child.

Two little girls were on the slide. One would stop so the other could bump into her on the way down. High-pitched laughter, racing up the steps to do it again. On a bench was a young, blonde-haired woman. Swedish accent: "You be careful, girls. I don't want you missing any arms or legs when we get home." More laughter.

Margaret dropped her book onto the playground sand. Watching the girls on the slide, she began rubbing both knees. Bending forward and back—a slow davening. Her lips were moving. I could hear the faint trace of a tune. Then her dark eyes narrowed, and a single glistening path formed across each cheek.

She had resisted crying with Walker, but now she was letting it happen. I felt so much for her then. I would have given anything for the arms to comfort her. Instead I helplessly watched, minute after minute, as tears coursed down her otherwise still face.

After a while the wind came up. And the Swedish lady gathered her children, retreating up the block. A squad car bombed out of the police station across the street, lights flashing. The kids laughed and pointed as they walked.

When the family finally passed out of sight, Margaret picked up her book and shuffled back to Taraval. Where she started waiting for the streetcar. On this line, I should explain, riders stood on narrow islands in the middle of the street. And each island had a ramp for wheelchair access to the trolley. Margaret walked up the ramp to stand on the elevated platform.

There she began to dance. Slowly turning. Reaching one arm out, a gesture of supplication, the other still holding her book. Then bowing and rising again on half point. She moved from the ramp to the edge of the platform—compressing herself beneath tented arms, then leaning out over the tracks. Eyes closed. Beautiful in her abandon.

On the island, three or four people waited for the streetcar. They watched Margaret in silence as the streetcar approached and hit her.

Margaret's shoulder took the blow, which spun her into the handrail, where she crumpled. The book went flying, to be ground beneath the back wheels of the trolley.

I understood immediately what happened. It was the same blind dance I'd seen on Market Street when Walker hit her with his Porsche. It was Margaret offering her body to fate, letting big, moving objects do what they would with her.

A thin, Asian woman started up the wheelchair ramp. She moved reluctantly, as if forced by some unwelcome social code. When Margaret rolled to her knees and stood up, clinging precariously to the rail, the woman stopped, retreated. Now Margaret did an awkward, drunken walk down the ramp and across Taraval toward the library. No one offered to help her.

When I was young, my father used to play a game with me. As we'd walk down the street, he'd say, "What's that person?" Meaning what obvious thing about them betrayed a hidden, deeper flaw. In my father's lexicon, I learned over time, there were six basic categories everyone got divided into: *pretenders* (meaning they had some kind of phony persona), *lemmings* (meaning they had no will of their own and would follow anyone to their destruction), *sweeties* (meaning they'd been put on this earth to serve and take care of others—but deserved no respect), *upright* (meaning they were honest and "had spine"), *fools* (too stupid even to discuss), and *gamers* (meaning they were selfish and manipulative).

My father could find evidence for any of the six types after a few seconds' study of a passerby. His judgments were instant, absolute, and irrevocable.

"Look. What's that person?" I never knew, and then he'd pretend disappointment. In fact, he was delighted to pronounce about the subtle cues only he could observe, which had led him to the diagnosis.

"He walks with his hands in his pockets, eyes on the ground. Helpless lemming."

"Look at the giddy smile. And the colors that don't match. A fool."

"See how he watches everyone, how he says what they want to hear? A real gamer."

I loved to listen to my father say this stuff. It made me feel like we were better than everyone. Like we had blown their cover.

When I was old enough to think, I knew my father was a pretender.

Margaret was a gamer. Not by nature, but because of the scars. And it was destroying her.

26

Tuesday night Margaret persuaded Walker to have dinner at The Grill. Liver and onions with slabs of greasy bacon on top. She could barely raise her left arm, but she wouldn't tell him why. Later, the pair took flashlights and went walking on Ocean Beach. Also Margaret's idea.

It was cloudless, with a thin scatter of stars. The couple played their beams on churning breakers. Margaret's little girl voice

commented on the smell of salt air, the chill, and other banali-
ties. She told Walker his lips were too cold as he kissed her.

After a half hour, and about the time I thought they'd go
home, Margaret found a piece of driftwood and began writing
with it on the sand. It was a poem. She formed each letter carefully, using two hands to guide the stick, while Walker held the
flashlight.

> At night
> girls who will survive
> the war
> assume the names of refugees
> so they can forget
> the killings
> by the dresser
> and the armchair;
> so they can walk
> unknown
> through the gardens
> of the enemy.

The poem was signed *Corine*.

When the twelve lines were finished, Walker went back to
the top and read it again. Margaret sat with her light off, watching the inky waves.

"I won't ask who Corine is," Walker said.

No response. Walker, catching Margaret in a wavering
beam, moved to sit next to her.

"I think the girls are angry. Is that right?"

Margaret shrugged, kept staring out toward the breakers.
Finally she said, "No. Not really."

"What do the girls feel then, these survivors of the war?"

Margaret looked at him, leaned back. Her crossed legs began
to do the scissor thing.

"Nothing."

"I don't believe that."

I didn't believe it either. The poem said one thing to me. That Margaret was alone. That she had given up relationships to be invisible. And of course there were the voices—drawing men in and pushing them away. Each voice helping to confuse and keep them from seeing her.

27

Margaret dumped the sand from her shoes in the toilet. Then she turned on the shower.

"Why didn't you want to write it down?" Walker was in the living room, pressing his voice over the sound of the water. "It was rather lovely. Disturbing and lovely."

"Things come to me. Then I let go of them." She shut the bathroom door.

"Why?" He shouted it.

The door opened a crack, and she peeked out.

"Because when I write, I forget. If I keep what I write, then the forgetting doesn't work at all." Her voice was sad and soft.

Her face disappeared, but after a moment the door opened further, allowing one breast to be visible. "If there's somethin' *you* want to forget, Ah know somethin' that might help you."

Walker waved her back to the shower. "We're waiting on that. Remember? Had a big ol' conversation about it."

She smiled. "Ah'm not sure if Ah recall."

"Bye now, see you when you get out." He walked toward the window.

Margaret lingered in the shower. When she returned, Walker was dozing in one of the overstuffed chairs.

Margaret knelt before him and pulled his laces. Gently she removed his shoes, socks. She observed the hairless ankles, the longish nails. And finally, delicately, touched the ridges of his toes with a slow, brushing gesture.

"Wake up now." Walker's eyes snapped open. "Do you want to sleep in a chair or a bed?"

He stared at her a moment. "A bed, I think, bodes for a better rest."

"Then you shall have it." Margaret made an ushering sweep of her arm, and mock-assisted him to the bedroom.

As they settled under the coverlet, Walker spooned Margaret. Then lay the customary hand across her abdomen. After a moment, in a very ordinary voice, she said: "Thank you. I need you to be just like this. Don't listen to—you know. She loves to get excited. But she ruins things. By pretending." Margaret touched Walker's hand. "You are the kindest person I've known."

Margaret's wind-up alarm clock went off at 6:00.

"Do we get up now?" Walker was trying to focus on the window, which was still ink black.

"In a minute, I guess. I like it in the morning. They don't have the television on next door." It was the little girl. "They're sleeping."

Margaret turned herself toward Walker, the fingers of one hand testing the hollow under her cheek.

"Maurice always came to our parties dressed as a clown."

"Who?"

"My dance teacher."

"Maurice was in costume?"

She nodded.

"These were children's parties? Young students?"

Margaret didn't answer. Eventually she tapped the bridge of her nose. "He had a red thing—here. Everyone laughed because . . . he did the *Dance of the Sugar Plums*, like he was dizzy. I knew that clown. I saw him before."

"Did you like him?"

"No. He was different when we were alone; he wasn't funny."

"Margaret?"

No answer.

"Your teacher dressed up as a clown—when you were alone with him?"

She nodded. "He had big white buttons."

"Why wasn't the clown funny?"

Silence.

"What did the clown say—when you were alone?"

"He said I was a beautiful dancer."

"And?"

"He said, 'The clown knows.'"

"What does that mean?"

Her eyebrows went up. There was another long silence while Walker studied Margaret. Now she put her finger in her mouth.

"What's the name of your big clown—the one on the chair?"

"Maurice."

With a rising inflection, as if it were a question. "Do you like him?"

"No."

"Everybody likes clowns."

Walker pulled Margaret's finger out of her mouth. "How old are you?"

"Nine."

28

That morning, getting ready for work, Margaret did something I no longer thought possible. She surprised me. For a full minute she hesitated, staring down at Maurice, then took the clown with her. The doll was a good three feet tall, and had the loose joints of a Raggedy Ann. Margaret carried it under one arm down 21st, and propped it up in its own seat on the trolley—while commuters were standing in the aisle.

A heavyset man in a suit and tie asked her why the clown rated its own chair.

"It's a fucking old clown. Maybe he's dying. He needs a seat."

"Then he can hold my briefcase," the guy said, and dumped his satchel in Maurice's lap.

Margaret shoved the case on the floor. Then she made a mild, sideways punch at the man's crotch. He bent forward like he was on a spring.

In a deep, grainy voice she said, "Pick up your case and fuck with somebody else. Otherwise," she smiled up at him, "You can look forward to more of the same."

At work, in the ballet ticket office, Maurice was carefully arranged on the top of a low bookshelf. The clown's hands were crossed over his lap, and a small printed sign was placed between the arms: "Don't ask, won't tell."

But that didn't stop anybody. An anorexic-looking woman, wearing a tweed suit and a necklace made with finishing nails, addressed the clown. "What shouldn't I ask you, big fella?"

"Why he's here. Don't ask that."

"'Cause he won't tell, I guess." She laughed like she'd made a sidesplitting joke.

"Right, it's a secret," Margaret said. "He's thinking about something he needs to do."

"Maybe he's planning to run away and join the circus." The woman cracked herself up again.

Thirty minutes later the mail came. It was Manuel, the boy who had expressed so much interest in Margaret's underwear.

At the threshold he paused, throwing out his hands. "Margarita, Margarita. So much beauty. *Tu belleza,* it fills the room."

"You're so full of crap, it's gotta make your belt tight."

"*Mi amiga*, I speak only what is so. What I see and what"— he tapped his forehead—"I remember."

"It was *un tiempo poco. Muy poco.* I can hardly recall it."

"It is, how can I say it, a light that shines."

Margaret held up two fingers in a pinching gesture. "That's the amount of patience I have today, Manuel. Bye-bye."

"*Un momento*. What is this *payaso*? He is keeping watch for you?" pointing to the clown.

"Read the sign."

Manuel picked up the neatly printed card.

"*Señor Payaso*. It is wise for you not to trust women. The beautiful ones, *las bellas*, will kill your heart; the ugly ones take everything and give you back *mierda*. So you can tell me *tu historia*. Speak, *mi amigo*."

Margaret's lips tightened. She brushed something invisible off her desk. "He's thinking of committing suicide. Bye now."

"*Verdad*? He is a sad clown?"

"He isn't sad. He disgusts himself."

"Why is that?"

She shrugged. "Perhaps things he has done."

Manuel took a long look at Margaret. He touched his chest — delicately — with just the tips of his fingers.

"I would miss him — you know? Because he may be a sad clown, or a clown who has done some things he regrets. But he is a good clown — you know? I can tell that."

"How can you tell, Manuel?"

"Because he is sitting here with you." He turned to the clown. "I will leave you to think carefully, Señor. You are a *payaso*; perhaps there are people you can make happy."

"He's never made anyone happy in his life." Margaret stood up and took the boy's arm. "You are sweet, Manuel. Come back with the mail tomorrow. We'll see what he decides." She lightly pushed him out of the room.

After work, Margaret let herself into one of the service doors of the opera house. She was carrying Maurice by his polka-dot clown suit. I was afraid, now, helplessly watching while Margaret ascended a series of concrete flights. Her ring, a thin silver band, clanked on the railing with each step. The sound echoed down the shaft.

Her face was expressionless, eyes staring up toward each landing. As Margaret climbed, her breathing became more labored, and I realized she was humming *Waltz of the Flowers*, the tune associated with her darker impulses.

The top of the stairs was dim, the concrete showing red alluvial stains from water leaks. Hundreds of crushed cigarettes textured the landing. On the steel-sheathed door, a padlock was broken. Margaret stepped into the twilight.

The roof was silver colored, cluttered with dozens of ventilation shafts. Wooden planking led to a flagpole in the distance. Margaret pulled Maurice up to look at him, seeming to study his features.

"Does the clown know . . ."—she was speaking in a slow, melancholy voice—". . . how to make a little girl feel happy?" She shook the doll slightly. "Does he? Can he make her feel good? I don't think so."

Margaret started walking in the direction of the flagpole. Now she circled the doll's waist, and pulled its arm around hers. She moved the clown's free hand so it was resting on her breast.

"Is that right?"

She was getting close to the flagpole. The doll's hand moved to her crotch.

"Is that your opinion? I thought it was."

By now she was standing just beyond the pole, at the edge of the roof where a thigh-high parapet guarded against falls.

Many stories below were the six lanes of Van Ness Avenue, head- and taillights glowing where it descended steeply from O'Farrell Street. Some wind caught the flag. Not much. I imagine the night chill would have been cutting at Margaret's hands.

Now she pulled the clown away from her body, too far for its arms to reach her.

"Do you want to dance, Maurice?" She began swinging the

doll in a mock waltz, tilting and lifting it overhead. "Ooo—it's a long way down. Do you trust me?"

I was terrified. Margaret seemed full of sadness. And though I had learned to see the pictures in her dreams, it was impossible for me to read her intentions.

Suddenly she took the clown by one arm and made a full turn—discus thrower style—flinging the doll in a long arc toward the street. Maurice landed in the middle lane—just as the signal turned. A moment later, a wave of traffic swallowed his gay polka dots.

Margaret knelt on the parapet to watch. When the signal changed again, and the street fell briefly quiet, the clown was torn and marked by tires. The smiling head was gone.

I am reminded now of something my mother said. When I was seventeen, shortly after my father's heart attack and funeral. The back window was open. She was pulling in the laundry—off a clothesline that stretched to a tall post in our yard.

"So that's it," she announced, apropos of nothing.

"What?" I asked.

"Something I decided to do . . . that I don't have to do anymore."

"What's that?"

She pinched open a pair of clothespins, pulled in an undershirt, and folded it.

"Stay with your father." Now she was folding a blouse, running her hand down the collar, pressing the cloth in place.

"I was going to leave him because . . . but I decided . . ." She looked at me; kept patting the blouse. "He was . . . a bitter man. He had contempt."

"For everything," I said.

She nodded and turned back to the clothesline.

"I'd have risked it if I was alone. But not with you."

Mechanically her fingers pressed the clothespins. Continued the ritual of folding.

"I'm going to buy a dryer now," she said. "He liked his clothes to smell of the sun. But I . . . "

She didn't finish. And now I'm thinking what that cost. Her slow death in the kitchen. Knitting, knitting, knitting. While my father flipped the channels, hoping for a show with a little action.

29

On the way home, while the streetcar rumbled between dark storefronts, Margaret clasped and unclasped her hands. Her head was on a swivel—she'd look through me at the neon signs, then turn to watch the overcoated workers plodding toward their rooms. Her face seemed slack. Empty.

That night Margaret slept fitfully. Clown images—both the doll and a slender, white-faced man—slipped into her dreams. And the prison camp showed up. Most disturbing, judging from her staccato breath, was a scene in a huge exercise yard. It was dusk. Prisoners had been lined up in long rows, facing an officer in charge.

The dreamer, standing almost opposite the man in uniform, seemed weak, listing. Her hands pressed her lower abdomen, which was full of sharp, moving pain. The dreamer had no thoughts, save the fear of losing control, or falling.

The officer, whose face was indistinct, almost cloudlike, pointed to people in line. The riding crop would snap upward. He'd shout a single word in a language unknown to me. Then the prisoners who were chosen shuffled toward a covered lorry, and disappeared inside.

After a few moments it became obvious—he was choosing the sick. The weak. I could sense Margaret's fear that soon the riding crop would point to her. The eyes of the officer worked down the row, pushing closer.

At this point I started trying to change the images—do something to soften her fear. But the course of the dream seemed fixed, unalterable.

Now Margaret felt it. The hand of the girl next to her brushed her wrist. It was the most delicate touch, but Margaret instantly felt a surge of hope, of belonging. She straightened. And though her legs had been trembling with the effort to stand, they now quieted, seemed stronger. Margaret turned; the two women locked eyes. It was the girl in the photograph— the older sister.

Now I heard a noise, and realized I'd lost track of the man in uniform. He was pointing the crop at Margaret, red-faced, the sound exploding from his mouth as if each word were a grenade.

Margaret quailed. Her body seemed to grow thinner—as if a vacuum was collapsing her inward. Then I heard a sweet, high-pitched voice weaving between the shouted commands.

"She must stay with me."

The black-booted officer stopped talking. And there was silence. Except for bird song coming from the eaves of a bar-rack. Now the officer moved closer. Short, precise steps. When he was in front of the girl, he unsnapped the cover on his holster and extracted a Luger. The gun rose slowly until it was pressing against the girl's dark, center-parted hair. Now he said some-thing with a lilt at the end—a question.

"She must stay with me," the girl repeated.

The officer nodded, looked at Margaret, let slip a weightless smile. Then he pulled the trigger. The murdered girl blew side-ways, colliding with her sister, showering her with clots of tissue.

As the body fell, the dreamer reacted with a sudden welling of loss. But not shock. And I was surprised to sense that the bullet was expected, that the event had unfolded with a dread-ful certainty. Margaret had dreamt this before.

The officer moved his gun. Now it was pointed at Margaret. His lips stretched in the same ephemeral smile. Margaret stared back, oddly unafraid.

"Yes." She was nodding. "Do it." And after another moment while the gun remained fixed on her, "Yes, yes. Why do you wait?"

But the Luger never fired. The officer said something brief, guttural. The dreamer understood. He would deny them everything—even the hope of being joined in death. He would, in a perverse cruelty, let Margaret live.

The dream began to break up, like voices on a bad connection. Images of a town with brownstone row houses; tall, soot-stained chimneys; children playing in a brackish puddle. Margaret's breathing slowed, became shallow. She drifted deeper into sleep.

30

Dear Sister:

I could feel you last night. Standing somewhere outside of time. When will you come? I look for signs.

I've had the dream again. Where you gave up your life for me. So calmly. I want to be that good, to show that kind of love.

You would never have been weak like me—letting them suck you out of my belly. I hate myself for that, more than anything. If you come to me, I will love you. I will lay down my life for you. That's my promise.

Walker has gone to Denver. For another of his interviews. Though he has a plane ticket to return on Wednesday, I don't believe he'll come. I think he'll disappear, that he's grown afraid of me.

He can't help. Though he is good, though he tries, it will end the same. You are the only one who can touch me. Do you remember, when I cried, that you caressed my face in the barracks so I could finally sleep? I am still crying. Only you could make this scarred, awful place worth living in.

Love,

Corine

31

Margaret:

Hope this arrives before I do. The interview in Denver yielded more than I expected. Very rich in detail and drama.

This woman's husband was a medical researcher. The guy was completely driven. Spent years designing proto-types of a large vein catheter. Kept himself going on money raised from family and investors.

Most nights he slept at the lab, often not alone. His wife found out and left him.

The prototypes, which were tested on animals, kept running into problems — infection, vein damage, clotting. When he finally had a design that seemed to work, he couldn't get approval for human testing. So he inserted the catheter in his own jugular and wore it for weeks. During that time it was his sole source of fluids and nutrition.

Finally, he walked into the FDA office wearing the cath-eter and demanded that they reconsider his application for human testing. At the age of 52 he finally got a patent and a sweet deal from a manufacturer.

Here's the thing I love: in that same week the guy closes his lab and calls his ex-wife to ask her out on a date. They date for six months. In her words, he's "strangely attentive." Drives her wherever she wants to go, always available. Always interested. She keeps waiting for him to revert to his old self. But he never does. They move in together; they talk of remarrying.

One day, while he's backing out of the garage, she hears

a car horn. Because it keeps blaring, she investigates. He's slumped on the wheel. When the paramedics come, they remove his coat; a boxed wedding ring falls out of his pocket.

You can't make up shit like this. I feel like every story points to something. Not just a pattern, my *sunrise effect*, but something I can't quite see yet.

I asked the woman why she thought her husband died so young. She said, "He'd finished what he needed to do."

I'll be back Wednesday night if all goes well. Do you miss me? Forget it. You wouldn't tell me if you did.

Walker

It was Wednesday after work. The letter had been Fed-Ex'd. Margaret dropped it to the floor when she was finished reading. Though her face held its usual thin smile, I could see a muscle rippling in her jaw. Two fingers scratched relentlessly at the side of her trachea.

Now she was mumbling something, repeating it. I moved near her mouth, conscious that I could have felt her breath if I was still living. "Roses or flies," she was chanting. Like that day, weeks ago, when Margaret first met Walker. And now, because of the dreams, I started to understand.

I remembered a scene where the dark-haired girl laid flowers on a dead woman's face. And a more recent dream of the camps: the body hanging on the fence wire, insects walking the lips, the open eyes.

Roses or flies. Two choices for the faces of the dead. The chant seemed to imply that destruction was inevitable. With the only question being whether the dead were properly loved, honored.

But why now? What in the letter had brought this question up? It was as if Margaret expected to be destroyed. Emotionally murdered. And the only thing that mattered was whether Walker would love her while he did it.

During these contemplations Margaret went to the chrome

and Formica breakfast table. I didn't notice at first. By the time I drifted into the kitchen, she'd already crayoned several drawings on a large sketch pad. One was a monochromatic fence. Gray posts, gray wire. Now she was doing a red and yellow clown, filling in the polka dots.

"He needs his big buttons," Margaret whispered in the little girl voice. "I'll do them now."

Above and behind the clown, she drew a crude-looking guard tower, bristling with guns. All in gray again.

Now Margaret tore off the first sheet and ceremoniously began brushing, almost caressing the new page. On this sheet, over the next twenty minutes, Margaret drew five rough human figures, one in each corner and one in the middle of the page. At the top left was a figure I'd seen before—an adolescent boy with a crew cut, huge biceps, and a tattoo. Plus stick legs that wouldn't hold up a four-year-old.

Bottom left was a little girl with an overdrawn smile, freckles, and straw-colored pigtails. She resembled Pippi Longstocking. Bottom right was perhaps an older girl with long, center-parted black hair. She had a flowing dress, big eyes, and a mouth turned down in a caricature of sadness. She was wearing ballet slippers. Top right was a woman with big breasts, over-rouged lips, and a dress too short to sit down in. Her yellow, shoulder-length hair flipped up in a tight, '60s-era curl.

In the center was Margaret, crudely rendered with long hair and vague, undifferentiated features. What nailed her identity was the checkerboard shirt and short denim skirt. Margaret also held the faint, fixed smile.

There was one other odd thing about these drawings. Margaret's arms and legs pointed to each of the four surrounding figures. Giving her the look of a pinwheel.

Watching the five figures emerge in her sketch pad was oddly exciting. I had the illusion that she was drawing them for me. As a favor—so I could finally know her. See into her heart.

I'm not sure why, but it led me to recall a moment when I was in the early grades. We had just seen the film *Black Beauty* and got assigned the task of drawing a horse. I'd no idea how to do it, but a girl—someone who never before spoke to me—leaned toward my desk.

"You make the neck and back on a curve like this," she said. And then drew the hindquarters and legs. "You can do the head yourself—it's easy. That way it'll still be your drawing."

I can never explain the joy of that moment. There was a sense of warmth in my face—as if I were blushing. And a tingling in my chest. I was acutely aware, perhaps for the first time, of being given something.

I remember, as the girl drew, her concentration. And the rhythm of her breathing. Our heads were close—almost touching—as her pencil made the final mark on my page.

"See? It's easy," she repeated as she pulled back to her own desk.

In retrospect, I'm not sure whether it was a moment of great generosity, or merely a chance to show off her horse-drawing skills. But that feeling—of a need seen and answered—is rare. And at the time, it seemed to me the deepest, the most precious kind of intimacy.

When the last crayon mark had been made, Margaret got up and turned off the lights. Then she dropped her skirt to the floor and crawled into bed. In the dark I could feel her eyes searching the room, prying the shapes from the shadows. One hand kneaded the silken edge of the blanket. The other, almost protectively, lay between her legs. Her breathing came in short, thin bursts.

Margaret didn't sleep. When Walker buzzed from the street, she got up immediately and opened the door in her underwear. He kissed her, their lips just touching. Then he pulled back to see her face. "Is this the same Margaret I left?" His fingers brushed her lips, her cheek.

Margaret turned on the lights in the kitchen. She inquired if he'd like some frozen ravioli while temptingly shaking a bottle of store-bought marinara sauce. Walker demurred, asked about the drawing on the table.

"It's nothing," Margaret said.

"No, it's something. It's four girls and that weird-looking punk you drew before. Who are they?"

"I don't know." The angry voice. She shrugged and turned off the light.

32

While Walker slept, Margaret stared at her wind-up clock, at the ballerina music box. She was still held by him—one arm around her shoulders, the other her waist. Yet instead of comforted, she seemed afraid. Over the hours, her limbs grew rigid beneath the covers.

Long past midnight, Margaret pulled off her underpants. She rolled on top of Walker and began to kiss him, pressing against his body.

"What are you doing?" Words slurred with sleep.

"Ah need this. Don't say anything."

"You know what will happen."

"Ah know, OK? Ah just need . . . "

She didn't finish her sentence, instead reached down to pull his pants and try to guide him inside her.

"Forget it." He pushed her off. "This has to stop. Be real. Talk to me like a real person.

Margaret touched him. "You're ready. Ah can tell."

"What do you need, Margaret? It's not this. Stop the charade and tell me."

"She needs to stop being a pansy." It was the rasping voice. "Come on, do what you're here for. Do it. Stop pretending all your sensitive shit. She doesn't believe it. Just unload. Do it."

"Margaret!" She'd turned away, and now he pulled her face so she had to look at him. "Cut the shit. Whatever that is, I know it's trying to protect you. OK? But stop it. I'm sick of it."

He shook her head. "OK?"

"Fuck her and get it over with."

Walker's face was less angry now. But I think he was at wit's end, and it drove him to attempt something he hadn't done before. He directly addressed the voice.

"You're trying to get rid of me. But we both want the same thing. For her to be safe."

"Fuck her. Do it. You're gonna lose your hard-on."

Again Margaret tried to look away, but Walker held her head in place.

"I promise you, I will watch over her. I will keep her safe." He kissed Margaret. "She doesn't need to be fucked right now. She needs to be safe. You know that."

"You're gonna lose your hard-on."

"Say you know it. She doesn't need to be fucked, she needs to be safe."

Margaret twisted against Walker's restraining arms.

"I'm not taking anything from her. Because that's the old story. People taking things. People using. That's the old story. That's not going to happen anymore because we want the same thing. For her not to be hurt. Right? We're going to keep her from being hurt."

A tear dropped onto Walker's cheek.

Now he let Margaret's head rest against his face. And he moved his arms to hold her—shoulders and hips. For a long time her body spasmed against him.

"It's OK," he said.

"I need you," Margaret finally whispered. "It's too much. Inside."

After a long time she rolled to her side and Walker folded himself against her back, returning to their original positions.

"Did you like my drawings?" It was the little girl voice. "She didn't want me to draw that."

"I'll look at them again tomorrow," Walker said.

There was a long silence and I thought perhaps they'd fallen asleep.

"I made them for you," the little voice said.

33

I had never seen a relationship like this. I don't mean Margaret's broken parts. I'm talking about Walker's intention: to do only what was best for this woman. And the more I saw, the more embarrassment I felt. For my own life. Because the one relationship I'd ever had was purely mercantile.

It started with a headache, and the girl massaging the muscles on my neck till the pain went away. We slept together that night, and occasionally for the next three months. But she was always busy, an artist consumed by the need to sculpt. I was convinced I bored her. So I lived suspended in the drama of whether I'd see her or not. All I cared about was the hope that she would answer the phone—and show me her ivory skin.

When I couldn't see her, I was petulant. I'd accuse her of not caring. Then I'd find flaws in her pieces, her style. For the whole time, I simmered with anger. Because she wouldn't give me enough. Because she was a commodity. Looking back, I remember her as rather sweet. Which is odd, because I had no sense of it then.

34

During a pathetic breakfast consisting of bottom-of-the-box cornflakes and skim milk, Walker looked again at Margaret's sketch page.

"Who are these faces?"

Margaret shrugged. Two fingers traced circles in a small puddle of milk. Then she licked them.

"Do they have names?"

Margaret brushed imaginary crumbs off her gray pinstriped skirt. Her jaw muscles bunched. "She doesn't want me to tell you." High, breathy voice.

"Who doesn't?"

Margaret pointed to the drawing in the middle.

"Could you write the names—under each picture? That way you wouldn't have to say them out loud."

Margaret picked up a brown crayon.

"I like brown," she said, "except this one isn't pointy anymore. You have to write big."

With tall, irregular letters, Margaret wrote "Millie" under the pigtailed child. "That's me. I like my hair like that. I only get to wear it that way at home sometimes."

"Corine" appeared under the black-haired girl with the sad eyes and downturned mouth. "She doesn't like it here."

"Louisa May" was printed under the blonde with flipped-up hair. "She has to look nice," the child voice said. "She always wants lipstick. Except we don't like it because it's waxy."

"Does she have a Southern accent?" Walker asked.

"Yes." Almost inaudible. "Sometimes."

Beneath the punkish boy with stick legs, she wrote "Keg." "That's not his real name, but he wants us to call him that. He likes to drink beer."

Now her finger pressed the face in the middle. "That's—you know. She doesn't drink beer very much."

"Why?"

"Because he gets . . . angry."

"Keg?"

"Uh huh."

"Do you all live together? When did this start?"

But Walker had asked too much. He could see her face get alarmed.

"I have to go now."

Margaret's eyes flickered. Then she abruptly got up and headed to the bathroom.

"I'm late." Voice echoing off the tiles.

"Do you want me to take you?"

Margaret's head popped out. "That'd be nice. But don't ask me anymore about those . . . people. OK?"

Walker agreed, and within ten minutes they were heading for the Civic Center in his old Porsche. Morning light glinted off windows of the stucco flats and houses of 19th Avenue. Stoplights caught the traffic in staccato waves. As they turned right on Lincoln, Margaret began talking about a dream.

"I saw the clown last night. I didn't like it. He was throwing me up and catching me. I was trying to hold my skirt down."

"What happened then?"

Margaret looked out the window. At a motorcycle cop who'd stopped a black man in an old Cadillac.

"They always give tickets to the people who can't afford it," she said.

"What happened with the clown, what did he do?"

"I'm not sure. I've lost the thread of it. I don't like dreaming about him."

Silence. They were on the curve at the east end of Golden Gate Park that leads into Oak Street. Margaret was leaning forward, looking far to her left.

"I like it over there, at the Arboretum." She waved a hand. "I go there sometimes when I don't know what else to do. It's warm, tropical. I feel like I'm somewhere else."

"It's good to get away—from the demons, or whatever."

Margaret folded her hands and raised them to her forehead. "I don't like you knowing about . . . I'm scared now."

"You were always scared."

She gave a mirthless grunt.

"Who are they?" he asked.

"My friends."

"Is it a story you keep making up in your head?"

"No."

"Were they real people, or always . . . imaginary?"

Margaret allowed a thin sigh, kept pressing knuckles into her forehead. "How long are you gonna do this? This thing?" The word *thing* shot out with distaste.

"Like I told you." His voice held an edge of annoyance. "Until you drive me away."

She pointed to the building that housed the ballet offices, then turned to Walker. She gave him a long kiss on the cheek, nuzzled him.

"I'm sorry," she whispered. "You're good to me. I don't know why . . . "

35

My father used to say, "Every dream will break your heart. The good ones kill you because they never come true. The bad ones kill you 'cause somehow they are true."

Margaret didn't have any good ones.

This dream, on a Thursday when Walker wasn't there, caught me by surprise. It seemed lovely. Margaret was dancing. Her body felt very young—twelve or thirteen maybe. A short man with thick, marcelled hair was guiding her, telling her how to step, a voice deep and sonorous.

"There you are—good. Arms up for the plié." His hands lingered across her breasts. "No, you're making an *S*; your body's like an *S*. Be straight. Stomach in, bottom in." Hands pressed her buttocks and abdomen. "No, in, in! They don't want to see your ass. The ass is for striptease, not ballet." The hand pressed harder on her buttocks, fingers sliding into the cleavage.

It was then I felt Margaret's distress. A wave of revulsion passed through her. With something else. She felt aroused. Then the flash of desire was followed by the deepest, most searing self-hate I have ever known. It burned her, even while she danced.

"No, no, no. You are back to being an *S* again. What will they think—the people who paid to look at you? They want beauty, they must see *through* your body to the ideal." He was running his hands down both her front and back. "Straight, yes. Yes. Your body is the wand of God, showing them, opening their eyes."

It went on and on, and I could do nothing to stop it. In her sleep, Margaret moved her hand between her legs.

The little man was wearing a white silk shirt with baggy sleeves. They flapped as he gestured now, toward some imaginary audience. "What do they see when they see you?"

At that moment, she had a memory of performing—an image of the lights, the ascending rows of faces. And now, faintly, the notes of a tune. This was my chance; I gave my energy to those images, allowing the touch and voice of the little man to fade.

Her disgust subsided now, replaced by the muscle joy of runs and turns, of perspiring limbs slicing the cool air. She kept dancing till the dream ended.

When Margaret awoke, it was clear that I hadn't stopped the ugliness in time. As she lay in bed, her lovely, full lips pinched into a thin line. Her eyes were fixed, unfocused. The little man had followed her.

A wan light collapsed on the hardwood floor, turning the rich oak to the color of frost. Margaret ran her hands across the coverlet, then up over her stomach and chest. Much the same way the little man had done. She was humming something.

After a moment, still staring at no object in particular, she slid her feet to the floor. Margaret stood in her underwear, waiting a moment as if to steady herself, and stepped to the dresser. Without looking, she clicked on the music box. The precise, tinkling notes of *Waltz of the Flowers* pierced the chilled air.

Margaret's hands, which had rested on top of each other

above her pubis, now stretched outward in a lovely movement suggesting petals opening to the sun. As they extended, her fingers assumed a half-curl. Like God's hand in the Sistine Chapel. Now all movement stopped.

I expected to see her hit herself, but nothing happened. The waltz slowed down, ended in the middle of a phrase. Margaret dropped her arms. Her fingers ran across the ornate backs of her brush and mirror. Then she swept everything—even her beautiful music box—to the floor.

Something about Walker's presence was stirring the past. Each dream was a shiv. The objects that had been reassuring links to childhood or dance were now symbols of betrayal. And she was bleeding.

Two hours later, Margaret was taking calls about group ticket plans for the ballet. On the desk was her journal, open to the letter she had just finished.

Dear Sister;

Where are you? Are you coming? I threw the clown away. I don't know why. But now, with it gone, I am remembering him. I remember his hands.

Love,
Corine

36

For some reason Walker wanted Margaret at a party. It was a solstice gathering hosted by John Madrone, a psychologist friend of Walker's, who'd been the subject of one of his "weird science" pieces. Madrone's condo was in the Marina district, with wide picture windows offering a stunning view of the bay. It was furnished with leather couches, cushions soft and heavily creased with use. There were two old-fashioned floor lamps—one with a fringed shade and the other with a Tiffany-type stained glass.

The walls were cream-colored, holding what looked like original Hopper paintings on opposite sides of the room. End tables and a large bookshelf were in dark mahogany. Against the wall facing the windows was a mohair armchair, with a beautifully stitched lace doily pinned to the headrest.

I loved the room. It had a warmth, a feeling it could be lived in.

The group was small, and Walker was the last to arrive. Madrone pumped Walker's hand at the door and announced loudly: "This man is the best damned writer I've ever met. Ask him about the book he's working on called *The Sunrise Effect*." At this moment Margaret stepped close to Walker, clearly expecting to be introduced. Madrone turned, and headed toward a little group of people near the window.

Walker did the best he could with the introductions. He already knew Madrone's wife, Julie, and he presented her to Margaret. Julie was in her thirties, with long, black hair, an oval face, soft lovely figure, and fragile-looking hands. She seemed cautious, even guarded, as she exchanged greetings.

A lesbian couple, Holly and Jan, introduced themselves next. Holly was in her early forties, still pretty, with straight, shoulder-length, blonde hair. She was tall and strong limbed. Jan was a trifle butch with short, dyed black hair, overalls, and suspenders. She was thin and walked with a slight rolling gait, suggesting injury. Both joked and seemed friendly.

Franklin Riles, a sixtyish black man, was tall and thickened with age. He wore a tan suit with a chartreuse shirt. "Thought we'd have to carry on with only the usual shit to talk about," he said to Walker. "Glad you could spare us from boredom."

When he was introduced to Margaret, Riles took her hand and did a slight bow. "Ain't you *fine*. You're cheerin' me up, darlin'."

"That's good," Margaret said, "'cause cheer is all Ah got for you. Ain't nothin' else." She bowed back, gave him a dry smile.

The next solstice reveler was a stout, middle-aged woman, introduced as Dr. Strite, history professor. Her specialty was "early-twentieth-century U.S." Spoken with a slight separation between words, as if she suffered a fear of being misunderstood. Strite was dressed in banker's pinstripe, garnished with tortoise-shell glasses.

"What do you do, dear?" she asked Margaret.

"Ah answer stupid questions. It's fun if you remember sometimes to give stupid answers."

Strite was silent for a moment. "Was that one of them, dear? One of those answers?"

The evening was going to be interesting. I longed to introduce myself, to sit down and look at them over the rim of my cocktail glass. I was remembering fondly the bitter taste of alcohol.

In front of the window, Dr. Madrone lifted his glass. "To the best of friends."

Walker told Margaret that Madrone was forty-five—but he looked older, weathered. He was tall, six foot three or four, with gray eyes and salt and pepper hair. He had a sweet smile.

Hors d'oeuvres were served, and Margaret was persuaded to have a Manhattan. "It's a drink," Riles said, "that always gets excellent results—'cause it's 100 percent liquor."

For a while conversation flourished, led by Dr. Strite, about neoclassical architecture. Then it shifted to cultural changes brought on by the radio. Strite again. This segued to the social impact of TV. And finally to evolving parenting styles, led by Madrone.

Margaret had a second Manhattan.

The quality of modern versus old-school parenting sparked a sharp debate. Jan argued that there was a positive movement—except in the fundamentalist churches—toward teaching respect for individual differences. Madrone agreed and suggested that rigid, church-based parenting sometimes led to the abuse of kids who didn't fit the norm.

"Just honor your kids; respect them," Holly slurred. "That's what counts, no matter what age you're raising children in."

That set Riles off. "Children need parents who don't take shit. What parents do now is give in, give in. Till the kid thinks the world owes him anything he wants."

"Historically," Strite said, "children were an adjunct labor force. They existed to serve their families. Whatever father or mother needed . . . "

"They were chattel and had to give." It was Margaret's angry voice. "Fourteen hours in the fields, give it. Sold into slavery, why not? Mom needs a char girl—sure. Dad needs a fuck. Sure. Give it. Give it."

The group drank their cocktails in silence.

"I'm just saying . . ." Strite's voice reached a high, belligerent note. "I'm saying that we've come a long way. The process of civilization has yielded—"

"More clever excuses. Like Freud who said girls make up the abuse because they want to fuck their fathers. Right, Dr. Madrone? Isn't that what he said?"

Strite tried to cut in, but Margaret kept talking.

"And we've reached a civilization zenith where a third of little girls are sexually abused. Right, Dr. Madrone? Right?"

Madrone looked helplessly at Margaret. "We haven't done very well protecting our children."

Margaret was breathing hard. She and Madrone locked eyes for a moment; then hers slid away.

"But there *is* progress," Holly said. "Forty years ago all of this was hidden . . . "

Margaret stood up. She looked at a spot in the corner of the ceiling. Then the rasping voice launched out at them, at their crossed legs and printed napkins (reading *shortest day of the year*), at all their clever, useless knowledge.

"Fuck progress. When the police show up at all these ass-holes' doors, and they take them out and . . ." She headed to the foyer. "Then I'll celebrate the progress."

Margaret pointed back at Walker. "Stay. Don't you dare follow me." Then she was gone.

I watched her safely board the F streetcar before I returned to the party. I wanted to see how Walker tried to clean it up. I arrived with everybody looking at him.

"She's been through a lot," he said. "It's all very personal to her."

Walker's face bore an embarrassed little smile. He looked like he'd just wet himself and was hoping nobody had noticed.

"There are boundaries," Strite sputtered. "Norms."

"Maybe it happened to her," Holly offered.

Riles was looking at the bottom of his glass like it had sprung a leak. "Of course, it did. You don't get that much heat without a fire."

There were murmurs of agreement.

"Is there something we can do for her?" Madrone was addressing Walker.

"She'll go home. I'm sure of it. That's where she feels safe. But maybe we could talk—later."

The psychologist nodded.

"A lot of people can't stand a free exchange of ideas." Strite's fingers were steepled, and now she was gesturing with them. "You know what I mean? We probably need to be careful who we invite to these things."

Madrone's wife, Julie, who'd said very little all evening, put her drink down. Now she smoothed her long skirt with both hands, pushing tiny wrinkles down her lap. "She's in a lot of pain. John's right. If we can do something, let's do it."

But nobody knew what to do.

"Here's to the winter gods," Holly held up a swizzle stick. "Time to call it a night."

37

Julie was sitting in the mohair armchair, biting her nails. Madrone was lying on one of the leather couches, propped on a bedroom pillow. His frown gave the impression of someone who'd shouldered a great burden.

Walker was at the window, watching a low, crude-filled tanker navigate the Golden Gate. A pair of tugs left churning wakes as they sped to rendezvous with the ship. The rest of the bay was black, rimmed by the lights of Richmond and Sausalito.

"She has names for them," Walker said, having just explained Margaret's four drawings. "And some of the voices she slips into—this southern belle, and that harsh voice you heard tonight—seem related to the drawings. There's a little girl voice called Millie who wants to befriend me, who's trying to help me understand what's going on."

Madrone groaned, but didn't say anything.

"When she's scared—particularly if she's touched sexually—all hell breaks out and the voices start shifting. You don't know who you're talking to."

"Was she a victim of sexual abuse?"

"Yes. A ballet teacher, whom she lived with from age nine to I-don't-know-when."

Madrone sat up a little. "Does she ever complain of finding herself somewhere and she doesn't know how she got there?"

"I don't know."

"What about losing time? It's 4:00, and the last she remembers it was noon."

"I think she's mentioned that."

"Does she do impulsive, out-of-the-blue things?"

"Yeah. She hits herself. And . . . she used to go out a lot and do one-nighters. I had to get her out of a situation one time. A guy who scared her."

"And the voices seem to have distinct personalities? They each relate differently?"

"Right."

"I've got to ask you something, and you're not going to like it."

"Why am I with her?"

"Yeah. Because rescue things don't work. They blow up in your face. Read Maugham—*Of Human Bondage*. People never stay with someone above their level of health."

"I believe you. I know it's gonna crash." He began shaking his head. "But I can't stop. You have no idea what it means to me . . . to watch her open. She was totally closed, walled off. And now she is coming out. Bit by bit. Starting to trust me with the names of the voices. Beginning to let go in my arms."

As he was talking, I had an acute moment of envy. Because it is what I'd wanted. The sense that I had unlocked someone. Finally pushed through the indifference. The uncaring.

"To finally be let in," he continued. "To know I am the first. You have . . . no idea." Walker shrugged helplessly.

"That's lovely." It was Julie's first contribution to the discussion.

"I'm trying to make a point here." Madrone craned his head around to look at his wife.

"You made it. And he made his. The real point is: can you help, John?"

Madrone fell back on the pillows and began massaging his forehead. He sighed.

"She has dissociative identity disorder, what we used to call multiple personality. Those voices are alter personalities who each might hold abuse memories, or carry out certain functions. Like asserting her needs, saying things she's afraid to say. The belle may procure men for her. Etcetera, etcetera. There may be more of them than you know about. Or even the little girl—Millie—knows about.

"Some alters could be fun, playful. Others could be depressed, or even suicidal. You don't know what you're getting into here, Walker. Believe me."

Walker shuffled to a couch under one of the Hoppers and dropped into it.

"What does she need, John? Make a plan." Julie pointed to her husband. "You are an expert on this. You've worked with a very serious case."

"Studied. Didn't work with."

"The point is you know about it. You need to stop warning about how serious it is and help Walker and Margaret."

"I can't do that. Think clearly, Julie. You may be a little identified with the situation."

Julie's eyes flashed and she turned to Walker. "For your information, I was *not* abused as a child."

Madrone held up his hand. "I'm sorry."

"You're afraid to help. I see it. That's why you were cruel. You don't want to deal with this again."

Silence. Everyone was looking at the floor.

"But these are people right in front of us, John. You know? Right here. And you have the knowledge."

Madrone sat up on the couch. "You're right. I'm afraid . . . to get near it." He stared out toward the bay.

After a while Madrone roused himself. "The therapy is extraordinarily difficult." He began counting off on his fingers. "It takes years . . . mapping the alters. Uncovering memories. Working with post-traumatic stress. Stabilizing. Integrating one alter at a time. Each personality needs to agree to let go and join the whole, in effect to die."

Walker said nothing.

"Here's what I'll do. Send her to me. I'll see her once. I'll confirm the diagnosis and explain as much as I can—given some of the alters may be afraid and not want to listen—about the treatment. Then I'll refer her."

"How much do I tell her?"

"Just give her my number. Tell her I can recommend ways to get help for the memories and fears. And the pressure inside that makes her do things that hurt her."

"Should I say anything about the alters?"

"Probably not. Less is more in this situation."

38

Margaret didn't go home. There was no answer when Walker called. And nothing happened when he rang her bell sometime after midnight. Now Walker was racing west on Taraval, letting the car go weightless down every hill. At 48th, where the tracks turn south toward the zoo, he slowed to study both directions. The salt air was doing its work on the peeling houses. In the street light I could see rust stains fanning from hinges and nails. No one was on the street.

Now Walker hit the gas again. A block later he pulled next to a hydrant, jumped from the car, and began a loping run to the beach. At the entrance to a dark pedestrian tunnel that burrows under the Great Highway, Walker clicked on his flashlight and plunged inside. Each footstep echoed like a rifle crack; the beam danced on the seeping walls.

Arriving at the far end, he stood for a moment to survey the sand. The beach sloped down for a hundred yards, succumbing finally to moon-silvered water. Muffled thunder marked approaching waves.

Walker scanned the surf line, bending slightly forward as if to improve his sight. Now he cast the beam of the flashlight in a wide arc. Nothing. He took a few strides south, then turned and began uncertain steps toward the faint lights of the Cliff House.

A quarter mile north, Walker found the poem. Eight lines.

In sand still smooth and wet from the receding tide. Margaret was nowhere to be seen, so he paused, sweeping his light across the neatly printed letters:

Easy anger
fills the mouth.
Another tide:
foam
flecking the lips,
hair swaying
toward the self-made
undertow.

Walker clicked the poem into darkness. A silver wave slid almost to its edge. He started north again, focusing now on a shadow in the surf line far ahead.

As he approached, Margaret was kneeling, facing seaward, clothes wet from the waves. He watched while she let them hit her—water foaming across her bare legs, slashing her waist, forcing her arms behind her. The battering continued. Blow after blow.

I wanted Walker to do something, to lift Margaret up and take her home. But he stood motionless. Shoulders slumped. A mirror of her surrender.

After a while a wave came, bigger than the others, slamming Margaret mid-chest. Tumbling her. Head submerged, skirt forced up her waist, legs high and thrashing.

She lay where it left her. Coughing. Brushing the hair from her face. And now another one was coming. Margaret raised her hand as if in greeting. Or acquiescence.

Walker was suddenly in motion—scooping Margaret up just as the wave hit. Keeping her head above the foam. He was kneeling behind, bracing as the force of the water crushed her into his chest. Then he shifted, digging in his heels, ready to keep the back churn from sucking them out.

"What are you doing?" Walker shouted it against the roar of the next breaker.

Margaret's body drooped doll-like in his arms, limbs drifting in the current. Walker was suddenly intent on pulling her skirt beneath her underpants. As if decorum might fix what was happening.

"What are you doing?" he repeated.

"They can't do anything right."

Margaret spoke in a voice I'd rarely heard. Slow and sad sounding. Another wave hit them.

"You mean at the party?"

No answer. Walker used the next wave to pull Margaret further up the beach.

"Can I take you home? It's cold."

She shrugged.

"Do you want me to take you home? Say it."

"There is no home." The sad voice again. "And all they do is make it worse."

"Do you know how to make it better?"

Silence. They were high enough on the sand now that the spent waves barely reached Margaret's feet. Her head began to loll on Walker's arm.

"Please take us back." The little girl voice. "Corine wants to stay here, but we're shivering."

39

In the bathroom, Margaret stood passively while Walker stripped her wet clothes. Tub water steamed into the cool air. Her eyes were closed, hands spread slightly outward while garments dropped to a small mound at her feet.

"OK, in you go." Walker supported Margaret's arm as she stepped over the rim and settled into the hot water.

"This is nice," the little girl whispered. "It makes my feet tingle. I couldn't feel them before."

Walker brushed damp strands back from Margaret's face. "I've got to change into a robe or something to get dry. I'll be back in a second."

When Walker returned, he was festooned with a skin-tight T-shirt and a sheet wrapped several times around his hips. Margaret giggled.

"That looks like a dress. I want to wear long skirts, but Louisa May won't go out unless it's a short one. But sometimes she's nice and lets me wear corduroys."

Walker began rubbing soap in his hands; getting a lather. Then he gently held up each of Margaret's arms and washed them.

"Did Corine make you go out there—in the waves?"

"Yes. She doesn't like it here. She wants to be with her sister."

"The one who died during the war?"

Margaret nodded. "And she hates Louisa May. All that going out to the bars. She thinks that's disgusting."

"Does Corine hit herself?"

Silence. Walker soaped her forehead and cheeks with small circular movements of his fingers. Then shifted to the neck and shoulders. Finally, he rinsed the lather with a washcloth.

"Come on, Margaret. Talk to me."

"That's not my name. You know my name."

"Fine . . . Millie. Does Corine hit herself?"

"Sometimes. But you told her not to."

"So now she makes you kneel in the surf? To drown or die of exposure?"

No response to the sarcasm.

"Is Corine trying to kill herself?"

"No. Just trying to go to her sister."

Now Walker touched Margaret's shoulder. "Kneel up for a minute. I want to get the rest of you."

Margaret folded her legs and knelt on her haunches. Walker used his hands to soap her back and breasts.

"Don't touch there . . . I don't like that."

"It's just a part of your body, Millie."

"*Her* body. I don't like them."

Walker took his hand away.

"Kneel up all the way." He gave her the soap. "You do your back side and between your legs."

"OK. Are you mad?"

"No." His voice softened. "You can decide those things. I'll go by whatever you say."

She soaped vigorously, using the bar instead of her hand. Then slipped back into the water. Now Walker carefully lifted her legs, lathering and rinsing.

"More hot water?"

Margaret nodded. He moved her feet out of the way and ran the faucet for a while.

"That's good." It came out as a sigh; she let her eyes close.

"You feel safe now?"

"Yes. You're always nice." She sank deeper into the water. "But Keg thinks you're gonna leave. Soon as you're tired of us."

Walker had lifted Margaret's foot to the surface of the water and was massaging it. "I love you." He said it softly, looking only at his moving hands. A moment later he repeated it in a whisper.

No response. Margaret may have been asleep.

I was ruined by the sweetness of it. By the respect he showed Millie. By his giving without taking. I wanted, with a deep yearning, to have been that person while I lived.

Thirty minutes later, Walker lifted Margaret to the bed; dressed her in a T-shirt and underwear. She did a fetal curl.

"I talked to Madrone."

"Uh huh."

"He wants to meet with you. He says there are ways to

help . . . so you won't get so upset. So you won't have to do things that hurt you."

"Ah don't need help, dahlin'. Ah need you to be a man." She rolled toward him and raised her eyebrows. "Know what Ah mean?"

"He said you don't have to be . . . the victim of this stuff."

"He's full of shinola."

"You felt bad about what happened at the party. I know you did."

"Ah did not."

"Some of you did. Some of you feel bad about the bars, and all that."

"Ah don't care what they feel, dahlin'. If they don't like mah life, they should get one of their own."

"John could see you, give you some ideas. What could it hurt?"

Silence.

"What's to lose by talking to him?"

"The whole kit and caboodle." She gave a glittering smile.

"Think about it."

"Ah think better with somethin' between my legs."

He caressed the hair out of her face and kissed her cheek. "The others aren't ready."

She did a fake pout. "They're stupid."

"Did you hear what I told Millie?"

There was a pause. "Oh, Ah heard it. Ah heard it before and Ah'll hear it again."

Margaret rolled over. After a moment or a two, a little voice said, "Sorry."

40

Madrone ushered Margaret into his consulting room with a sweeping hand. The office was small, with a thick forest-green rug framing a red-hued afghan throw. A scarred mahogany desk with Tiffany lamp occupied one wall, and a creased leather couch ran along another. Opposite the desk was a red leather armchair and floor lamp. The lamp had cut-glass dragonflies with jade-colored wings.

Margaret sat on the couch while Madrone dropped into a swivel wooden chair.

"I suppose I should thank you for offering to see me . . . but I'm not sure I feel that way. Walker wanted me to come, so I . . ." Her voice trailed off as her eyes lit on a framed etching— what looked like a child with somber dark eyes.

"So it's more Walker's idea—you're not certain if you want to be here."

Margaret smiled, but said nothing.

"Walker tells me you sometimes struggle with moods and . . . impulses . . . that put you in danger. From your point of view, is that true? Or is maybe Walker overreacting?"

Margaret was now looking at a statue of a galloping horse— front legs suspended in air.

"It's true." Almost inaudible.

"Now I'm going to ask you a very important question. Think about it for a moment before you answer. Would you like help with that? Is that something you want to change?"

Margaret was rubbing a finger across the nap of her black corduroys.

"Sometimes it scares me." High breathy voice.

"Yes, it's scary when you do something that ends up putting you in harm's way." The doctor paused, observing Margaret for a moment. "But what I wondered is this: do you want to change what's happening? The bad moods, the pressure inside that makes you do stuff that hurts you?"

No answer.

"Margaret?" He waited till she raised her eyes to meet his. "Do you wonder why these things happen?"

"No." The voice was deeper, sharper.

"I think that maybe you do."

"*I* wonder where you learned all this fake concern. What school teaches this shit?" Margaret opened her legs and crossed her arms.

Madrone leaned forward, resting elbows on knees. He laced his fingers. "I want to talk to the part of you that wants things to get better. I know there are others inside who maybe like things as they are. But somebody wants things to be less sad, less scary. I want that one to come out, to talk to me."

Margaret closed her eyes. When they opened again, one finger entered the corner of her mouth.

"Sorry." She said it in the small voice. "That isn't nice."

"Are you the one who wants to get better?" Madrone asked.

"I don't know. Maybe."

"What's your name?"

"Millie?" It was said with a lilt on the end, like she wasn't sure she should answer.

"How old are you?"

"Nine."

"Are you comfy; do you feel OK here?"

Margaret looked around. "I like that lamp. With the dragon-flies."

"Could I ask you some questions? And if you didn't want to answer anymore, would you tell me, Millie?"

A small shrug.

"How many are there—inside?"

No answer.

"Are there more than you—inside Margaret?"

"Yes."

"How many?"

Again she was quiet.

"OK, Millie, I'd like you to close your eyes and take a deep breath. Get comfy on the sofa . . . good. Now take another deep breath . . . "

Madrone hypnotized her. When he finished the last count-
down, he suggested that she was feeling very safe and relaxed.

"Millie . . . how old are you? I've forgotten."

"Nine." She spoke as if the air was barely moving through
her throat.

"What do you do when you want to have fun, Millie?"

"Draw . . . the beach . . . swings."

"I like watching the waves at the beach. Do you like watching the waves?"

"Yes."

"It's very peaceful. It makes you feel very peaceful. When
I'm at the beach, I like to take a deep breath, and just let go. Just
relax. Just take a deep breath of all that sea air . . . and relax."

Margaret took a deep breath.

"How many others are inside Margaret?"

"Three." She sounded like she was talking at the far end of
a tunnel.

"You and three others?"

"Yes."

"Do you get along?"

"No."

"Do they do things you don't like?"

No answer.

"Millie, what do the others do that you don't like?"

Long pause. "Dress up and do things . . . with men. I go
inside."

"What else don't you like?"

"Keg's mean . . . people get mad at us."

"What else?"

"Corine."

"What does she do?"

"Dances."

"Do you like that?"

"No."

"What happens when Corine dances?

"She tries to hurt us."

Madrone sat back in his chair and looked at his hand. Turning it from front to back. Stretching out the fingers.

"Who likes to dress up and do things with men? What's her name?"

"Louisa May?"

"That's everyone? Corine, Keg, Louisa May, and you? Those are the only ones inside?"

"Yes."

"Millie? I want you to go back in time. Go a long way back. Keep going and going back till you arrive . . . at the first thing you remember. Go back . . . to the first moment you recall. When you get there, I want you to take a deep breath."

After a minute, Margaret took a deep breath. And her face began to cloud. With sudden lines forming at the corners of her mouth.

"Are you there? At the first memory?"

A furrow appeared between Margaret's eyes. But she said nothing.

"Millie, you're safe here with me. You're safe in my office. But you are looking at something that happened a long time ago. From this safe place you can look back and see what happened. In a moment, you can take a deep breath and watch what happened, all the while completely safe with me. Go ahead and take the breath—watch the scene. Like on television. Just watch the scene unfold."

After a pause, Margaret took a deep breath.

"Good, Millie. Just watch the scene. Like it's on television. Watch and listen. And when it's over, take another deep breath."

Margaret began to breathe more rapidly, her face contorting. She looked like a child caught in that moment before tears come. But her mouth opened without sound. Without the relief of sobbing.

"You are safe here with me," Madrone chanted. "Watching something long ago. Watching as if it was on TV. When you've seen and heard what happened . . . take another deep breath."

Margaret's eyes raced back and forth beneath her lids. One hand rose, as if to protect herself. Then she made a small sound, and the hand plunged between her legs.

Silence. Margaret's face stayed frozen, compressed. A few moments later, her head turned. Slowly, as if she was tracking distant movement. She closed her mouth and took a deep breath.

"On the count of three, you can tell me exactly what you saw and heard. Remember, you are watching from here, protected by time. Safe and protected."

Madrone counted slowly. Then silence.

"Tell me your first memory, Millie. Say it out loud."

"I wet my pants." The words were slow, slurred.

"Start with the first thing, Millie."

"The clown."

"What does the clown do?"

"He pulls up my skirt." Margaret's hand, which had remained between her legs, pressed tighter against her crotch. "Now I can't hold it."

As she let herself tell the rest of the story, all I could think was that I wanted that man snatched from the earth. From that moment. So he could do no harm to her.

Madrone told Millie she was a brave girl. And that the clown was a bad man who should never have done those things. He went on and on about how Millie was good, that she should be cherished and protected.

It all seemed too late. The damage was done.

But I was wrong. Madrone was about to damage Margaret further.

"Millie, I'm going to tell you some things. And the others can listen if they want. Or they can go to sleep if they don't want to hear.

"When Margaret was a little girl, the clown did things that were so scary that the only way she could survive was to divide into parts. Parts that have the memories and parts that have the feelings. We call them alter egos—alters for short.

"Millie, you have the bad memories, and I think the others have the feelings—sadness, anger, sexual feelings. Each alter holds a piece of Margaret's experience of what happened.

"At different times, different alters get in control. That's why Margaret's feelings can change suddenly, or she can start doing the scary things you told me about. If Margaret is going to get better, a therapist will have to work with each alter, helping them deal with all the bad memories and feelings."

"But what about me?" The little voice was scared and plaintive.

"The therapist will take care of you and keep you safe."

A few moments later, Madrone brought Millie out of trance. He inquired how she felt and then, too quickly I thought, asked to speak to Margaret.

"Did you hear?" he started.

Margaret nodded.

"What you have been struggling with, what triggers the moods and impulses is a dissociative disorder. There are four alters—did you hear that, do you know who they are?"

Margaret nodded again.

"Like I told Millie, you dissociated, divided into parts to deal with overwhelming pain. Something too big and scary for a little girl to face. If you hadn't done that, it could have destroyed you. So dissociating helped you survive—*then*. But now it's different. The alters exert a lot of control over what you do. They affect your ability to form good relationships. And sometimes they put you in danger." Madrone hesitated, looked down at his fingers, then returned his eyes to Margaret's face.

"I can refer you to a specialist, someone who has a lot of experience with this. In time, I feel certain you can recover."

"How?" Margaret cocked her head.

"By exploring all the memories and feelings until you understand them. And you don't need the alters to keep them anymore."

"What happens to them?"

The doctor paused. "I'm going to be honest, because you need to know where this is going. Their identities dissolve into the whole. They let go and become you again. It's called integration."

Madrone leaned back in his swivel chair, looking very pleased. His manner suggested he had made a rabbit disappear.

Margaret stood and, for a moment, looked around the room. She stepped over to the floor lamp and touched the cut glass dragonflies. Then she moved next to Madrone, bending to speak in his ear.

"Ah don't think . . . that will be acceptable."

41

My father greatly distrusted the virtue of honesty. People preach honesty for two reasons, he said. To excuse mistakes and disguise meanness. I don't know how many bad sitcoms and westerns he had to watch to find that jewel, but I remember the exact moment when he revealed it.

I was struggling with a paper on Horatio Alger while my father enjoyed a particularly violent episode of *Miami Vice*. I couldn't concentrate. Through the doorway to the living room, I could see a box of Cheezits balanced precariously on his stomach. I started to feel angry—not merely about that moment, but the thorough way in which my father was wasting his life. After some minutes of fuming and preparing a little speech, I marched to the TV and shut it off.

"Can I tell you something honestly?" I started. My father nodded and placed a cracker on his tongue—no less carefully than a priest does the communion wafer.

"All night, every night, all you do is watch television. You're not *doing* anything. It makes me lose respect for you. Why don't you leave the TV off now and find something . . . productive."

I remember hesitating about the word "productive," afraid that it might inflame him. Whether that was what set him off, I don't know, but a moment later he gave his brief discourse on honesty. At the end, very calmly, he said, "You can switch it on now."

My father was an idiot, but no fool. I think his analysis of honesty applies to Madrone. The doctor would argue, I suspect, that he must give his patient an accurate report about her problems and their cure. Including the expectation that the alters would integrate, and essentially die. It was *honest*—the classic excuse for incompetence.

The night following her session with Madrone, Margaret got a call from Walker. He was going to be late. A new letter had come in for his *Sunrise* project, and he was trying to work it into the manuscript.

"This is a good one," he told her. "A man ties his boat up to a dock in Chicago. Some homeless vet panhandles him. The vet's obnoxious, and the boat guy tells him to fuck off. Then the vet says, 'I'm only trying to find peace, man.'

"The boat guy walks away, but after a few minutes comes back. 'I know the way to peace,' he says. 'You have to help children.'

"'How?' the vet asks.

"The boat guy stands there for a minute. He has no idea— he's just running his mouth, being self-righteous. After a minute, he says, 'Go down to the bus station. Find the strays, the ones who are wandering. They need to go home.'

"'How?' the vet asks again.

"'I'll pay you to do it,' the boat guy says. And right then, the two of them start this place for runaways. Still going, except the boat guy's dead. Of course. The letter was from the vet—they help 500 runaways a year."

"Will I see you tonight?" Margaret wanted to know.

"Late. But I'll be there before you go to sleep."

Though he knew Margaret was scheduled to see Madrone, Walker failed to mention it.

"Ah'll be waitin', then. But Ah'm not sure—when Ah really think about it—what Ah'm waitin' for."

Walker laughed and hung up.

During the hours she waited, Margaret dusted. Then she went through the dresser drawers, extracting what seemed to be mementos from her dance career. She read some letters and threw them away. By the time Walker arrived, Margaret was mechanically drinking tea—raising the mug, setting it carefully down—while studying the cabinets in her kitchen.

Walker's first ten minutes brought a fuller recitation of the new *Sunrise* story. Then he fussed through the brewing of some Earl Grey.

"I saw Madrone." Margaret let steam from the fresh tea brush her face.

"What did he say?"

"That I'm a house divided." She spread her fingers on the Formica. "That I need help to glue together again."

"Did he suggest what you can do?"

"He gave me a referral." Margaret's eyes worked one corner of the ceiling.

"That's it?"

"Yeah, that's it. Why did you send me there?"

"Because he said he knew what was wrong. He seemed very certain."

Margaret took another sip of tea. "Yeah, he's certain. But

is that what you want? To get me all glued up. Because if it is, we're done."

"Why?"

"Because then I'm just some broken piece of shit." She stood up, eyes glistening. "Something you're trying to fix. Do you understand?"

"You're in a lot of pain, Margaret. You're destroying yourself."

"No." She shouted it, pointing at him. "No. I'm just trying to do one thing. Not be alone."

Walker reached for her, but Margaret pulled away. She was at the stove now, burner lit, moving her hand up and down above the flame.

"Just tell me one thing," she said. "Is that what you want? Are you just trying to get me better?"

"No, John asked me a lot of questions, and then he told me . . ."

"I don't want to get better—do you understand? I don't want to look at you, to have you in my bed knowing you expect that."

Silence. Walker looked stricken, his mouth in a rictus of alarm.

"He told me that the cure is to kill them. To puncture and drain them like a cyst, like an infection. Did you know that was the treatment?"

"No. He said a lot of things. I didn't understand it all."

Margaret was still heating her hand, turning it from front to back. "The cure is to be alone. Isn't that funny? The cure is what I have always tried not to be."

She gave a tinkling giggle. "I suppose you'll want to go in there and sleep in a minute. Spoon, hold me around the stomach? Right?"

Walker raised one hand, as if in surrender. "So don't listen to him, Margaret. Let's just go on as we were before."

"Except," she said, "I know. All this has happened and I know."

42

In the morning, Walker found the note stuffed in his under-pants.

> The wall
> between life
> and disease
> is a radio
> playing
> to a couple
> in armchairs,
> their children
> waiting
> in the back room.

He read it, put it down, read it again. Then, assuming Margaret was at work, went home to continue efforts on his manuscript.

But Margaret had already called in sick and boarded the 28 bus, transferring to the 5 Fulton, on her way to the Arboretum. Her face was the usual half smile as she walked two blocks down Stanyan Street and west into Golden Gate Park. There was a faint mist that morning rising from the lawns and circling the empty branches of the elm and maple. Margaret walked in her odd, tilting-forward gait. Her leather car coat was open, billowing behind as she pressed into the fog.

The Arboretum, dating from the late 1800s, was built with a delicate latticework of white wood and glass, topped with high, Victorian cupolas. Margaret pulled the front door and turned right. Once she reached the narrow, concrete walkways of the east wing, she slowed, turning and bending to examine the exotic species. Jeweled rivulets descended each pane of glass. Illumination from high above washed Margaret's face with a filtered, gray light.

"This is the place," she said to no one and stopped moving.

Margaret was beneath the high arch of a fern that brushed thin stems of a flowering joewood. She closed her eyes. In the far wing, high voices of schoolchildren echoed off the glass.

Now Margaret's arms reached out, hands cupped. As if beseeching. Or making offerings to some god. After a moment she bowed, dropping her fingers to the moist earth. Then her arms rose again, extending, her body starting to turn.

As the turn accelerated, the schoolchildren filed in. No sound. Except for a faint humming. They were rapt, crowding forward, the little ones pressing for a view while Margaret whirled. She went on, oblivious, at last ending in a slow fold— arms across chest, kneeling and bending, touching her forehead to the concrete.

When Margaret's eyes opened, twenty small faces ranged across from her. They broke into applause. For a moment, she looked uncertain. Then she stood, made a slight bow, and gently pressed between them to the exit.

"Why do you wear that coat?" a little girl said. "Dancers don't wear coats."

Margaret touched the child's shoulder. "It tells grownups I don't take shit. But you're right. I should take it off when I dance . . . see you, sweetie."

Margaret's next stop was the wharves—south of Market where the pilings jut from the water like rows of broken teeth. It took a while to get there on the 5 and then a streetcar. She seemed to grow more agitated as she sat, running fingers through her hair, pressing on her windpipe to make a lot of red blotches.

At the wharf she perched on a railing, back to the bay, letting a teenage boy in his orange Grand Am look up her skirt. Then she turned around to watch the container ships, tall and massive, get herded by a fleet of tugs.

After a while, Margaret paced. Then threw pebbles from the dock. As dark fell, the water turned silver. Pressing the final light into thin, luminous waves. Now the ferries, throwing high, white plumes, began to take commuters home. Men could be seen looking shoreward from the decks, lips touching the rim of a cup.

Margaret put her hands in her pockets, crossed the Embarcadero, and set a brisk pace up Harrison toward the City Zoo. When she got there it was 6:00—opening time, but long before the arrival of the band. I was disturbed to see the place again. The scene of my lost life. I drifted to the soundboard where I had worked, seeing the familiar knobs and gauges. No one was in the booth now, and again I felt the helplessness of that place. Of watching the laughter and conversations. Rarely speaking, never touching.

Margaret ordered a beer. The bartender recognized her and gave her a few rays of sexual sunshine. About an hour later, a guy came in who was short, sporting a thin, gray mustache. He was physically powerful, with a dense, restless energy. His forearms were tattooed and tanned, his face seamed with tiny fissures running from eyes to chin. The man wore a Greek sailor's cap, peacoat, and black work pants.

"You're lookin' good, honey," he told Margaret as he let his eyes drift down her body. "You look like you could give instructions on havin' a good time."

Now he put his hand on Margaret's shoulder. "Could I sign up for the class?"

"Maybe later," Margaret told his crotch. "This class has certain prerequisites, and Ah'm not sure you qualify."

Sailor didn't like that. "You can examine my qualifications any time you want. But until then, honey, you shouldn't talk about somethin' you know nothin' about."

"OK." Margaret touched him between the legs. "Now Ah know somethin' about it. Ah'm really not excited. But maybe it'd help if you bought me a drink."

Sailor ordered two beers.

"Do you believe things should be equal—between the sexes?" he wanted to know.

"Sure, whah not?"

"'Cause we have a situation here—between us—where things have gotten definitely unequal."

"What do you mean?"

"I mean you touched me. You checked me out. And I didn't get to do that with you."

Margaret just looked at him. Doing her Mona Lisa smile.

"I'd like to see what you got to offer. 'Cause I'm somebody who likes a woman to be real. Know what I mean?"

Margaret's eyebrows rose. She picked up Sailor's hand and put it on her flannel shirt—over her breast. Then quickly removed it.

"That's good," he said. "There's females I know, doctor gave 'em some fucking battering rams. Some bricks. I don't like that."

Sailor smiled. "You feel nice. We could get somethin' goin'."

"Is that supposed to be some big compliment? Do girls get all wet and go home with you when they hear that?"

Sailor's eyes narrowed. He pressed a thick, stubby finger into Margaret's forearm. "You funnin' me? Or you fuckin' with me?"

"Ah'm definitely fuckin' with you." Margaret moved her arm away and sipped her beer.

Sailor lifted his hat, ran a hand through his hair. It was salt and pepper, trimmed in a crew cut. Now he looked up and down the bar, as if assessing other prospects. The stools were empty.

"Where do you live?" Margaret asked.

Sailor turned slowly to look at her. He took a long time to answer, and gave the air of boredom. "Berkeley. Near the Marina. I crew for a fishin' boat over there."

"You like that?"

He shrugged, drained his glass. Now he began to button his peacoat.

"You give up easy," Margaret said.

"I don't give up when somethin's worth it." A thin stretching of the lips. "But when it isn't . . . "

Margaret nodded while guitar tuning started coming through the speakers, then a sound check.

"What do you catch? What kind of fish?" She flashed him a brighter smile.

"You interested?"

"No."

An hour later, Margaret left with Sailor.

43

Sailor's place turned out to be an Airstream trailer housed in a shed. The shed—three corrugated walls and roof—was insufficient to the task because the trailer protruded a good five feet. A tarp was duct-taped to the Airstream's top, covering the front window.

Margaret held to her escort for support as they threaded a narrow, debris-choked path along the side of a warehouse. A hard wind, straight off the bay, riffled her hair. As they approached the shed, Sailor made a thin gesture of welcome.

"Home sweet home and all that shit," he said.

In the half moon, his face looked pasty and swollen.

"Ah love a man o' means." Margaret was slurring. "Ah can tell this is gonna set all records for excitement."

"I have something that might help," Sailor said, as he wedged in the narrow passage between shed and trailer.

He fumbled with the key, then banged the aluminum door into a support stud on the shed. Margaret sidestepped after him, climbing on a plastic milk crate to reach the threshold.

The Airstream was Spartan: one each of an overstuffed armchair, lamp stand, and TV on a leaning metal table. A black fishing rod was by the door, bending acutely where it hit the roof of the trailer. On the floor, an open tackle box displayed an assortment of weights and lures. The bench dinette had torn red cushions with strips of foam showing through. Breakfast dishes were still on the table.

"Nice," Margaret said. "You must need a maid to keep up a big place like this."

"Look at this." Sailor took her arm, fingers pressing deeply into the flesh, and guided Margaret to the kitchen. He pulled open a drawer next to the stove, extracting a box of matches and some badly knotted twine. Then he reached far in the back of the drawer to get a small Tupperware dish.

It was a kit—spoon, needle, tourniquet, and rolled Baggie containing some kind of powder.

"What's this?"

"H."

"What?"

"Horse, smack, shit, whatever. It's good once in a while. It relaxes." He paused, looking at Margaret. "I think you'd like it."

Margaret bent to examine the contents of the kit. She prodded the Baggie with her finger.

"Whah would Ah like it?"

"Because it helps you not care. You know? The world can go take a big fucking jump."

"You got anything to eat? Any moldy bread or anything?"

"I'm serious about this, honey." He snaked a hand around her shoulder and squeezed it. "'Cause when you shoot a little H, it makes your body like what it feels. It likes everything. Even if something's rough, it likes it. H makes everything good."

"Does it make this place good?"

"This place is a fucking palace on H."

Margaret swayed over to the dinette and sat down.

"Ah don't like rough." Her voice was lower now, hard-edged. "If Ah'm gonna be hurt, Ah'll do it myself."

"You'd like it rough. On H you would. But forget that. If you don't go that way, then forget it. I'm just telling you, everything feels good." He held up the rubber tourniquet, swaying it back and forth. "What do you think?"

"Where does it go?"

"The H?"

"Yeah."

"In your fucking vein, what do you think?" He pointed to the crook of his elbow. "Right there, unless I can't find a good place. Then we do the back of your knee or something."

Margaret stared out the window at the wall of the shed. Then around the room, letting her gaze settle on what looked like a couple of bills lying next to a cigarette burn on the rug.

Sailor followed her eyes. "Somebody I brought home did that. Too fucking drunk to watch her cigarette."

He sounded like he'd been betrayed after doing someone a favor.

"Yeah, those drunk, fucking women. They really should come here sober." She waved her hand in an inclusive gesture. "To appreciate all this."

Sailor wouldn't be deterred. Now he was picking up the Baggie and the spoon. "Want some? Takes a second to cook."

Margaret stood up, as if she was thinking of leaving. Then sat down again.

"In here?" She pointed to her arm.

"Yeah, I promise it won't hurt."

"Ah don't care about the needle . . . Ah don't care, period. That's whah Ah came with you." She made a grunting laugh. Then held out her arm.

Sailor got busy lighting the burner with a match.

"Fucking pilot light won't stay on. Somebody cleaned it once, and it never worked after that. Plugged the hole up, or something. I was gonna stick a pin in it—to clean it. But I can never remember to bring home a pin."

While he prattled, Margaret kept flexing her arm, looking at the place the needle would go. Her insouciance was scaring me. She was drunk, and that was part of it, but there was also a sense of detachment. A letting go. I was reminded of that night of suicidal oblivion when she had danced into traffic.

"Are veins green or blue?" she asked. "Ah can't tell."

"Who the fuck knows—they're probably some other color entirely underneath your skin."

"People say they're blue, but they look green to me." She was rubbing the crook of her elbow. "You don't realize you live in . . . this machine. It works . . . so beautifully," she slurred.

"Not that beautiful. Not when you're my age."

Margaret didn't look up. "It works perfectly—giving you this chance . . . to live. Till you fuck it up."

"That's the way it is, honey. We're all kids. Just having fun till we wreck everything." He threw the tourniquet at Margaret. "Put it on, high up your arm—near the shoulder."

Margaret pulled the rubber tube around her biceps, but couldn't get it to stay.

"Do it tight. Gotta get a vein popped."

Sailor was sucking the cooked heroin into the syringe. He looked over at Margaret.

"Oh, you don't know shit. I'll do it."

Holding the needle in one hand, he expertly tied Margaret's tourniquet with the other. Now he started patting her veins.

"Good, good, we're getting a beauty. Like a rope. You got veins, honey. Perfect for mainlining. Close your eyes now, and look away. It'll just take a second."

As soon as Sailor inserted the needle, he loosened the tourniquet.

"Feel that? Feel the rush?"

Margaret opened her eyes and looked at him. She took a deep, hesitating breath.

"Oh." She let the sound trail into a whisper.

"Did I lie to you? Is that God's own medicine? Everything's gonna feel all right now. Even pain's gonna feel good. I didn't lie."

The needle came out of Margaret.

"Oh," she said again, and leaned back against the cushion. "Shit." Her legs opened.

"Just go with it, honey. Just relax. Let the river take you."

"Shit." Margaret braced herself with one arm on the table, sending a dish clattering into the windowsill.

"The river's gonna take you anyway. So you'd better give in to it."

Margaret closed her eyes and slipped backward till her head was on the bench.

"Good, now you're on the nod."

When Margaret regained awareness, she was face down on the dinette table. Her skirt was around her waist, underpants at her ankles on the floor.

"What?" she said in a thick voice.

She looked around. Sailor was behind her, Greek cap still on his head, lubricating an erection. I wanted to hit the man.

"What are you . . . doing?"

"What it looks like, honey."

Margaret put her forearms on the table and started to pry herself up. Sailor, pushing above her spine with spread fingers, sent her horizontal again.

"You were already in the absolute best position. No use changing." He touched her buttocks. "Like I told you—relax and go with it."

At that moment, Margaret shot up, switchblade quick, throwing her weight backward. Sailor grabbed at the table and missed; they both fell with Margaret landing hard on his chest. A plate clattered to the floor and broke. Now she rolled off, reached for a shard of the broken dish. She crawled toward the armchair and pulled up her pants.

"Fuck this." It was the raspy voice. "And fuck you."

Sailor rolled heavily on his side, then got to his knees. "There's no reason . . ."

"Get away, fucker." Screaming, brandishing the shard like a knife. "There *is* a reason. You dosed me. You undressed me."

"Calm down." He was standing now, zipping his pants.

"I'll calm down when you back way over there. So that's what you like? Fucking people who are asleep? Fucking people who are helpless? Is that what gets you up?"

"Whatever you say." Sailor raised his arms and moved into the kitchen.

"Keep going. Go back to your skanky bedroom and close the door."

Margaret tried to get to her feet, but she toppled to the rug. A second attempt brought the same result.

"Get in the bedroom. I'm gonna sleep over here by the chair. That mickey made me too fucked up. But if you come near me tonight, I'm gonna cut you. Then I'll get the cops. I'll talk about the H, the horse, the smack—whatever I have to tell 'em to put you away."

Sailor waved. "I guess I won't make breakfast." He turned and disappeared down the hall.

44

Margaret slept curled on the floor. The trailer was cold, and she repeatedly turned and shifted in what seemed like an attempt to get warm. For a while she drifted in dreamless slumber, due perhaps to the combined effects of the heroin and alcohol.

Around 2:00 a.m., Margaret began a series of short dreams.

Images mostly. Vast horizons, an empty, curving road. Then she saw a dark-haired girl walking down an aisle between pews or benches. The face was pale; in her arms was a bouquet of white roses. Drops of blood were swelling where the thorns had pierced her skin.

Now I realized this was the child Margaret believed to be her sister.

The girl's head was bowed as she made passage down the aisle—walking with measured solemnity. She stopped in front of a casket, and carefully laid the roses on the bottom lid. Now she snapped two stems short—near the bud—and placed them over the eyes of the deceased. I saw, at that moment, that it was Margaret's body, half-revealed by the open upper lid. One hand on her stomach, one lying open at her side, the usual half smile still on her lips.

Within seconds, Margaret was awake, at full alarm.

45

Margaret crawled into the armchair and wrapped herself in her car coat. Her eyes paced the room.

"White roses," she whispered.

I had always fared better at seeing the imagery of Margaret's dreams than reading her thoughts. This moment proved no exception. Margaret brooded, and I had no idea what was going on. The image of her face in the coffin had sprung too quickly for me to change it, and now I was anxious about what the alters might do. Particularly Corine, whose letters had all seemed preoccupied with joining her sister.

About an hour later, Margaret rose to get a drink of water. Then she went to the bathroom in the trailer's cramped little toilet. I didn't like that she was humming *Waltz of the Flowers*.

When she emerged from the toilet, Margaret gently turned the handle on Sailor's bedroom door. A small night-light revealed a clutter of VCR boxes and a collection of unwashed mugs. At the base of the bed a plastic basket spilled dirty clothes.

He was on his back, gently snoring. Several sex magazines lay scattered across the mattress. "Wake up." Margaret spoke in a soft, sad voice.

She shook one of Sailor's feet. His eyes opened, but it took a moment to recognize Margaret in the half-light.

"Oh no. I thought you were going to sleep and then get out of here."

He threw a tattooed forearm across his eyes.

"I had a dream," Margaret said. "And now this will be your lucky day."

"What?"

"I made a decision I think you'll like." The voice was modulated and sweet sounding—decidedly unlike Louisa May's bantering style. "You could have what you didn't get last night."

"You're fuckin' with me again. We already know you don't like what I like."

"That's true, but I know a way you could do what you like— with me."

Sailor pushed himself to a sitting position. He discreetly pulled up the blanket.

"I'm listening."

"It's simple, and it would be good for both of us." Margaret paused.

"OK, say it. I can't wait."

Sailor reached up to turn on a light. It was in the shape of a squat vase. Faux antique. One of the ceramic handles had been knocked off.

"I would like to die," Margaret said pleasantly. "I can't quite make myself, but I could turn it over to someone else. The H was nice, it was just . . . slipping away. I'd like you to do like you did last night—but use enough so I don't wake up."

"No fucking way. You're crazy."

"I've been told that. But wait, you're not considering the advantages."

"Which are?"

Sailor was squinting his eyes as if Margaret had gone out of focus.

"Two of them. First, you get to finish what you started last night. Imagine—you could do anything you want. Things you've only dreamt of. It doesn't matter. Just as long as I'm unconscious, and heading out."

Margaret smiled, spread her hands. "I see I have your attention."

"I'm not killing you, honey. I'm not fucked up like that. Go home and . . . "

"But you haven't heard the second advantage." She squeezed his foot again. "The second advantage is I don't go to the police and swear out a complaint that I was drugged with the intent to rape. I think having me dead so I don't do that could be a real positive, don't you?"

Silence. Sailor rubbed the slight turkey flap on his neck, then looked at his fingers as if something might have come off.

"God, why did I sit next to you at the Zoo?"

"Because you wanted to fuck me. And now you can."

"This is a helluva thing. Kill somebody or get sent up."

"But the point is I *want* you to do it. It's not killing. You're just assisting with a suicide."

Sailor's eyes shifted around the room, landing finally on a mug that said *Vegas*.

"OK," he said. "But I'm hungry. I can't do shit like that on an empty stomach. You up for me treating you to a last meal?"

Margaret's eyes narrowed.

"You were hungry last night," he reminded her.

"I know, but . . . it's early. Where would we go?"

"Denny's. Perfect place; I expect a lotta people take their last meal there."

"Why don't we just get on with it?" Margaret was clearly uncomfortable with the breakfast idea. "I'm not hungry anymore; I'm just going to have to sit there and . . . "

"But I am hungry. I told you. If I'm gonna do this, I want my strength."

Margaret finally agreed. Sailor drove her, in a multi-dent, white Corolla, down San Pablo and then east on Dwight Way. When they were almost at Shattuck, he started to park.

"Where's the Denny's?"

"Around the corner. I like to park here because there are a lot of homeless assholes who'll fuck with your car up there."

They got out. A hulking building occupied the entire block on their left. A lit emergency sign presided over wide double doors. Farther up the street was a sign that said *Oncology*. Sailor took Margaret's arm and started steering her toward the emergency doors.

"What's this?"

"You'll see."

"No, I won't."

She tried to pull away, but Sailor had a vise grip.

"Where are you taking me, you slippery dick fucker?" The deep, harsh voice must have been Keg.

Sailor kept dragging her. Margaret stumbled, her shoes scraping across the concrete.

"Let me go, fuck bag." Keg was screaming.

Now Sailor shoved Margaret, face first, into the double doors, and pushed her toward the receiving desk. A large black nurse surveyed them with hands on her hips.

"This is the psych unit, right?" Sailor asked.

"Herrick Psych Emergency." She pointed to a sign. "Says so right there."

"OK, good. This woman is suicidal. She asked me to kill her. She's crazy as shit."

Margaret tried to turn for the door, but Sailor violently whirled her back to the counter. "She met me and came home with me. Then she gave me this." He put the syringe and Baggie of heroin on the counter.

"What's that?" The nurse's eyes shifted from an agitated Margaret to the powder.

"It's junk. She said somebody gave it to her, and she wanted me to do her—kill her. She heard I'm an ex-junkie and I know how to fix."

The nurse was looking at the needle mark on Margaret's elbow. "Looks like she already fixed."

"I don't know about that. That must have been before I met her."

Margaret leaned toward the nurse. "You gonna listen to this shit? It's *his* heroin. He tried to dose me." Keg was still talking. "Let me the fuck go. I'm out of here."

"Did you ask this man to kill you?"

"Who cares if I did? Do you care? You don't care about shit. You're just waiting to get off. You just wanna get home to your fucking TV."

The nurse turned and gave the nod to a Sumo-sized orderly behind her. "I think we need you, Shig."

Sailor gave a thin smile. "See what I mean? She got like this as soon as I said I wouldn't do it."

Shig was behind them now, putting strong hands on Margaret. She kicked back at him, then tried to butt him with her head.

"I'm leaving. This man tried to dose me. What kind of stupid fuck can't understand that?"

The nurse looked at Sailor with suspicion.

"You leaving that?" She pointed to the Baggie.

"Of course. It isn't mine."

Margaret dropped to the floor and tried to punch Shig in the crotch. The orderly responded by expertly rolling Margaret on her stomach and placing her wrists in soft-cuff restraints.

"Got a live one here, now don't we?" the nurse said. She looked at Sailor. "We'll need to interview you—find out what's what."

"Fine by me, but the girl's got some stuff in my car. A paper bag full of clothes. I'd better get it."

"OK. I'll call upstairs, have somebody come down and talk to you."

Margaret's cheek lay against the floor. She had started to cry, and tears were smeared on the linoleum. "Please," she said in a little voice.

Sailor left and never returned.

I felt both relief and a corrosive sadness. For the moment Margaret was safe, but I had been witness to the falling apart. Now her pain was inside me. And I had no vessel to hold it. Even alive, I knew nothing about holding pain—mine or anyone else's. I just watched. Judging, detached. This was different because the woman crying on the floor in some way belonged to me. Somehow her tears were my own.

46

Margaret's restraints were removed within half an hour of her arrival. She had stopped crying and hadn't tried to hit anyone since the episode with Shig. She was now talking to a thin, fiftyish social worker named Tara. The woman had short, dyed black hair with gray showing at the roots. Her face, still somewhat pretty, was a map of tiny smoker's lines. Heavily mascara'd eyes seemed sad.

They were seated on either side of a long table in the day room. Several patients—some in jeans and tees, others in hospital robes—milled by the window. It had bars. The room was painted gloss gray—a lovely color, I thought, to treat depression. Along several walls, travel posters had been taped up. In the far corner, Shig was talking to a girl with a bandage on her wrist. He pointed to the bandage; she hid it behind her back.

"How's it feel to be alive right now?" Tara asked.

"Fine."

"Fine, you like being alive? Or fine, you'll tell me anything to get out of here?"

Margaret didn't answer.

"The guy who brought you in seemed a little sketchy. He disappeared before we could talk to him. How did you hook up?"

"In a bar."

"You go home with him, like he said?"

She hesitated. "Yes."

"He's kinda low class—you go for that? Or is there some other reason you chose him?"

"I chose him because he was there—next to me."

"So he was available and you needed some . . . comfort?"

Silence.

"'Cause he says you knew he was a junkie, and you asked him to OD you?"

"I already told you. He dosed me. He tried to rape me while I was out. Whatever else happened, it's not your business. OK? Those are the facts. Stick with that."

"Is that how you got the needle mark?" Tara pointed to it with a nicotine-stained finger.

"Yeah."

"Did you consent to the fix?"

Margaret nodded. "It seemed like . . . it would help."

Tara looked at her watch.

"Shift over soon?"

"Uh huh. We got to decide what to do with you."

"When you leaving?"

"Seven, but I got to give report first." She looked at her watch again.

"Let me go. I'm fine."

"Yeah, you said that. But you got some heroin and . . . "

"That's his. He lied."

"Why would he make it up? Give away his stuff?"

Silence.

"See what I'm saying? We got a problem here. I don't want to take a chance you still want to hurt yourself."

"It doesn't matter. You know that. I'm just another psych case. Pretty soon they're gonna let me out—you, somebody. It doesn't matter."

"It matters to me. A long time ago I had a boyfriend kill himself. Off the bridge. It left me . . ." She shrugged.

"OK. You care. I'm sure that's true." Margaret took a breath. "But I just got into a bad situation. I feel fine now. The world looks brighter."

She gave her half smile and looked toward the barred windows.

Tara leaned near her patient. "Margaret, if there's one thing you're not, it's fine.

"What makes you so sure?"

"The way you came in here, for one, screaming like a banshee. I think we should 5150 you—check you out. If you're depressed, Margaret, medication could help."

"What's 5150?"

"A 72-hour hold. Gives us time . . . "

"No . . . no." The little girl voice drew the vowels into a keening sound. She lowered her head into her hands and started to cry.

Tara sent outstretched fingers toward her patient's arm, barely touching.

"Wait!" Margaret bounced up again, tears no longer spilling. "What if I had a friend, a very reliable friend, who could take me home and watch over me? Someone who could make sure I'm safe, make sure I'm feeling all right?"

Tara looked at her watch.

47

They let Margaret call from the office. Shig was there, his massive body draped over a tiny office chair. And there were several other staff members, all congregating to chat and escape the patients. Plastic-sheathed charts—in cheery orange—lay at various angles on the counters.

Tara pressed a button on the phone. "There you go. Let's see what he says." She leaned against the Dutch door separating the nurses' station from the day room.

When Walker answered, Margaret's face lit up.

"Hi. You'll never believe where I am . . . I'm in the hospital."

A tightening in Margaret's lips suggested Walker wasn't particularly surprised.

"It's Herrick—over in Berkeley . . . it's a psych hospital. They think I'm suicidal."

Margaret listened for a while with her eyes closed.

"No. Ah'm fine. It's a long story. But, Walker, Ah was . . ." She hesitated, eyes suddenly wide open. "Yes, OK . . . the point is . . . I'm fine. Could you take me home? They seem to think I need a responsible person."

There was a long pause. Margaret kept pulling the cord and letting it spring back.

"So you'll come for me? I'll wait." A little giggle. "I can't do anything else."

Tara, who'd been tapping her nails against the Dutch door, now reached her hand out for the phone.

"They want to talk to you—my social worker's here—to

make sure you aren't some figment. To make a . . ." She turned to Tara. ". . . what is it? A discharge plan?" Margaret giggled again.

Tara took the receiver. "Mr. Anderson? Do I understand correctly that you're our patient's . . . boyfriend?" She said the word like she didn't think it was possible. "Margaret came in last night very agitated; we're concerned about releasing her without someone—a friend or family member—who will be responsible."

Long pause. "I understand she lives in San Francisco . . . If I give her a referral to the Sunset Mental Health Clinic, will you make sure she follows through and presents herself there for a psych eval? . . . Because, like I said, we are concerned. We have reason to believe she might be a danger to herself. Do you understand what I'm saying, Mr. Anderson?"

Silence.

"Because if you don't, if you don't want to take responsibility for keeping an eye on her and getting her over there for treatment, she might be better off staying with us for observation."

Tara looked at the wall clock. Compared it to her watch. Then she moved over to a pile of charts and began smearing them around till she located the one she wanted.

"OK. I'll do her discharge papers. We'll be waiting for you."

Margaret was reaching out her hand, but Tara hung up.

"There's plenty of time to tell him everything when you see him. Or some. Or nothing." She shrugged, put three fingers lightly on Margaret's arm. "We're letting you out of here. But take my advice. Get treatment. I'm not sure you'll make it if you don't."

Now the fingers gave Margaret a little shove. "OK, back to the day room. You can wait for him there. I gotta do your chart before . . ." She closed the Dutch door.

A skinny patient with a three-day beard made a beeline to

Margaret. "Be careful," he warned. "CIA." He pointed toward the nurses' station.

While Margaret waited to be released, I drifted into the street, letting cars pass through me. Watching the drivers' slack, expressionless faces. Behind steel and safety glass. Consumed with some errand, with the illusion of direction. Perhaps it was my sadness about Margaret, but I felt how alone they were, all seeking some ephemeral dream that must sooner or later be lost.

48

When Margaret emerged from the elevator, Walker was standing near the intake desk, his coat pockets sagging from the weight of his hands. He shrugged, lips tightening. Then he pulled one hand out to make an infinitesimal wave.

Margaret took a few steps toward the desk and handed its current occupant—a thick-set Asian woman with a silver wig— a folded piece of paper.

"Would you give that to Tara?"

The woman nodded, and while Margaret was looking, unfolded and read it. The missive turned out to be a poem:

We are all
helpless,
except some
pretend otherwise.

Now Margaret continued in Walker's direction, looking past him toward the door.

"What asshole fucked you up this time?" The hand was back in his pocket.

Margaret's eyes narrowed. For a moment she looked hurt.

"Same guy. They're all the same guy." She pushed past Walker and out the double doors.

A moment later he caught up with her on the sunlit pavement. "What guy is that?"

"A guy who's looking for a hole." The harsh voice. "Good-bye."

She started walking toward Shattuck, where a steady stream of cars was crossing with the light.

"I'll take you home," he shouted after her.

"I'm not going home."

"Why?" He was half-running, trying to keep up.

"Because there's nothing there. It's just a place."

"Then where are you going?"

She turned around, pushed a hand out in a stopping motion. "Walker, no. You don't want me. We already figured that one out. You want somebody broken, but fixable. Somebody you can turn over to Madrone and watch while she recovers. While she gets all melty and dependent."

"Not true. I just want . . . to be trusted."

"Why?"

Walker hesitated. "I don't know. For Christ's sake, stop walking away."

"And do what? Get in the car? Have you drive me somewhere? So you can think you're taking care of me?" The words *taking care* were thick with sarcasm.

"Yes."

"You're trying to redo the scene with your mother—you know that? Find some sick person you can lead around the block, somebody you can feed and comfort and give pills to. But unlike your mother . . ." she pointed at him, ". . . will never leave you."

Now Margaret put her hands on her hips. "That's what all this trust shit is. Getting me so I'll never leave."

Silence.

"Walker, listen." Margaret stepped closer. "I'm going to stay exactly like this, the person you see right now. I don't want your help—to get better. Or even to stay alive. All I ever wanted from you . . . is this." She touched beneath his eye. "To look at me. That's it. Just to look at me."

"OK . . . that's all you want. Just see you—without changing anything."

She nodded. "No matter what I do. Or decide."

"OK. I can do that."

"You're so full of shit."

"Try me. Get in the car. I'll take you wherever." He gestured down the street toward the Porsche.

After a long moment, Margaret nodded. "OK. I want to rent a room. Some place that looks out on the water. That's peaceful. I'll go that far with you."

Walker thought about it. "There's a hotel at the Berkeley Marina. Looks out on all the sailboats they've got tied up there. The rooms have little balconies. You can go out and smell the salt air."

Margaret nodded. "Looking out the window will be fine. I don't have to get all involved in the place."

On the way, Walker got into a long monologue about a woman he'd known while working as an editor in Omaha. I wasn't sure what launched this—maybe it was an oblique response to the accusation that he wanted to clip Margaret's wings.

The woman had lost her husband to some extreme skiing mishap. She was an in-house writer for a Sunday supplement magazine specializing in new cultural phenomena (of which there were none in Nebraska). She'd moved to Omaha because her husband was in the Air Force—worked in one of those missile silos they've got buried in every cornfield.

After the funeral, the woman was too distressed to write. So Walker ghost-wrote some of her articles. They had a lot of lunches, and eventually he started spending the night. But she was abstracted—which at first Walker took for grief, and finally understood as boredom. With Omaha, with her life.

They stayed together seven months while he helped her recover. Then he supported her to find a job closer to her family in New York.

"So that's what you like?" Margaret's eyes narrowed as she watched him from the passenger seat. "Little ruined people?"

Silence.

"I'm sorry. OK? You helped her; you don't deserve . . ." Margaret touched a finger to his shiny glove box. Leaving a print. "Did you love her?"

"Yes. Enough not to hold her there."

"Why didn't you go with her?"

"I knew what would happen."

When he didn't say anything more, Margaret prompted him, "Please finish the fucking story."

"Her gratitude would have turned into something else. *Was* turning. I sent her off while we were still . . . "

"She didn't love you."

"I told you, she was grateful."

49

"This is good," Margaret said, as she pulled open the drapes of a second-floor room at the Radisson. I was concerned because she'd just spent ten minutes in the bathroom throwing up. But Margaret was now oddly cheerful. Almost ebullient.

Stacks of gray cumulus pressed the hills above the bay. But a cleft in the clouds poured brilliant sunlight on the balcony. Below them, masts of a hundred sailboats swayed to various rhythms in their slips. Chime-like notes and dull clanks came from the slapping of ropes and pulleys. Waves triggered a faint groaning from the wooden docks.

Now Margaret tested the bed, bouncing on her hands and knees.

"Yes, this will do."

I noticed a style of speech that had been more evident recently. Words came slowly, deliberately. The voice held a richly modulated, blue-blood tone.

"It'll do—for what?"

Walker sat in the desk chair, watching Margaret continue her inspection.

"As a place to . . . let go."

Walker rolled his hand in a "keep talking" gesture.

"Let go of this life."

Silence. Walker began rubbing beneath his eyes. Creasing the skin in little folds.

"Are you talking about killing yourself? Here?"

"Don't be dense."

For some reason, despite having no luggage, Margaret was methodically checking the drawers.

"Here's the Bible." She held it up while she walked to the balcony. "Won't be needing this pile of shit. 'The Lord is my shepherd, I shall not want.'"

Margaret made a good heave, and the book splashed in the water.

She continued, "You know what I hate about religion? If you can't take what life deals you, it's always your fault."

Margaret took a deep breath of the marine air. "Smells good. Cold and good."

For a while, she chirped about the light, the wind, and a couple of the big yachts moored at the far end of the harbor. Walker said nothing; he wasn't even looking at her.

Then Margaret went to his chair and knelt. Very gently she picked up Walker's hand and kissed it. The gesture had a dense formality. As if Margaret wanted to solemnify what she was going to say next.

"You have been good to me. Better than anyone. Better than I deserved . . . but it's time."

Margaret replaced Walker's hand on the arm of the chair. She caressed it a moment. Bowing and letting her raven hair spill as she touched him.

"I need one last thing," she said. "For you to accept this. Accept that I don't want to integrate. I don't want to lose the others. And that I have lived this life long enough—believe me."

I wanted to shake Walker. He seemed mesmerized. His eyes wandered the edges of the wheat-colored carpet; his shoulders had collapsed in a slump.

After a minute or two of silence, Walker roused himself enough to meet Margaret's eyes.

"Who am I talking to? Who is making this decision?"

"Corine." She said it in a soft whisper, as if the name might be dangerous to utter aloud.

"How do the others feel—about this? Millie and Keg and Louisa May—how does Margaret feel?"

"Louisa May is a fool whose opinion doesn't matter." She stretched her lips in distaste. "Keg—he's a chip of flint. A fragment. His whole life is anger. Millie is scared and tired. All these years she just wanted a child's life. To make castles in the sand, to draw, to throw her feet up high on a swing. But she doesn't get it. Instead, she has to feel the hands of the men—touching her between the legs. Or she takes refuge in sleep."

"Corine, let Margaret come out. Let her talk to me."

"No." Her body shivered, and she started to close her eyes. "No. Margaret is empty. She is nothing without us."

"I don't believe that."

"Margaret is a basin, a container. Just bones and skin. We fill her up. Believe me, Walker."

He shook his head but said nothing.

"We are tired. Not just Millie, but all of us. We need to leave this."

"For what?"

"To be with my sister."

"Where is she?"

No answer.

Walker abruptly rose, headed to the balcony. He opened the sliding glass and leaned on the rail. Stretching out both arms. Bowing his head.

"So you want me to—what—watch while you kill yourself?"

"You don't have to watch. But you said once you love me. If you love me, I need you to see that we've reached the end. We can't do this anymore. The pain won't stop. The loneliness won't stop. I need you to believe me that we're tired."

She came up behind him, put her hands on Walker's shoulders, and rested her cheek against his back.

"This is . . ." Walker didn't finish.

"You can't stop me. You know that. I will do this one way or another. But it would mean so much if you could see . . . that I need to. Really see that. Love me enough . . . to let me. And not be angry. And not try to stop it."

Walker's eyes glistened. "You're right," he said finally. "I can't stop you."

"Thank you." She leaned around his shoulder and kissed his cheek. "I've got to go out and do a few things, but I'll be back tonight. Will you be here?"

Walker nodded.

"Thank you," she said again.

50

When Margaret left, I felt something break open in me that was hard and barren. Like the valleys of granite I once walked in the high Sierra. With only the sound of wind combing the fractured rock.

If Margaret died, there would be nothing holding me. I imagined the emptiness of her rooms, her bed. I imagined rising, weightless, higher and higher, until I was beyond reach of human sound. Margaret's death would complete my own. I knew it would thrust me out of my limbo—into the emptiness, into the cold distances between stars.

My father, I suddenly remember, sometimes went to the window during commercial breaks. He'd stare for a moment into the evening sky. "Think I'll stay here," he'd say to nobody. "Looks cold and lonely up there."

I was afraid—for Margaret and myself. But she had said she'd return to the hotel that night. We had that long—Walker and I—to keep her. And perhaps she'd change her mind, or maybe Walker could get smart and persuade one of the other alters to take charge.

Margaret took a cab from the Radisson, telling the driver to drop her on Telegraph. "The part with all the street people."

"You serious? Is that where you go?" He had a thick Pakistani accent and a Free Kashmir sticker on his dash.

"Can you take me there? You know where I mean?"

"I take."

He hit the gas like he was in a hurry to get the trip over with.

On the corner of Dwight and Telegraph, Margaret got out and started working her way down the street. Clots of men lay or sat against the storefronts. A few had quiet, undernourished dogs; most had a sleeping bag or duffel. The faces were young, unshaven. Eyes were alert, wary with an admixture of defeat.

In front of the urine-stained facade of Moe's Books, Margaret knelt by a guy who was trying to play an old National guitar—with no E string.

"Hey," she said. "What's happening?"

He gave her the once-over. There was an angry-looking boil just to the left of his Adam's apple. He had a thin nose, and thin blond hair. Grimy fingers began pressing the perimeter of the boil. His eyes narrowed like he was doing a difficult calculation.

"Nothin'," he said finally. "Want to hear a song?"

Without waiting for a reply, he started a rather strident rendition of "I Fought the Law." Margaret put a hand on his strumming arm.

"Maybe later. You're pretty good." She offered a blistering smile. "But I was wondering. I need a doctor."

The guy broke out a couple of quick power chords. "I don't know any doctor. You sick?"

"Not exactly."

He looked disappointed. "Why d'you want a doctor?"

Margaret got closer. "I need a . . . scrip," she whispered. "For pills because . . . you know, to get well."

The guy shrugged. "I've heard a name . . . a doc who's got an office up near Ashby—sometimes helps people out. You got any money for strings? It's fucked trying to play like this." He ran his fingers up and down the frets where the string was missing.

Margaret gave the guy ten dollars.

"That's cool. Thanks." He put the bill in his sweatshirt pocket.

"What's the name of the doc?"

"I forgot. But he's near Ashby—like I said."

"That doesn't help—I need a name."

"I know." He started playing again. A three-chord riff that sounded like the intro to about a hundred punk songs.

Margaret stood up and headed for a threesome that were sitting on a blanket. One was a woman with fleshy, sunburned cheeks and cinnamon-colored dreads. She was smoking a hand-rolled cigarette. Sucking in with relish—exhaling twin streams through a flat, simian nose. Her companions were two long-haired men who were trying to teach their dog to sit.

"Abby? Sit the fuck down." A guy with painted fingernails

was pushing the dog's hindquarters. Now he lifted the mutt's ear and shouted, "Sit!" The dog barked and tried to bolt.

"Stupid dog—doesn't understand English." High, wheezing laughter. "Sit *down*. Fucking dog has the fidgets." More laughter.

Margaret bent over them; put her hand out for the dog to sniff. The woman blew smoke in her face.

"I was wondering," Margaret said, "if any of you know a doctor . . . who could write a scrip."

"Sit." This was the second guy—festooned with tattooed bats on each hand.

Margaret started to lower herself. "No, I mean the dog."

"Fuck off, narc," the woman said.

"I'm not a narc." Margaret was indignant.

"Suck my ass. Get out of here." She kicked Margaret's shin.

On the next block, a light-skinned black man was selling stapled poetry at a card table. By his side was a woman who looked like Mrs. Doubtfire—doing Tarot readings.

Margaret asked her question while Doubtfire flipped cards and studied them. "See that," she said, pointing to a card with goblets on it. "That's trouble."

"What kind of trouble?" Margaret asked.

"The kind that has a shortening affect—on your life. Just some free advice."

Margaret had gone four blocks, and was almost at Bancroft when she bent to talk to a guy who was sitting huddled in a sleeping bag. His hair, in tight ringlets, hung like a curtain across his face.

"You on the wrong street," he told Margaret. "People here don't have no money for drugs. We all just sleepin' out. Tryin' to get by. You want drugs and scrip docs and shit like that? Go hang outside the Free Clinic. On Durant. They know about that shit. They all tryin' to score down around there."

His hand moved inside the bag—as if attempting to point. "All that shit takes money. You go on down there."

Margaret nodded. "Thanks. Maybe I'll do that. You need anything?"

The guy looked at her for a couple of beats, and gave a phlegmy little laugh.

"Do I *need* anything? I need every-fucking-thing. That's why I'm here. You think I got a flat screen and a zebra-skin couch somewhere? You think I'm just visitin' the street?"

Margaret straightened to her full height. She brushed imaginary dirt from the front of her coat.

"But if you want . . ." he looked up at her, hair falling away to reveal pouting lips, ". . . you can give me money."

Without saying anything, Margaret stuffed a twenty in the top of his sleeping bag. She gave something between a wave and salute—then walked away.

Berkeley Free Clinic was in the basement of Trinity Methodist Church, a peeling, stately relic of the twenties. An entrance sign warned, "No crashing or camping." Thick wire mesh protected the lone window. Across the street, a needle exchange truck boasted a pair of green Chinese dragons.

Several men squatted next to it under a billboard that read, "Is God Still Speaking?"

As Margaret approached the group, I saw a flash of money exchanging hands. One of the men turned to check her out, eyes lingering on her breasts. He had a long, pale scar descending his cheek. Fright-wig hair framed red, sun-damaged skin.

"Well, who do we got here?" He smiled up at Margaret.

His three companions suffered a flurry of putting things in pockets and backpacks. They looked unhappy with the intrusion.

Margaret asked the scrip doc question. Straight out. No pretense she wanted a conversation.

"Well, look, you don't need a doc. There's people around here . . ." he smiled suggestively, ". . . who could help."

"I'm sure you're right. But I'd like to be certain what I'm getting."

"I could get you something."

Margaret squatted next to him. "I just need a hookup. That's all. D'you know anybody?"

"I know whatever you need . . ." he gestured to include his friends and the street in general, ". . . is here. See what I'm saying?"

Margaret hesitated. She studied his three companions.

"Fuck sake, Louis. You don't know her." It was a guy with a bandana tied around his shaven head. And thick, squared-off fingers that he pointed at Margaret. "Look who you're tellin' your shit to. You never seen her. Bitch might be fixin' to slam your ass."

Louis stood up, saying, "I'm tryin' to do some business here. I don't need you fuckin' with my business." He touched Margaret's arm. "Let's talk over there."

"Hey!" The guy with the bandana again. "Jimmy Dale. Got an office on Shattuck. He'll write. But don't be seein' him if you're not straight up. He can smell shit. If you're wrong, he won't give you an aspirin."

Louis was on high bake. "What're you doin' in my business?"

"I'm getting rid of the bitch."

Margaret started to slide away, but Louis grabbed her coat.

"Wait, I want to show you somethin'. You don't need Jimmy Dale. Fact, I never heard of no Jimmy Dale."

Margaret yanked the coat out of his grasp and started to half-run across Durant—in the direction of the clinic.

"Thanks for everything," she shouted over her shoulder. "You're a great bunch of guys."

51

Dr. James Dale's office was a walk-up over a fabric store. The gray front door had scuff marks near the bottom, where it looked like someone once kicked it. Dr. Dale had answered

Margaret's call himself and offered to fit her in. He told her he kept the waiting room door locked, and she should buzz when she arrived.

A nasal-sounding electronic voice—also Dale—requested Margaret's name before a loud click indicated the door had been unlocked. Margaret climbed a straight flight of terrazzo steps that led to a windowless waiting area. The room was framed by four rows of molded plastic seats—an unfortunate chartreuse. Walls were sand-colored and covered with matted photographs of winter scenes. A man—who turned out to be Dale—was captured with goggles and poles in front of a snowbound lake. Track lighting splashed bright pools on the photos and chairs.

A thirtyish woman, with stringy blonde hair and a foot that kicked restlessly, was the lone occupant of the room. She looked up when a frosted glass door opened on a short, thick-set man. He had bushy black eyebrows and about ten hairs still growing on his widow's peak. I didn't like him, and I didn't like the radiant smile Margaret blasted his way.

"Elise," he addressed the blonde. "Can you wait a couple of minutes? There's something I got to deal with here."

"It's OK." She looked like being put off was an accepted part of life. "I gotta pick Phil up at 4:00. Other than that, I got time."

Dale's eyes slid to Margaret. He made a slight "come in" gesture toward the door.

"Just don't forget me," the blonde said.

"Not possible." The doctor threw her a molten glance. "Forgetting you isn't something that could happen."

As Margaret walked in front of Dale, her body grazed his abdomen.

"Sorry," she said with no tone of regret. "Nice of you to see me."

They were in a glossy white hallway with two small exam rooms opening on the other side. Jimmy Dale led Margaret to his office, a generous, wood-paneled room that looked out on Shattuck Avenue. There were photos of more ski scenes on the walls, plus the usual diplomas and certificates of training. From what I could see, Dale had completed a residency in gastroenterology.

Dale gestured Margaret to a Bank of England chair, while he slid behind a desk cluttered with charts and magazines. On the corner of the desk a globe, dotted with red pins, touted the doctor as a world traveler.

"How can I help you?" Dale's voice was shriveled and high-pitched. He cleared his throat as if trying to break into a lower register. "You said you were in a lot of pain."

Margaret smoothed her corduroy pants. "I've had ulcerative colitis . . . since I was a teenager. I just moved here from L.A. and had a flare-up. I was better for a while and it gave me confidence I could make a change. But the stress, I guess, of moving . . . "

Dale was nodding rapidly. Several hairs had come free on his comb-over, and were whipping around as his head moved.

"I don't have a doctor here yet, and someone gave me . . . recommended your name."

"How has your colitis been treated—pharmacologically?"

"Valium. To control stress. I get very anxious and then . . . everything gets worse."

"Worse in what way?"

"Bleeding. Pain. Running to the bathroom. The whole colitis mess."

"Valium isn't the first line of defense against colitis. There's pain management. And Prednisone to reduce the inflammation. Now we've got Remicaid. Have you ever had a trial of Remicaid?"

"Valium is the only thing that really helps me. I guess because flare-ups are always so stress-related."

Dale had lapsed into heavy duty nodding again. "So Valium is all you want . . . for the colitis."

"Right. I'm so anxious, with the move and everything; it's ripping up my guts. I need something to calm the whole reaction down."

There was a tightening at one corner of the doctor's mouth. "How many will you need—Valiums—to calm your gut down?"

Margaret hesitated, looked at her fingers as if she was considering counting on them. "Sixty. I think sixty would get me through."

"That's quite a lot." Dale sat back, lacing his fingers behind his head. "People can get in trouble with that much Valium." The chair groaned as he tilted it. "*Beaucoup* trouble."

"I won't get in trouble," Margaret said sweetly. "I'm trying to get out of trouble."

Dale said nothing, stared at the ceiling.

"How much does it cost? An office visit of this nature? I'm happy to pay whatever."

"We're talking about a medical issue here. Has nothing to do with fees. Is this an appropriate treatment for your problem? Is sixty Valiums too loose a tether, in terms of monitoring? You have to realize—Valium is an abused drug, and these prescriptions are monitored by the feds. So everything has to really make sense medically."

"I need this, doctor. I'm going to be very sick without it. Is there a way to avoid . . . the scrutiny?"

Long pause. Dale's chair groaned upright, and he began to slide around the contents of his desk.

This was the moment of choice, and I wanted so much for Dale to rise above things sleazy and venial. I wanted him to honor his oath—and do no harm.

"I could call it in to a pharmacy I know," he said. "That way we wouldn't have a paper trail. But, of course . . . that's an additional service . . . "

"And has an additional fee," Margaret finished.

"Of course."

"What's the name of the pharmacy?"

"Sinclair. Over in Oakland. Bit of a problem neighborhood. You driving?"

"No."

"Take a taxi and have it wait."

Dale found a billing form under a magazine. The front cover showed some fool snowboarding down a 60-degree slope. He scratched a few notations and handed the form to Margaret. The consultation cost $400.00.

"In situations like this . . ." he coughed delicately, ". . . it's cash or plastic. No checks."

Margaret handed him a credit card. Dale swiveled to a gun-colored credenza behind him, swiped the card through a dial-up verifier. Now he returned the card and signature slip to Margaret.

"Very efficient—considering . . ." Margaret was looking at the rat's nest on his desk.

"In some things, one can't afford to be sloppy."

Dale phoned in the prescription and wrote the pharmacy address on note paper that advertised Remicaid.

Margaret stood, waved the yellow credit card receipt. "Isn't this a paper trail?"

"Not the kind anybody cares about. It's just . . . money."

52

Now, as Margaret's cab pressed between the gated liquor stores and broken cars, I was sick at heart. I sat next to her in the cab, as if I were another passenger. As if I were her companion. I felt an almost physical heaviness. A sadness flecked with helpless anger.

I remember as a child when our cat got sick—poisoned probably—and my mother called my father at work. He didn't think a vet was necessary and had us wait till he got home. We bundled the cat in a blanket and kept holding and talking to her.

The cat wouldn't open her eyes by the time my father got there. He lifted her paw and let it drop.

"She's a goner," he said. "Put her where it's warm by the stove and let her be. This is why you can't get too attached to animals."

My father folded the blanket around our motionless cat, and got up for a pre-dinner snack—*Le Petite Ecolier* cookies, dark chocolate, engraved with the likeness of a schoolboy. He turned on the television and began mechanically bringing the cookies to his mouth. I could hear the snapping sound of every bite.

It was the same feeling now—with Margaret. The same bitter surrender to a loss. I watched while she headed into the pharmacy, fingers brushing the bars over the front window. Nothing I could see in her face gave me reason to hope.

53

When Margaret returned to the Radisson, she found Walker sitting on the balcony. The chair was tilted back, his feet on the railing.

"You've been here all day?" she asked when she finally stood behind him. It was her melancholy voice.

"No."

Walker didn't elaborate—his eyes stayed fixed on the swaying masts.

Margaret touched his shoulder. "It's a lovely view. Thank you for choosing it."

She stepped to the rail, looked at him while leaning against it. Walker was crying.

"I thought maybe you wouldn't come back. Maybe you changed your mind. But then I heard you come in." He shrugged.

Walker's fingers laced and dropped into his lap. He looked

down, studying them, while his thumbs caressed each other. "Now I realize . . . "

Margaret knelt then, kissing his cheek where the tears were streaming.

"You're a sweet man. I'm sorry," she whispered.

Now she kissed him on the lips. Tentatively at first, and then with more passion. Walker turned his face away.

"No. Please let me." She drew his face back, pressed her finger over his lips. "Please let me."

Margaret kissed him again. Their mouths were open now, taking each other in. Walker's arm encircled her shoulders, and after a while he just held her, stroking her forehead and cheek.

"I . . . I would like to," Margaret said.

"Like to what?"

"You know."

"No. Say it. It's important to me."

"Make love." She whispered. "I've never . . . done it before."

"What are you talking about?"

"Louisa May does that. And Keg comes out. But with men, I'm always . . . sleeping." She kissed him again. "I never did this before. I never wanted to. They were disgusting."

"You have no memory of those . . . men?" His voice was incredulous.

"When Louisa May was out, I had to be inside. I could watch. I saw her tease them. All the games and innuendo. But at a certain point, when their hands began to touch her, I went to sleep. I had to." Margaret rested her face on Walker's shoulder. "Afterwards . . . I felt vile. With no way to wash. No way to be clean again."

She lifted up to look at him. "But I want to know what it's like. With someone sweet . . . Could you show me?"

"Where are the others, Corine?"

"Inside. I won't let them out. I've always been the strongest." She said it with a note of pride.

"Stronger than Margaret?"

"Yes. She could never stand up to me."

She kissed Walker again. A full, deep kiss. "Will you show me then? There never was anyone like you . . . before. I waited, but there never was anyone."

Walker picked Margaret up and carried her inside. But he didn't lay her on the bed. Instead, they stood facing each other. Quietly looking.

"This is the way we undress," he finally said. "I unbutton your shirt . . . and open it. And then you unbutton mine." He brought her hands to the top of his shirt.

"Then I kiss you to show that you are safe and cared for. I hold you a moment—like this—so our skin touches. And we feel each other's warmth."

Walker knelt. "Now I undo your pants and kiss your stomach. To show I will be gentle with each vulnerable place. And now I take off your pants, but not your underwear. Because you aren't yet ready."

He stood. "You can do the same. Slowly."

When Margaret had unbuckled and pulled down his pants, she stood facing him. "Now what?"

"Now I hold you till you feel safe—ready to take off the rest." He circled his arms around her, pulling tight so that the full lengths of their bodies were touching.

"How will I know?"

"Your body will tell you."

After a long time she said she was ready.

When they were undressed, he kissed her again—a delicate, slow touching of their lips. "This is so you know that you are lovely. But more. That I can feel you beneath your skin."

"You're a writer," she said, and continued to kiss him.

"I love you . . . beneath your skin. I love how much you hurt. I love your different selves, your voices. I love how you struggle with each other. I love your loneliness. I love how you mock me.

I love all your sharp places. I love that you dream about your sister—and won't let her go. I love that you're tired and want to stop living in this empty place. I love how hard it is to trust."

They lay down then, and he pulled the covers around her. Walker asked permission for each place he touched.

"Tell me how you feel that," he said. "Tell me if it feels OK."

And she kept answering him in that soft, melancholy voice. Her breath came quickly; her eyes were on his eyes.

"I am empty there," she said when he caressed above her pubis. "It's like a place no one has ever been."

When Walker entered her, there were no other voices. Just a low keening sound. Of grief or letting go. She kept her eyes on him—as if his face was a harbor.

He said later, "Now we aren't empty. Do you feel that?"

Margaret nodded, touching his jaw with the tips of two fingers. Taking a slow, shuddering breath.

When it was over, they lay for some time without speaking. I imagine Walker was hoping that Margaret would rethink her plan. He might have felt that her openness would bring a new kind of trust.

But then Margaret said, "I just wanted to know how it felt. Just one time before . . . thank you."

54

"I hear you wet everything when you overdose," Margaret said as she placed several layers of towels on the bed. "I don't want to make a mess."

Walker slumped on the desk chair, watching her. He was tearing strips off a note pad.

"That's considerate of you."

"Please don't be like that. All sarcastic. I have to do this—I need you to see that."

Walker changed the subject. "Why won't you let any of the others out? I'd like to talk to them."

"They're scared. They need to stay inside."

"They're afraid because you hijacked them. You're taking them to their death."

"No. They're all tired; they want to let go. It just scares them to do it. So I have to."

Margaret held out her hand. "Let me have your key. You shouldn't be here when I do it. And I don't want you changing your mind and coming back."

Walker handed her the plastic key card. I wanted to slap his sad, stupid face. I wanted to pull a string at the back of his neck and make him say something miraculous, something to change her mind.

Margaret carried the cards to the bathroom and flushed them down the toilet. Then she closed the door.

"I'll be out soon," she called to him. "We can talk for a few minutes and then you have to go."

Margaret threw up. She seemed so calm, so sure of herself, I was surprised to see again this sign of anxiety. Perhaps even Corine had doubts as she made a choice where there was no going back.

Margaret rinsed her mouth. Then peed. Then methodically—five or six pills at a time—took the sixty Valiums. She watched herself in the mirror as she swallowed, rubbing her face now and then with a pair of outstretched fingers.

She came out of the bathroom with her hand on her stomach. Pressing slightly.

"Made me a little queasy," she said. "I'm gonna lie down and let it settle."

Margaret climbed into bed, carefully arranging herself on

top of the towels. She patted the blanket, gesturing for Walker to join her.

When Walker moved to the bed, she asked him to hold her hand. And, of course, the fool did it, sitting there in silence and waiting for the pills to take effect.

"This is good," she finally said. "Please, Walker, listen to me. There's no recovering from what I have. I'm not talking about Maurice or any of that. I mean that I can't . . . stop being alone."

"We were together an hour ago. I could feel it."

"Only because I'm leaving. Not otherwise. It could never happen otherwise. Listen—there is no cure for this white room I live in. It's got no windows or doors. I am shouting, trying to be heard. But even if someone hears, it doesn't matter. There's no getting in or out.

"For years I waited for some force—something outside to knock it down. But I know now that will never happen."

"You don't know that, you haven't given the two of us a chance."

"I knew that when you sent me to Madrone." She released Walker's hand. "I knew you couldn't live with this, that you would try to . . . change it.

"It's weird. It took finding someone really good, who cares for me, to finally know I can't leave the white room."

Walker leaned closer. "I could be the person who breaks into that room."

"No. To get in you'd have to understand this. How much I need to do it. You would have to see how tired I am. How alone I am. And accept it."

He gave a low grunt. "You mean the only way to prove that I love and accept you—the only way to break into your solitude— is to watch you kill yourself."

His voice had an edge of anger, but all his spineless waiting made me sick. Call the police. Run to the balcony and shout for help. Something. But no, he was going to reason with her. He was a total waste.

"Right now," she said, "I'm thinking about when I was nine. After my mother kissed me, she drove away down the street, waving the whole time. I had on my pink jacket. Her arm was bare and it was cold. But she kept waving. When I turned to go inside, Maurice was . . . waiting. At the door. His hands were against his chest, one holding the other. The room, like all the rooms of his house, was white. From that moment to now, I have been . . . lost. I have been unreachable. Believe me.

"For years I would visit my pink coat. In the hall closet. I would take refuge in its fleecy feel. The smell of my old house. I would dream of putting it on and running away. But I would never wear it—not even when it was cold. Because I was saving it. For my deliverance.

"When I was older, I took it down one time. To smell it. And put an arm through the sleeve. Just to feel it over me, just one arm. And then I saw it was too small. My wrist pushed far out of the sleeve. I had waited too long."

Margaret adjusted her legs under the blankets. "It's nice and warm."

"Because you couldn't escape Maurice, you think you can't change now?"

"Listen to me. It *never* . . . got better. You understand? From the day she waved and disappeared into that other life. With her farmer in Merced. All the way to now, where the anger and loneliness—which we turn into lust—poisons every meeting with a man. And I'm still the little girl wishing the coat would fit, that finally I could run away. But to where? To what? There's no leaving the white room."

Walker looked away from her—night was falling on the Marina.

"Do you understand?"

Silence.

"Do you understand?" Her voice was dark. "Answer me."

"Yes. If I love you, I am supposed to let you do this. So the pain can end."

"And more than that." She started whispering now. "So I can be with my sister."

"You said that before. What do you mean?"

"She told me in a dream. What I have to do."

"She wants you to die?"

Margaret nodded. "I was in my coffin."

A flash of panic touched Walker's face. Tightening it. His eyes ricocheted around the room.

"I want to talk to Millie, say good-bye to her."

"She's too scared. She . . . "

"Please. I love her. I need to say good-bye."

"You're going to have to leave soon. I'm getting sleepy."

"Let me talk to Millie."

Margaret closed her eyes, and I thought she might be succumbing to the pills. But a moment later they slowly opened. Her voice, when it came, was high and breathy.

"I'm tired," Millie said.

"Do you know what Corine is doing?"

No answer.

"Corine is committing suicide. Do you understand that, Millie? If she dies, all of you die. Keg, Louisa May, Margaret—and you. Do you want that?"

"Corine is the smartest one. She likes to read. All those history books." Long pause. "She writes poems."

"I know. But this doesn't make sense."

"She says we won't have the men anymore. We can be with our sister."

"You'll lose me. Do you want that, Millie? If you die, you'll lose me."

Margaret's mouth opened, but she said nothing. Her lower lip had begun to tremble.

"I love you, Millie. I want to take care of you. We can go to the beach. We can draw together."

Walker kept talking for a while, describing a world where Millie could be safe, could have a father.

"She's gone to sleep," Corine finally said.

"Why? I was trying to tell her something."

"That you love her? She heard you."

Walker looked in the direction of the balcony. The sky was ebony—the boats had disappeared.

"Let me talk to Margaret. I want to say good-bye to her." His words spilled quickly. "Margaret, please. Come out and tell me if you want to do this."

"Walker?" She covered his hand. "It's time now."

Walker tried another tack. One that was—if anything—more pathetic. Because he was now playing on Margaret's sympathies, pulling for guilt.

"My mother was considerate," he said, rubbing half-circles under one of his eyes. "When she killed herself, she left a note telling me not to go in the garage. The garage was detached, and we used it for storage. Never for the car. On this night, when I went outside, there were boxes and furniture all piled along the edge of the house."

Walker paused here. His voice had been a slow monotone, but now, as he resumed talking, it seemed thin. Reedy. The words were twisted with emotion.

"I could hear the engine running from outside. I understood immediately—she'd cleared a space for the car so she could go in there and do it. And I wouldn't have to find her. Smoke was leaking from the bottom of the door and . . . I felt compelled to go in. See if she might still be alive.

"Her mouth was open. The fumes were all around her face, undisturbed by the faintest breath. And . . . we never went to church, but she had a rosary in her hand. Some stupid talisman to help her face death. I don't know."

Walker's face seemed to compress. His voice abraded to a hard whisper.

"I don't know," he repeated. "And now . . ." A vague gesture toward Margaret.

"Would you kiss me before you leave?" She gave him a sad, downturned smile.

Walker didn't move.

Now Margaret sat up and pulled Walker's face so he had to look at her.

"I love you," she said, "as much as I know how."

She kissed him and fell back.

"Go. I need to sleep now."

She closed her eyes, let out a little sigh.

"I forgot. Would you call the hotel in the morning and tell them? So a maid doesn't come in and get scared? And put 'Do Not Disturb' on the door."

Walker got up finally, brushed his fingers over her arm.

"Thank you," she slurred. "Bye."

And Walker—that consummate ninny—let himself out the door.

55

I felt alone on a cliff ledge. With no one to help me. The responsibility for keeping Margaret alive was now solely mine. Helpless to touch her or make a sound, I had only one weapon. Her subconscious.

As Margaret crossed into sleep, she started to fall. Like a heavy object drops through water. Slowly accelerating, her spirit letting go to the waiting depths. And I knew I had one chance to catch her—when she descended to the point where she could dream.

Past that point she would be lost. And I would have to watch her breath slow, her body give up.

I lay next to her—as I had done the first night I was discarnate. My arm touched hers, but I couldn't feel the warmth. My finger traced her lips, feeling neither skin nor breath.

Familiar losses. But now I was about to lose the one I loved. Not love of the flesh, not a fascination, but a love I had learned. By paying attention. By knowing the beautiful, broken places.

The first dream arrived less than five minutes after Margaret closed her eyes. It was the clown. Dancing with a drunken tilt. Then there was another dream. Of a room with spindly, old-fashioned furniture. From somewhere came the sound of crying. Margaret began to race through darkened halls, pulling open door after door. But the crying only seemed to recede.

Now the dream turned, or perhaps another was beginning. Margaret was in a bedroom. It was spare, with a straight-backed chair, chest of drawers, and a bed with a pink coverlet. Dim light was emitted from a ceiling globe.

The room had an odor—like food that had spoiled—and quite suddenly I could sense Margaret's nausea. I also realized that the queasy feeling wasn't new, that she'd been struggling with it throughout the dream.

Margaret walked deeper into the room—she was looking for something. She stopped at the chest of drawers, began opening them. First the twin drawers at the top, then several beneath. They were empty.

Now Margaret checked a narrow walk-in closet. It held wire hangers and, in one corner, a tangle of chewed or torn newspapers. She kicked the little pile and the paper seemed to explode, scatter. Drifting in slow, unnatural patterns through the air.

As Margaret turned back to the room, the odor intensified. I could feel her stomach begin a series of little spasms. Now Margaret walked to the bed and lifted the coverlet. Nothing.

I don't know what drove her to continue searching—perhaps she still looked for the crying child—but what she did next gave me the chance I'd been looking for. Margaret lay down to look under the bed. It was dark, and she couldn't see anything. She reached in, and began sweeping her hand across the smooth hardwood. It hit something, and she scooped whatever it was into the light.

The object was a lifeless rat. Gray in color. Lips drawn back to reveal the long incisors. The odor was intense, almost like a physical blow. Margaret recoiled, scrabbling backward across the floor.

For all the effort to get away, Margaret couldn't take her eyes off the rat. So I went to work making small alterations in the scene. There were tonal variations in the animal's fur—and these I exaggerated into a mottled gray and white. To the white areas I added movement. Until Margaret suddenly saw the gestalt—a dead rat crawling with larvae. Now I turned up the smell by linking it to the maggots.

In the bed, Margaret kicked suddenly and rolled to her side. Her stomach began to tighten. I kept the scene in front of her, kept the maggots moving, kept the fetid death stench at the center of her awareness. Margaret threw up. With projectile vomitus that cleared the bed—followed by a spectacular series of wretches and dry heaves.

When it was over, she lay peacefully by the pool of discharge, breathing slowly, steadily. The rat dream was gone. In its place was a window—boarded up—that Margaret was trying to open. I made the boards loose, rotten. She pried them off with her hands. Now she could see the glass was broken—cool night air pressed against her face.

Fifteen minutes later Walker let himself in the door, courtesy of a replacement key from the front desk. Even now, I don't know whether he returned to summon help or watch Margaret die. Maybe it doesn't matter. I'd already gotten the pills out of her. When she woke up, he could say what happened was natural. He hadn't betrayed her, hadn't tried to stop her decision to die.

When paramedics wheeled Margaret through the double doors of Alta Bates Hospital, she was still unconscious. An oxygen mask covered her nose and mouth. And they'd started an IV in the back of her hand. Walker was next to the gurney, talking to her, trying to wipe the clots of vomit from her hair.

"You're OK, you're OK," he said. "It wasn't your time. You're OK now."

He kept chanting. And though I knew it wasn't the truth, I enjoyed it anyway.

And I enjoyed something else. That my love had done something, given something. I had stopped being the watcher of lives. Instead, I had saved a life, which is something I'm still proud of. Something Walker, for all his generosity and sweetness, seemed reluctant to do.

56

Margaret regained consciousness sometime after midnight. Her eyes wandered the white curtains of her stall. Then she studied the monitors, the IV lines. She raised her hand, turning it, observing where the needles pierced the vein.

After a while, Margaret reached beneath the sheet — feeling first the wires to the heart monitor, and then the Foley tube between her legs. Her eyes closed again, and the tears began. In streams across her temples to her hair.

When the nurses checked on her, she answered questions with a single word. Voice empty. Someone took blood; someone checked her urine bag. Around 4:00 a.m., they took off the monitors and moved her to a private room. At 6:00, Margaret threw up on her bed. Yellow bile.

Walker called her — to say he would visit at noon. And a physician came in to discuss the results of Margaret's blood tests. At 11:00, the excellent Dr. Madrone arrived. Walker, no doubt, had filled him in about events at the Radisson. The doctor said nothing for a moment. Just stood and watched. Finally, he cleared his throat and stepped closer.

"Hello, Margaret."

She turned to look out the window. At a haze of leafless branches. "What do you want?"

"Walker asked me to look in on you."

"Forget it. OK? You've both done enough." Her voice was a whispery paper cut.

Madrone's head thrust forward and his eyebrows got an elegant little arch. "You angry at Walker?"

"He made the call; he put me here. Let's say I'm disappointed."

"He made the call—but only after he found you in a pool of barf. You'd already thrown up the pills."

Margaret glanced at her visitor before letting her eyes dart away again. "You mean Walker . . . "

"Your body made the decision, Margaret. The fact that you didn't die has nothing to do with Walker."

"Oh." She sounded like she was at the far end of a long hall.

"I can't say what he would have done if you hadn't thrown up. Maybe he would have called it in, maybe not. I don't know."

Margaret started nodding. She pushed the button on her remote to turn on the television. "Thank you for coming," she said over the foamy sound of a beer commercial.

Madrone reached up to the set, turned it off manually. "I'd like to stay a little longer and ask a couple of questions."

Margaret's lips pinched; she turned again to the window.

"Let me start with this. Can you tell me if you are disappointed to be alive?"

Silence.

"Please answer. I'm not going away till we finish. The questions are necessary."

"So you can figure out which loony bin you'll ship me to?" She gave a small, contemptuous laugh. "But, fine, I'll answer. I felt disappointed to be alive. But that changed."

"Changed? How did the feeling change?" He sounded disbelieving.

"Because . . ." She lifted her knees and seemed to stretch, then dropped them again. "I had a tube with a bag for the pee. I didn't like that."

"You were saying why your feelings changed."

"Because I had a blood test. After I threw up this morning for no reason. The doctor told me the results a little while ago. I'm pregnant."

Madrone caressed his lower lip with a fingertip. "And that's what changed how you feel?"

Margaret nodded.

"You want the baby?"

She nodded again. "For a long time."

I could hear a slight trembling in Margaret's voice. Her eyes glistened, and she looked to the ceiling, trying to stop the tears.

"There's no way . . . I would do this again. Not with a child." A single tear spilled and she wiped at it. "If you're here to figure out how suicidal I am, what the chances are, they're zero. I'm going to have this child. I'm going to take care of her."

I found myself doing a mental jig, just watching her and flooding with this feeling of relief.

The slightest smile pulled the corners of Margaret's mouth. "If you'd come in here a few hours ago, I couldn't have said that. I would've danced around and bullshitted you—trying to get out of here. So I could find a way to get myself dead."

She hit the "on" button again for the television. "If you don't mind," Margaret said, "I think you have everything you need to know."

"You keep trying to end the conversation. How come?" He was talking over the sound of a car chase.

"Because the last time I talked to you, I didn't like it. And I don't like it now." She turned to look at him. "I don't want the shit you have to offer. Your *treatment*. To be probed. To have parts of me killed off."

"That's not what I was saying." On the screen, a Mercedes hit a bread truck and turned into a fireball. "What I was trying . . . "

"I don't care. I don't want to hear it. I want to stay what I am. Do you get that?"

Madrone bowed his head. "I get it."

He started to speak softly, and I don't think she heard him because there were police sirens on the set. Margaret seemed absorbed in the program. She didn't look up when he turned to leave.

At the nurse's station, Madrone got the phone number for Margaret's attending physician. Ten minutes later, he confirmed the pregnancy.

Then Madrone did something odd. He returned to Margaret's room, and just stood there. By the doorway, leaning slightly back against a dough-colored wall.

"You checked to make sure I'm having a baby?" She didn't take her eyes off the screen.

"Yeah. You're about four weeks into it."

"Can I get out of here now?"

"When you're medically cleared. As far as I'm concerned, it's OK to go."

"Good."

Madrone kept his position, now putting his hands behind his back.

"I know what you're waiting for," Margaret said. "But you don't know how to ask it."

"What's that?"

A black-haired man flew through a windshield on the TV. "You want to know if Walker's the father."

"OK, maybe I do . . . is he?"

Long pause. Margaret adjusted the front of her gown. "Yes, Dr. Madrone . . . Now shall I say what you're thinking?"

Madrone raised his eyebrows.

"You're thinking, 'God help him.'"

57

Walker showed up with a book he'd gotten off Margaret's night table, and some changes of clothes. He greeted her with a kiss on the cheek. If he'd been expecting the lash of Margaret's anger, it didn't happen. Instead, she reached for his hand and drew him to her.

"Did Madrone tell you?"

"Tell me what?"

"Did you talk to him since he was here?"

"No."

Then Margaret told Walker about throwing up in the morning, about getting a blood test. She strung out the story for dramatic effect, explaining that she'd been nauseated a lot lately—which probably explained why she threw up the Valium. Walker nodded, didn't say anything. When Margaret finally got to the punch line—presented rather triumphantly—Walker remained expressionless.

"Are you happy for me? Tell me." Her face was creased with excitement. And what might have been the beginning of alarm.

"Sure, I guess so." He seemed hesitant. "Does it mean you're going to stop all the suicide shit?"

Long silence. "Yeah."

"You're not doing that again?"

"No. Not with a baby." Her voice had gathered a slight indignation.

"Good."

"You don't care much about the baby, do you?"

"If it gives you a reason to live, I'm happy about it. But the child, itself . . ." He shrugged.

A pony-tailed male nurse came in to check Margaret's vitals.

"I think they plan to discharge you this afternoon," the nurse said. "Somebody'll be in later to talk to you about it."

Margaret closed her eyes, and the nurse eventually bustled out. When she opened them again, her focus danced around the room, not lighting on anything.

"I had a needle in my hand," the little girl voice announced. "It hurt when I tried to hold anything." She held up her hand. "They took it out. See where it's black and blue?"

Walker suddenly smiled and kissed the top of Margaret's head.

"Millie, honey, are you OK? Corine wouldn't let you out."

"And I felt like I couldn't hold anything, like I was going to pee the bed. But there was a tube in me."

"It must have been scary," Walker said.

"We know who the baby is. Do you know?"

"You mean who the baby's father is?"

"No, you're the daddy. Corine says so. But I'm not talking about that."

Walker spread his hands.

Now Margaret's voice dropped to a conspiratorial whisper. She leaned toward Walker.

"It's our sister. The one who died?"

"The girl in the photograph."

"Uh huh. The one who's a little taller. She would have come a long time ago. But Maurice and our mother wouldn't let us have her."

The little girl voice held a shallow sadness. As if she were describing the demise of a pet salamander. Margaret lay back against the pillows.

"How do you know it's your sister? You seem very sure, Millie."

"Yes, we're sure."

Millie didn't elaborate on what made her certain, but now she pointed vaguely toward the ceiling. "For a long time she has been trying to come."

"Millie?"

"Yes."

"I love you."

"That's nice."

"I was afraid I was going to lose you."

Millie didn't answer.

Walker changed direction. "Corine was out for a long time."

"Yes."

"But she's inside now?"

"Yes. She was . . . doing everything, but now she has to rest."

Margaret's hand slid along the metal surface of the little rolling table where they put the meal trays. "There's nothing to do here. There's nothing to draw with."

Walker gave her his fountain pen, then ripped an unused page out of her chart. Margaret bent over the paper, beginning a crude, painstaking sketch of some animal. I couldn't tell what.

"I can't really draw with this thing."

"I know, Millie, it's all I have."

Suddenly her face brightened. "Corine's happy. She always wanted to leave before. She hated the men; she hated Louisa May. But now . . . "

Walker took his pen back. "We'll have some fun later. We can blow bubbles on my balcony and watch them scatter in the wind. Would you like that, Millie?"

"Yes."

"That's good. Millie? I need to talk to Margaret now. I need to figure some stuff out. OK? Can I talk to Margaret?"

"She has a headache."

"That's all right. I still need to talk to her. Maybe I can get her an aspirin."

After a brief flickering of the eyes, Walker heard Margaret's adult voice.

"What a lonely place this is." She gestured toward the corridor. "So many people. But they hardly talk to you. They touch a button; they shove a thermometer in your mouth." She gave a little laugh.

"You'll be out of here soon."

"I know."

"Are you hungry?"

"Yeah. I had only a tiny bit of breakfast because I was nauseated. And now my stomach hurts. I think that's what's giving me a headache."

"You were gone a long time . . . while Corine was running things."

"I know. I wanted to talk to you last night, but I couldn't . . . say anything." There was a pause while Margaret smoothed back her hair. "Walker? Can I go home with you? I don't want to go back to my place. It's too lonely there."

Walker nodded, touched her hand.

Now Margaret sat up, almost violently circling her arms around Walker's shoulders.

"Thank you. I promise I'll go to work; I won't be a burden. I just . . . don't want to see those shelves anymore, don't want to read those books. You know? I don't want to be reminded."

"It was a prison . . . that looked like an apartment. I know. I could feel it."

"Did you?"

Margaret kept holding him with a desperate grip. As if letting go would risk losing his promise. After a while, she asked Walker to lie in bed with her. When the social worker came to arrange discharge, they were still twined together. Margaret, face pressed to Walker's chest, didn't even look up. Walker gave his address. "I am taking her home," he said.

After the discharge papers were signed and Margaret started

to get dressed, Louisa May came out. She did a little striptease with the open-backed hospital gown.

"Ah do like it," she said, "when a man wants to take care of a woman. When he's ready to do his duty." The gown dropped to the floor, exposing her breasts. "And if he's kahnd—that's just frostin' on the cake."

Walker handed Margaret a bra and one of her flannel shirts.

"Better cover up, sweetie, before I forget my manners . . . and Mr. Keg pays us a visit."

"That boy does suffer," she drawled. "Ah never knew a boy that got himself more riled over nothin'. He just hates that any-body . . . would ever have a good time."

58

Louisa May's little performance reminded me of something my father did. Before he sat down to watch TV, he had to fuss and get the pillows on his Barcalounger just right. Then he opened a button or two on his shirt and fooled around with this little space heater he kept near his feet. Finally, he had to get his wine and snacks lined up for easy consumption.

"You building the Taj Mahal in there?" my mother called sarcastically. "Or just getting ready for a little television?"

"I'm taking care of myself," he'd say. "And, believe me, you know nothing about it."

Late in the afternoon, Margaret finally departed the hospital. Though it was cloudy and cold, she insisted they drive across the Bay Bridge with the windows open. And when they got to Walker's Fell Street flat, Millie immediately wanted to go up on the balcony and blow bubbles.

During the evening, they didn't talk much. Margaret fell asleep on the couch. As Walker carried her to bed, she woke up and recited part of the nursery rhyme "The Little Girl with the Curl":

"When she was good, she was very, very good; and when she was bad, she was horrid."

"Is that you?" Walker asked.

"No. Because I'm never really good. Just bad or a little more so." She giggled.

Walker pulled off Margaret's corduroys, then drew the blanket to her shoulders.

"I think good and bad are bullshit," he said. "They're words our parents used to keep us in line."

She nodded and closed her eyes. Walker slid under the covers on his side of the bed.

"Sleep now," he told her. "You didn't get much last night."

"Is it true—what you said? That we can stay here?" It was Millie.

"Yes."

"Did you believe me, when I told you it was yours?"

"Uh huh. But that's not why I said you could stay. I want you here, regardless."

"OK."

Walker rolled on his side, dropped one arm across Margaret's belly. "How's your sister doing in there?"

The next day, they went to Margaret's apartment for her clothes and a few personal items. Including pictures of her mother.

"Where is your mother now?" Walker asked.

"They sold the orchard and moved to Palm Springs. I visited a few times. She came down with leukemia when I was—I don't know. A year later, she got a stem cell transplant: died of massive infection."

"Do you miss her?"

"No."

"Did you ever tell her about Maurice?"

"No. She was too chipper for something like that. She would have gone, 'Oh my God, oh my God,' and then changed the subject."

"Incredible."

"Oh, yeah. She was that. A few days before she died, my mother called to say that she was sick. She prattled about snow she could see in the mountains above there. And about the flowers people had brought—a fucking description of every bouquet. Then she said, 'Sweetheart, promise me you'll fill your life with happy times.'"

After they left, I hung around Margaret's apartment for a while. It had been my home, too. My anchoring place. And my prison. Margaret's books were still there, two walls of shelves. The floor lamp and the overstuffed chairs cast shadows in the living room. From her window, I observed the siding of the house across the yard. And the sliver of street and sidewalk out on 21st Avenue. It was twilight. A few pedestrians climbed home from the trolley line. Wind searched through their clothes.

Downstairs a television was on. And somewhere—still early in its journey of pain—a child was crying.

59

The next morning they sipped tea and watched a storm slash the eucalyptus on the Panhandle. A great bough had fallen in the night, leaving a branch with torn, white wood.

"Bloodless wound," she said.

I suspected Corine was finally out again.

A half hour later, while Margaret was in the shower, Walker called Madrone and arranged a late afternoon appointment. Then he made some toast for Margaret to eat while he drove her to work.

At the ballet office, I watched Margaret on the phone. Selling tickets in a phony, singsong voice. Manuel came in with the mail.

"You are looking better than good, *mi amiga*. You shine so bright I need to hide my eyes."

He did a pantomime of covering his eyes, then peeked between two fingers.

"But I look anyway, even though it blinds me. Even though," now he gestured toward her with both hands, ". . . you could be the last thing I see."

"You're sweet, Manuel. I hope your eyesight recovers enough to sort my mail."

"I know. Because if it doesn't, I'd have to go on . . . the disability. And it would be your fault, *mi amiga*."

He ran a finger along the edge of her desk—as if checking for dust.

"I know what would restore my sight."

"What's that?"

"A kiss, *mi hermosa mujer*."

"I have a boyfriend, Manuel. I moved in with him yesterday."

"*Verdad?* You are not pretending?"

Margaret nodded.

"Then he is a lucky man." Manuel paused and his face tightened. "Because when it's late, when everything is quiet, perhaps you undress for him. And perhaps he holds you."

Manuel was looking at the floor. "I wish I was that man, *mi amiga*. I wish I was."

"I know, Manuel." Now Margaret stood. "Come here. At least I can do one thing for you." She reached up to take his head in her hands.

"I can restore your sight." She gently kissed each of his eyes. "Thank you, Manuel, for thinking I'm something. Now leave me my mail and I'll see you tomorrow."

At noon, while Margaret was in the bathroom, she raised her

flannel shirt to examine her abdomen. Then she bent to look from each side, running a hand over the flesh. Measuring.

During lunch at a greasy little French fry and burger place, Margaret wrote a letter—in the leather diary she'd always kept for these missives.

Dear Sister:

At the exact moment I gave up waiting, you entered me. And now I feel you growing. All the emptiness is gone—the minute I knew you were inside.

I promise I will take care of you, my sister. You will live the life that was taken from you. Walker can help me; he knows who you are.

Never in this life have I felt joy. I only imagined it. But now I know joy. Because I have you again.

Love,
Corine

While Margaret wrote, I formed myself to the shape of a facing chair. As if we had met for a meal. As if I had walked in and we had waved, greeting each other. And I imagined sentences I might use to begin the conversation.

"Did you know I see your dreams?

"Did you know I saved your life?

"Did you know you are all that matters?

"Did you know . . . I love you?"

When Margaret left the restaurant, quickstepping in the direction of her office, I drifted away. Up Polk Street where the young men sell themselves—in tight pants with colored kerchiefs, advertising their sexual wares. I dallied in the loneliness of the bars. Where the patrons studied each other, trying to imagine how the sagging flesh might still kindle passion. Then I swept by City Hall, watching men in suits climb the long stairways. Moths to the flame of power.

It was all in a minor key. All regrettable. Nothing held me;

nothing mattered. In one way, I continued to feel relieved—
Margaret seemed happy. Purposeful. Yet my own emptiness
had deepened. Inside it thrummed, like an undertone of loss,
of disconnection.

Now, after a morning lull, the rain started again. Drizzling
at first and slowly gathering force to a wind-whipped sleet.
No one was left on the sidewalks as I passed into the building where Madrone had his offices. But the sound of the wind
followed me. A muffled roar against the windows, rattling the
casements.

Walker had arrived before me. He was in his usual jeans and
sports coat, clutching a slender spiral notebook. Dr. Madrone
shook his hand with apparent warmth. Then he led Walker to
his private office, waving him to the leather client's couch.

Walker produced a fountain pen. "The reason I wanted to
see you, John, is I need to know more about how to handle . . .
these personalities. She's not getting treatment, so I . . . "

"What do you want to know?" Madrone shifted in his chair,
looking suddenly darker, more guarded.

"Answers, I guess. Strategies. For example, one of the alters,
Corine, thinks the baby is her sister." Walker explained Margaret's obsession with a past life in Holland. And the yearning to
rejoin a sister killed in the Holocaust.

"You want to know if that's healthy? Answer is no. You want
to decide whether you should go along with it? Answer is yes."

"Why?"

"Because you can't fight it. This alter has a fixed delusional
system. You're never going to change that. The best strategy
is to support delusions that are useful—like this one, because
they make her want to live and take care of her baby."

"So I play along."

"Have to. Corine is probably schizophrenic. You could only
treat that with drugs—which Margaret won't take."

Madrone laced his fingers across his chest, and leaned back.

"It's a scientific fact that different alters often have different medical conditions. For example, each personality may require a different correction for their vision. So a multiple might need three or four pairs of glasses. One alter might be manic-depressive, or have diabetes, or colitis—while the others do not. Certain alters may have unique allergies not shared by the others. Or require different dosages of blood pressure medication. See what I mean?"

"That's crazy." Walker was writing furiously.

"Exactly. And then there's the problem of each alter having unique needs and reactions. One might want to kill you; one might want to sleep with you. One might desperately try to get better, and one—as in this case—might decide to die.

"It's like relating to a big, squabbling family. You try to manage some weird, mumbling aunt, while also paying attention to the kids. You try to support one teenager's autonomy, while not letting another fall off the cliff. You have sex the way one alter demands, without offending another's sensibilities."

"I get it, it's bad. But I pretty much knew that. I'm hoping you can tell me how to work with it."

Madrone looked out the window, then rearranged some objects on his desk. He was forced to adjust the letter opener several times because it wasn't in quite the right place.

"I keep doing that, don't I? Trying to scare you off?"

Walker didn't respond.

"I'm going to say this one thing—then I'll shut up about it, OK? You found Margaret because you want to correct what happened with your mom. You want to make a different outcome, OK? But here's the catch. You won't ever save Margaret because she's exactly like your mom—someone whose course can't be altered. No matter what you do.

"See what I'm saying? You're trying to fix her, but you choose folks who can't be fixed. So you'll end up feeling all that familiar despair you had growing up."

"Fine." Walker scraped under a nail. "I appreciate the insight."

Silence.

"You want techniques. The good news is you only have four alters. Some people have dozens. It's a small enough group that you can check in with them regularly. See how they feel, what they need. You can usually get an alter on stage by simply calling his or her name, and insisting they come out.

"That'll also help you if one alter is out and doing something crazy. You can literally demand that a more stable alter take over. Or ask for an alter with skills appropriate to the situation."

Now Madrone was uncurling the cord on his telephone.

"Speaking of skills, some alters will have executive abilities to help Margaret deal with challenges. One might be socially adroit, one might be a good problem solver, one might be assertive, one capable of hard, focused work. See what I mean? So your job is to encourage and strengthen those skills—and when Margaret needs them, help the right alter come out and be in charge."

Walker put his pen down. "Corine is smart; she likes to study; she likes to write."

"There you go, perfect example. Probably there are lots of situations where you'd encourage Corine to take charge . . . On the other hand, if Corine gets a bit depressed, then you need to encourage a happier alter to come out, like Millie, or maybe even Louisa May.

"They all need time on stage. Just don't let them stay out if they're messing up, OK? Encourage Millie to come out and draw. Maybe give Louisa May a little time in a sexual situation. Get Corine involved in something creative, something that requires her to read and write. Maybe get Keg into a competitive sport. Ice hockey might be good—he could legally beat the shit out of people."

"What about when the alters want different things?"

"Then you have to do shuttle diplomacy. You go back and forth between the alters, finding out their needs, and brokering a compromise. Millie wants to go to the park; Corine wants to go to the ballet. (She's the dancer, right?) So maybe you get them to agree to the ballet tonight, and some fun on the swings tomorrow. See what I mean? You're going to spend some time doing these negotiations. Because if you don't, the family of alters will get mucho dysfunctional."

"What if one of them wants to do something really dangerous?"

"You straight up label it as such. Then you find out what need the behavior is designed to satisfy. And you work individually with that alter—or the whole family—to meet that need. Don't just try to shove it underground. Never works. It always comes back to bite later."

"What about Margaret herself? How do I take care of her?"

"Keep her out as much as possible, OK? Confide in her. Get her advice about the family conflicts and negotiations. Try to strengthen her with intimate conversations, expressions of love, that sort of thing. But be careful—don't neglect the alters. They'll freak if they don't get time. And you'll see a lot of weird moods and impulses."

"And sex? You said maybe go along with Louisa May if she comes out. But Keg is nuts; he's hostile as hell. Turns the whole thing into a nightmare."

"OK, talk to Keg. Negotiate. Tell him it's really hard when he comes out during sex. Ask what you can do for him so he isn't compelled to come out. Maybe he needs reassurance that Margaret is safe, loved. Maybe he just needs to do some martial arts." Madrone gave a mirthless laugh.

"What if Millie comes out? Sex traumatizes her."

"Ask her to go back to sleep. Then name and call out another alter who can handle it. Also, try not to do things sexually that really terrify a particular alter. 'Cause if that alter suffers more trauma, they may get crazy."

Walker was tracing the veins on the back of one his hands. "So that's the drill."

"Pretty much. There are a lot of nuances, but those are the broad strokes."

"What about the trauma she already suffered? The abuse. Can I do anything about that?"

"If an alter wants to talk about bad memories, OK. Generally speaking, telling the story helps to work through trauma. But don't go looking for it. You don't know how to deal with that stuff, and she could regress. Get even more unglued."

They sat in silence for a moment. Madrone had a small collection of paper clips he was picking up and dropping.

"This is going to be a ride," Walker finally said.

"Already been one. But right now, since she wants to live, you and the alters may finally be on the same side. This is the moment to build your alliances."

"I'm going to need help as things come up. Can I call you?"

"Any time." Madrone smiled and spread his hands. "You're the one on the tightrope. All I have to do is shout up to you. Tell you to hold on, don't fall."

60

Margaret's move to Walker's flat was a watershed. An almost casual stepping from one life to another. From the life of impulsivity and running away to something quieter. Less desperate.

The next few months seem to happen in a kaleidoscope. With no linearity. Instead I see images, randomly arranged, of odd moments in their lives:

Keg screaming, "Fuck you, fuck you," at the pitcher while

they were at a Giants game and Walker promising that Keg could play Grand Theft Auto if he'd go inside and let them enjoy the baseball game.

Soft-voiced Millie begging to go to the Tennessee Grill for French fries and a shake. Or to the beach. Or the playground at Golden Gate Park with its high, twisting slide.

Louisa May coming out during an obstetrical exam to inquire, "Does starin' at mah privates makes your privates think it's party time?"

Corine dancing for Walker with her pregnant belly. And one time reciting a little poem while she did a bow:

My body holds
birth and death.
Two birds in a rain pool,
taking and taking.
Equally welcome.

Walker also pushed Corine to write. For a while she worked on a cautionary essay about children getting damaged by ballet, and later started a piece—in diary form—woven from the dreams about her sister.

On the other side of the coin, Louisa May often pestered Walker while he wrote, and he would solemnly promise to give her attention later. Which he did by holding her, or sometimes touching her between the legs while she watched trashy TV.

On these, and other sexual occasions, Walker always checked to make sure Millie was asleep. And sometimes he would offer her enticements of ice cream or to watch her draw if she would stay inside.

Intercourse was usually with Margaret, who arranged for Keg to stay out of it by letting him roughhouse at a later time. Which meant Keg "attacking" Walker while he rested on the couch. Or sneaking up on him when he tied his shoes. It would start with a punch in the arm, followed by straddling and wrestling him to the ground. Walker wasn't allowed to give up too early; a premature *no mas* resulted in a flurry of jabs or a wrenching headlock.

On one occasion, Corine asked to experience sex again, although I often suspected she was a participant at other times. Corine held Walker's face as they made love, staring at him, saying each moment what she felt. At the end, as she gave up to the release, she began to weep. Soundless, eyes large in surprise.

Softly she said, "You are there. I felt you, in the room."

"The white room? Did you let me in?" Walker asked.

"No. You were just there. I don't know how."

"I told you I could find a way." He kissed the tears. "Let's be quiet now; just be there together."

As Madrone had suggested, Walker asked often to be with Margaret—seeking her opinion on or help with the alters. It was usually with her that he shared feelings, expressed a need. And it was with her that he talked about the baby.

"Is this *your* sister, too?" he once asked as he caressed Margaret's belly, "Or only the alters'?"

"I don't know. That's what Corine wants, and I accept it. Whether it's true or a story . . ." she shrugged.

"Do you want it to be true?" Walker kissed her stomach. "Because I suspect that everything is just a story—until we decide it's real."

For a while, Margaret combed her fingers through Walker's hair. "Then I'll decide it's true," she said finally. "It makes them happy. It makes them welcome the baby."

"Do you know the story *I* want to be true?" Walker rested his cheek on her belly. "I want it to be true that you and I have a baby. It doesn't matter to me if it's your sister, coming back from that other life. All I want is for you and I to take care of this child. Together. Would you believe that story? Would you want it to be true?"

Margaret nodded. "Sure. We'll make that one true." A tinkling laugh. "We'll make it all true—every fucking thing we want."

Later that night, Margaret looked up from her book. "I like this 'making things true' shit. I'd like to make it true that I don't sell ballet tickets anymore."

"OK. So we need a new story—Margaret doing something totally different, something she likes."

"You know what I'd like?"

Walker raised his eyebrows.

"I'd like to teach dance."

"Who wants to do that—you or Corine?"

A tiny smile pulled her lips. "Me. And maybe Corine a little, too. I'd like to teach kids ballet. Not make it a total, lose-every-thing-else-in-your-life obsession. Just teach them the beautiful parts, the lovely ways you can move your body."

"Good. How do we make it true? Tell me the first step."

Margaret closed her book and looked away a minute. Then she told him exactly how it could happen.

61

Perhaps my most vivid memory from that time was an afternoon, early in her pregnancy, when Margaret was helping Walker put groceries away. She was on a chair, arranging cans on a high shelf. Walker was below, handing things up to her. Quite suddenly, Margaret dropped her arms.

"You OK?" Walker touched her leg.

"I was just thinking about this time . . . in Maurice's kitchen. I was high up like this—but on a stool—reaching for something in a cabinet."

"And?"

"It was the last day I lived there."

Margaret stepped down and leaned one hip against the counter. Her mouth lifted in a thin smile.

"Why was it your last day there?" Walker's voice rose with a trace of irritation.

"I don't know. He told me to do a half-point turn—on the stool. He was always doing shit like that."

"'Legs straight,' he says. 'Don't look at the stool. Look up. As if you see something beautiful.'"

"But I'm afraid of falling, so I keep looking at the stool."

"'Up,' he shouts. 'I'll catch you if you fall . . . Up, up.' He has his hands on me, under my skirt."

"'Let your feet tell you where the edge is. Look up.'"

"As I turn, his fingers trail against my legs. But then I stop. I don't know why, because . . . "

Silence.

"You don't know why you stopped?" Walker made a rolling gesture with his hand for her to continue.

"Yeah. Because he was like that. Always . . . So instantly he's all upset, and telling me to make the turn. That my balance is bad, and I should do this stool shit every day."

Margaret pulled a box of something out of a shopping bag and started reading the label.

"So I just . . . kicked him. In the face."

She shrugged, ran a finger across her forehead. I thought she was finished with the story, but a moment later Margaret moved over to the sink and lifted a dirty coffee cup. She examined it like she'd just discovered the Holy Grail.

"You never know when it's coming. The moment you're finished. I was 14. I was tired of listening. I was tired of his hands."

The cup swung sharply down on the edge of the sink, shattered. The little smile, which had remained throughout the story, left Margaret's face.

"Was that Keg?"

She nodded.

"What happened? After you kicked him?"

"He seemed afraid. I think I broke his tooth. After a few minutes, he called a cab and sent me to a friend's house. Said I was an ingrate and I should think about what I wanted. His plan was that he'd pick me up the next day and I'd be all contrite. Soft and willing again . . . I never went back."

Walker opened her fingers and removed the cup handle.

"Why then? At that moment? What finally made you able to leave him?"

"She would have been one."

Walker looked puzzled.

"I figured out the date she would have been born. And when she'd have her birthday. So I lit a candle."

"That day? When you hit him?"

"Yeah. She'd have been one. Except he killed her."

62

Walker finished what he *thought* was his last *Sunrise Effect* story in June—when Margaret was around sixteen weeks pregnant. It was about a guy named C. C. (short for Candy Cane), who'd been in and out of jail for a series of robbery and drug-dealing charges. One night, toward the end of a prison stint for possession of crack, he had a dream. In Walker's words,

> The dream inaugurated the most lucid moment in C. C.'s life. He was in a subway car. Two men were fighting at the far end, hitting each other with tremendous blows that sounded like smashing melons. Next to them, a skinhead went through several purses in his lap. Across from C. C., a woman snorted a line off the back of her hand. A second woman, big as a linebacker, went through an old man's pockets. She held a blade by the papery folds of his throat.

C.C. felt no fear. This was his world, populated by out-laws and victims. He watched as the train pulled into a sta-tion and the doors opened. No one got on or off. When the doors closed, and the train plunged again into the tunnel, C.C. had an odd thought. Maybe he should get off. At the next stop, as the doors reopened, he could simply walk away. Onto the platform, then up the stairs to the street.

The thought of cool wind held a sudden, irresistible allure. As if the ozone and the hot, pressed air were no longer toler-able. As if the people on the car, living their dark, stricken lives, were suddenly too painful to watch.

And it occurred to C.C.—in his dream—that this was a moment of choice. He could leave or stay. As the train slowed for the next station, he stood. The coke lady looked up at him. Nodded. The doors opened. He waved at her and stepped off.

When C.C. woke up, he knew the dream had been sent to tell him something. And now, lying on the thin mattress in his double cell, he began to imagine other possible lives.

When Walker read this story to Margaret, he paused here. "You know what happens next," he said.

"Sure, C.C. starts an orphanage."

Which was close. C.C. got released a few months later and founded an after-school program. A unique combo of sports and life skills. The kids got to be on teams coached by famous athletes, while at the same time learning how to make a budget and write a job app.

It was a wild success. But C.C. began to disrupt several local gangs as he lured away their members. His car got torched. Then, a month later, C.C. was gunned down in a drive-by.

"Ah love a story with no surprises," Louisa May said brightly. She touched Walker's chest. "Ah believe you've been workin' altogether too hard, makin' every word just right. What you need . . . is a little fun."

63

In July, Walker got great news. Harper Collins had agreed to publish *The Sunrise Effect*, and Dr. Madrone offered to host the contract-signing party at his condo.

I don't think anyone, including Walker, was expecting Margaret to come. But she decided to anyway, announcing at 6:00 p.m. on the evening of the celebration that she was "showing up, like a bomb in a letter box." This started a flurry of nervous activity while Margaret tried on several skirts and pinned a small gold dragonfly (once belonging to her mother) to three different spots on a turquoise blouse.

"Why are you putting yourself through this?" Walker asked while he watched her prepare.

"Because I don't like running away. Let them fucking think what they want. You know? If they think I'm crazy, fine. If Madrone avoids me like the plague, fine. I want to be there with you—'cause your book's a big deal. So we can all just deal with it."

Walker kissed her on the cheek. "Then let's do it. But if you're gonna go all kick-ass, warn me so I can hide in the bathroom."

"If Keg comes out, I'll hide in there with you."

Madrone's eyebrows flew halfway up his forehead when he opened the door to Walker and Margaret. But he pulled himself together and shook her hand warmly.

"You look very well," he said. "Pregnancy suits you, I think."

"Ah feel like the man who fell off the Empire State Building. Every floor he thought, 'So far, so good.'"

Madrone gave a slight bow and made an ushering gesture. "While we fall, that's what we all think. At least the people I know."

A small, grateful smile touched Walker's lips as they arrived in the living room. He waved to Julie, Madrone's wife, who sat deep in a mohair armchair, sipping her cocktail. Her long black hair fell forward as she launched herself to her feet, moving swiftly to embrace Margaret.

"Good to see you." She dropped her arm to circle Margaret's waist. "Stick with me; we'll face down this crazy crowd together."

Julie and her charge began to make the rounds. First to Holly and Jan, the lesbian couple. Who couldn't stop repeating their congratulations that Margaret was "cooking up a baby." Then to Riles, the older black man, purveyor of smooth contempt.

"Well, now, darlin', what makes you want to brave these dark waters again? You plannin' to teach us more about how parents ruin their kids?"

"Franklin!" Julie touched his arm with a warning gesture. But Margaret seemed unaffected.

"Ah left my soap box in the car. But if you want me to fetch it, Ah got some special things Ah could tell you."

Riles smiled; let his accent broaden. "Wouldn't wan' chu to go to no trouble."

Julie and Margaret moved toward a little group including Madrone and Dr. Strite. Strite had her hideous tortoiseshell glasses and a forest-green pantsuit bulging over her significant waistline. A fiftyish woman was next to her, with peroxide hair and squinting dark eyes that conveyed both hurt and generosity.

"You remember Dr. Strite," Madrone said. "And this is Sandra Becker, visiting from Seattle. She's an old friend who writes biographies of extraordinary teenagers. Joan of Arc, a kid who spied for the French resistance, that sort of thing."

Margaret shook hands with both women. "A pleasure," she said.

"I love that phrase," Strite remarked. "Comes from the Victorian era—when the only pleasure they could publicly admit was greeting someone. All other pleasures were secret and guilty."

"Well, it *is* a pleasure," Sandra said heartily. "Are you a writer, too, like Walker?"

"Just the occasional poem in the sand." Margaret gave a tinkly laugh.

"That's a good place for it," Strite said. "Most of the stuff that passes for poetry these days might as well wash out to sea."

Julie pushed Margaret along to the next little group—where Walker was talking to his editor from Harper, a woman with spiky blonde hair and fingers that danced in the air while she talked. A man stood with them who was tall, with sunken cheeks and long, white sideburns.

"My editor, Arlen, and her fiancé," Walker pointed as he introduced them.

Margaret leaned against Walker. "Did you acquire the book—was that your choice?"

The editor nodded. "I love the idea, I love the drama. This man . . ." she pressed her fingers into Walker's forearm ". . . is an incredible writer."

"She doesn't usually get this excited," Sideburns said. "Believe me."

"Ladies and gentlemen!" Madrone had his hands cupped around his mouth. "It's time for the author to give a reading. Take a seat."

The assemblage made their way to couches and armchairs. Walker drifted to stand near a Tiffany floor lamp and proceeded to read the story of a guy who owned a diner. It never made much, though it had a loyal clientele of families whose kids loved the electric trains that circumnavigated the restaurant. Eventually the owner reached an age where he could draw Social Security. He turned the diner into a chef school for teens from a nearby barrio.

Walker made a formal bow as he finished his narrative. The expected "Bravo" and applause broke out. Strite announced that diners were contributing to the nation's ill health. Riles said there weren't enough diners, and short-order cooking was a lost art. Margaret, in a raspy voice, said, "I'll drink to that," and asked for a beer.

"No," Walker whispered to her. "The baby."

"Time for a cold one." Margaret got up and headed for an ice chest.

"No." Walker took her arm and steered her toward the window.

He pointed to something—maybe Alcatraz, maybe a barge making its slow, weightless progress toward the Golden Gate. His arm circled Margaret's shoulder and he started whispering.

"It'll hurt the baby, if you drink, Keg. What do you need right now? What can we do for you?"

"Nothing." She sounded pouty.

"Something's happening with you. Something about these people or this place."

"They're all assholes—except Julie. They all suck."

"You want to get away from them?"

"I wanna stick knives in them. Where's my beer?"

Walker tightened his arm around her. "Beer's no good for the baby. I know you don't care, but the others do. Margaret and Corine. So let me make a deal with you. We'll be out of here in ninety minutes—watch the clock. Meanwhile, I need you to stay inside."

Big shrug. Margaret stuck her finger on the window—pointing randomly to fog-shrouded landmarks.

"What do you say, Keg?"

"They're packed with shit. I don't want to talk to them."

"Then let someone else come out. We'll just stand here together; I won't let anyone say anything bad. But you need to stay inside till we leave, OK?"

A few seconds later Margaret's body melted into Walker. With Keg out of the way, a conversation started with Walker's editor. Arlen delicately brushed a hand across her punji-stick hair while listening to Walker enthuse about his research.

"In the end," he was revving to a conclusion, "I feel it's given me a new way to make sense of death."

"Funny thing about death," Arlen shot back. "We always feel

the need to explain it. As if discovering some reason or pattern would protect us."

"Maybe there is a reason." Walker spread his hands.

A slight pulling of the lips—perhaps a look of disgust—hung for a moment on Arlen's face.

"When my baby died—my miscarriage—I tried to see a reason. I thought I'd done something to offend God ... Maybe if we'd been married, it wouldn't have happened. Then I thought it was because I hadn't sacrificed enough, hadn't really made room in my life for the baby. So it got taken away. For a while I got the idea that the baby felt how crazy I am, and decided not to stay with me, decided I'd be a crappy mother.

"What all those reasons added up to ... was me trying to take control. So I'd never lose anything again. Somehow I'd perfect myself, fix the wrong I'd done, the mistakes. It was too scary to think things like that just happened."

Arlen suddenly stopped talking; her hand went to her mouth. "Sorry. It's six months and I ..." She swept under each eye with the tips of her fingers. "And I ... "

Margaret's hand went beneath Walker's arm—seeking protection.

"I keep waiting, but I don't get over it."

Margaret was almost standing behind Walker now. Leaning against him. "It's too hard," she said.

Arlen nodded, her eyes scanning the light-rimmed bay through the window.

Margaret dug her fingers into Walker's bicep, pressed the side of her face against his corduroy jacket.

"Maybe Ah need to sit down," she whispered.

"You tired?" He excused them and led her to a couch perched below a painting of a north coast lighthouse.

"Are you OK? You feel sick?"

Margaret closed her eyes. "She scared me." It was the modulated voice of Corine. "Losing her baby. Somehow I never thought of that. I was so sure. But now ... "

Margaret's hand sought Walker's.

"But now?" he prompted.

"Now," she whispered, "I need you to hold me."

Walker did that, circling her with both arms. "How's that?"

"Will I keep her? Tell me."

Walker nodded.

"I'm not going to lose her? After all this . . . tell me. Say it out loud."

"No. You'll have your baby."

"My sister. Say it—I won't lose my sister again."

"You won't lose your sister, Corine."

Silence. Her body shook in tiny spasms as she tried to hold back the tears.

"You know something?" The whisper hardly escaped her lips. "Since I was nine I needed what you're doing. I never had anybody who could make things all right." She put her hand on his chest—half to take comfort, I think, half a caress. "Thank you."

"Ladies and gentlemen," Madrone raised his glass in an importune toast. "To a man who is helping us rediscover the beauty and completeness of a meaningful life. I have had the privilege of reading his manuscript, and I learned this: no life is so shattered that it can't be redeemed by a single choice. To Walker."

There was general glass raising and murmurs of "Hear, hear."

Margaret lifted her face to kiss Walker. A sweet touching of the lips.

"Congratulations," she said, loud enough for the room to hear, "on believing in something enough to make it true."

I think she was talking more about their relationship than his book. But no matter. There was another round of "Hear, hear," while Julie passed out plates of Courvoisier-soaked ladyfingers. A few moments later, Arlen presented Walker with a pen, and he ceremoniously signed two copies of his contract.

More applause. Which by now was getting tiresome. But I suspect jealousy on my part. Walker had Margaret, he had friends, he was about to publish a book. And, of course, he was alive.

64

The week after the contract signing, I left the Bay Area for the first time as a discarnate—following Walker's Porsche while he threaded his way deep into the Sierras. He was heading for an old hotel in Yosemite that Madrone had recommended as a peaceful place.

As we approached, the white, colonial-style buildings of Wawona showed up in a clearing next to Highway 41. Most of the structures were two-story, with wide verandas and thick, rough-hewn posts supporting peaked roofs. The buildings ranged around a vast, sloping lawn, shaded by cedar and sugar pine. In the center of the lawn was a looping carriage path and a fountain made of river-washed granite.

Opposite the hotel, on the far side of the road, was a long, tree-rimmed meadow. At the west end were the manicured lawns of Wawona golf course; and at the east, separated by a split rail fence, was a field laced with wildflowers.

"I want to go swimming," Millie's little voice insisted as they parked near a picket fence surrounding the pool. "We can change and go in right now."

"Let's get our room. Then if you want to swim, we'll do it."

"I like to float," Millie said, "and watch the sky."

But by the time they checked in and carried their bags to a room overlooking the fountain, Louisa May had put the kibosh on swimming.

"Ah look fat."

"That's 'cause you're 24 weeks pregnant."

"Ah look like Ah've been a piggy at mah plate. If Ah put on a bathin' suit, people gonna run from the pool."

After a good deal of discussion, they decided, with input from Corine, to take a hike. The two headed up Chowchilla Mountain Road, an unpaved stage track that climbs several miles to a crossing of Big Creek. At the bridge, Walker and Margaret headed upstream along a faint fisherman's path. It was a lovely place. Leaves of overhanging trees flickered in a slight wind. The creek rose, alternating from jade pools to steep cascades. Slashes of reflected light shot from water pouring between granite boulders. In the shallows, mica glistened. Sedge leaves, catching the sun, turned from green to blinding white.

The climb had been difficult, requiring constant navigation around fractured rocks and jutting branches. Margaret looked tired.

"The ripples are so bright," she said. Then mentioned a headache.

"It's hard getting here, but what a place."

She touched his arm. "I know. Thank you for taking me."

They were at a bend. Sand-covered shallows sloped to a deep pool, sheathed in granite. A pine leaned across the water.

"Could we rest here?" Margaret asked. "Stick our feet in?"

Walker pointed to a boulder. "Sit and I'll take off your shoes."

Without shoes and socks, Margaret's ankles looked red, swollen.

"That climb was tough on you," Walker said. "We'd better keep to things a bit less strenuous."

Margaret leaned down, one hand on Walker's shoulder, one rubbing her foot. "Pregnancy is death on your endurance."

"Glad I don't have to do it." He sat down next to her on the boulder. "Want to sit in the water and cool off?"

"We don't have suits."

"We got underwear; that's good enough."

"OK, maybe it'll help my headache."

They stripped down to T-shirts and underpants. Walker

settled himself in the shallows, whimpering as the snow-fed water rose to mid-belly.

"You sit between my legs," he said. "I'll be your back rest."

"Ah never heard such a proposition in mah life." Margaret struck the pose of a '40s pin-up. "Ah'm not sure it's at all proper."

Now she dropped into the water, letting Walker support her arms as she settled down. Margaret leaned against his chest while Walker held his water-chilled fingers to her forehead.

"Ah love a man with cold hands." She giggled, and pushed her hips into his crotch. "Your reward, Ah promise, will come later."

He dipped his fingers, cooling them again, and started a circular massage on her temples. Just beyond their pool, water slapped and gurgled down a short cascade. Small, blue butterflies lit on the damp sand behind them, drinking at the creek's edge. Now and then came a susurrant brush of air as wind sighed through the upper branches of the pines.

"Relax now. Let the headache melt away."

Margaret cupped her hands, pushing little waves across her rounded abdomen. Then she hooked them beneath Walker's thighs. "I love you," she said, letting the chatter of the cascade hide her voice.

"When I was a boy," Walker said, "my mother bought me this pine incense. It was cone shaped. Sometimes we'd light it and watch television; we'd pretend we were in a forest. The way this place smells reminds me."

Margaret rolled her head against Walker's chest. "If I was there, in your living room, what would I see?"

"My mother on our brown plush couch, propped up on pillows. I'm in a papasan next to her, curled up. I've got little soldiers and shit I'm playing with during commercials. Occasionally she gets up for something. Tea. These little plums she liked."

"What does it feel like—in your papasan?"

"Like if you walked out the front door, there'd be nothing. Empty space. So you'd better just be content with what there is."

Walker put both hands on Margaret's belly. "How's our girl in there?"

"Working to get ready."

Long silence; Margaret raised her knees and rubbed them. "Is that why we're together—the empty space?"

"I don't know."

She nodded. "It's OK—it's as good a reason as any."

Next morning—in the half-light—mist rose off the lily pads beneath the fountain. Margaret sat in a white Adirondack chair on the second-floor veranda.

"There you are." Walker poked his head in from the door of their room. "How come you're up?"

"The headache. Gets a little better, then it comes back." She closed her eyes. "I don't think my body's all that fond of being pregnant."

A row of pines posed in silhouette against the dawn sky. Beyond them, wide, deserted fairways pushed the edge of the forest. A jay landed on the porch railing a few doors down, started a long run of abusive chatter.

"I was thinking," Margaret said in the Millie voice, "about what you told me yesterday. The way your house felt. I wish I could have been a little girl on your block. And every time you were sad I would just *know*, and every time I was sad you would know. And then we'd go over to each other's houses."

Walker sat on the arm of her chair. "That would have been nice."

"Were your closets the sliding door kind?"

"Uh huh."

"I like that kind. You can play elevator in them. We could have gone to your room and pretended we were in the elevator of the Empire State Building. We'd go up and down, and not let anyone else on."

"Why not? But, Millie, that's why we came up here. So we can enjoy being together."

The jay was still making noise, and Margaret suddenly stood up and shooed it. "I know . . . but we had to wait such a long time."

I drifted out then, over the lawns, watching them from a distance. I yearned to smell the pines, and feel the cool morning air wash across my skin. Margaret was bending toward Walker. Perhaps kissing him. I felt the emptiness of the mountains, the truth that she no longer needed me.

65

The doctor's office was drenched in pink. Walls were flesh tone. The plastic cushions for the plastic chairs were a shiny, lip-gloss rose. A dozen photographs, framed in salmon-colored matting, depicted homeless children working the streets. Some were begging, some scavenging trash, some bathing in gutter water. On one wall was a piece of stretched silk, depicting an elephant lifting a child on its trunk.

Dr. Sanjeev's desktop had a small onyx slab with a pair of red pens. Jutting at various angles, they looked like lobster antennae. The desk also held an imitation kerosene lamp and a blotter edged with hammered brass and the initials MBS.

Margaret and Walker waited in identical plastic chairs. Except hers had a scarf with pink, stylized fish draped over the back. Dr. Sanjeev, who had just examined Margaret, was out of the room.

"It's really bad," Margaret said. "The more I pay attention, the worse it gets."

"The blurry vision?"

"Yeah. I can't even see what's in those photographs over there." She waved toward the wall. "It's just blobs of shadow and light. My eyes are seriously fucked up."

"Hopefully, Sanjeev has answers."

An intercom on the doctor's desk squawked something about an incoming call. I drifted outside the window to watch Dr. Sanjeev standing on the grassy verge of the parking lot. She was in a pink lab coat, sucking on a filterless cigarette. As she held in the smoke, each heartbeat sent twin plumes from her nostrils. A moment later, cigarette consumed, the doctor popped a breath mint. She smoothed her black, center-parted hair and the loose braid that descended between her shoulder blades. Now she hurried through the front door. In seconds she was bursting into the office where Margaret and Walker waited.

"Just give me a moment, please." The doctor had an Indian accent. As she gestured toward her patient, she managed to simultaneously knock a small plant from her desk and bang her thigh into a rolling table.

"Oooof." Sanjeev dropped into the armless secretary chair behind her desk. With manic energy she began to rub her injured leg.

"Let's summarize what we know. I already told you about the elevated blood pressure. And we have the labs back—you're spilling protein in your urine."

She was checking her earrings—dangling silver elephants. Then smoothing her coat, fingers lingering over her embroidered name.

"Then we have your symptoms. Headache, sensitivity to light, blurred vision. And edema in your ankles. This all tells us," her voice became more singsong, "one thing. This is something that happens in about 5 percent of pregnancies, for reasons we do not understand. It is called preeclampsia."

"What is it?" Walker broke in.

"Basically," (she said it ba-sic-al-ly) "it is a condition characterized by high blood pressure and water retention. You have the most typical symptoms, although some women may also get nausea or shortness of breath."

"What will happen? How's this going to affect Margaret?"

"It is a condition of pregnancy that resolves after your baby is delivered. By itself, it is not a problem. I will give you some Labetalol to control the blood pressure. You will need to rest more, drink lots of water, follow a low-salt diet. We will monitor you carefully, but in the vast majority of these cases everything goes veddy nicely."

Sanjeev wheeled herself around the corner of the desk and bent to retrieve the potted plant. Now she kicked some of the loose soil out of sight.

"I always seem to be knocking things over. I hear them call me," she gave a self-deprecating smile, "Dr. Hurricane."

Margaret leaned, placing just her fingertips on the edge of the desk. "Is there any danger with this . . . "

"Preeclampsia? In a very small percentage of cases, it progresses to eclampsia. But we will be careful and not let that happen."

"What won't you let happen?" Walker again, voice getting higher, thin.

"Ba-sic-al-ly, the patient develops seizures, and that is veddy bad. We have to deliver the baby, whether it is full term or not. If you are 28 weeks, or more, the baby will usually survive. Less than 28 weeks . . ." she shrugged, "we have to induce anyway because the mother's life is at risk."

"Because of the seizures?" Margaret's fingers laced together. Still pressing the edge of Sanjeev's desk.

"The seizures are veddy dangerous. Coma. Intracranial bleeds. But, as I say, we won't let that happen."

Silence. Sanjeev turned to get something on a credenza behind her.

"Here are some guidelines . . ." She handed Margaret a single

Xeroxed sheet, ". . . for management of preeclampsia. Just follow this when you're at home."

Margaret focused on the paper, reading a few lines, then looked up at the doctor.

"Twenty-eight weeks is the cutoff?"

"I would say 28 weeks is a dividing line, yes. If the fetus is too small . . ." Sanjeev held up parallel hands, ". . . then it is veddy difficult."

"Then let's not have it *veddy* difficult; let's have it *veddy* easy." Suddenly Keg was out, the voice harsh, assaulting. "Because basic-al-ly that's your *job*, that's . . . "

Walker put his hand on Margaret's arm. Then he stood. "We have confidence in you, doctor. As soon as we get home, Margaret's gonna start doing a lot of resting. We'll rent a good action flick and stretch out in front of the TV."

Walker touched Margaret's elbow. She rose now, eyes still locked in a menacing stare at Sanjeev.

"Thank you." Walker gave a big, "Ain't life beautiful" smile, and propelled Margaret out of the office.

66

Margaret took a leave from work. Which was distressing to Manuel, who on the last day told her, "*Mi amor* will keep you safe." Then he held her hand and touched it to his face. Not quite a kiss—more, perhaps, a caress. "I look forward to seeing *tu nina*."

He dropped her hand and walked backward out of the office, not letting his eyes leave her.

At home, Margaret began residence on Walker's couch. She read, and Corine worked on her self-help book for young dancers. Walker became a tea-making machine, brewing a dozen foul-smelling herbal cups a day to keep Margaret hydrated. Each evening, he hooked her to a home blood pressure cuff, and anxiously watched the mercury give them a reading. After the Velcro scraped open, and he was massaging Margaret's arm, Walker always said, "So far, so good."

At the end of Margaret's 26th week, while she was complaining that fried liver wasn't the same without a few slabs of salty bacon, she paused and said she needed to use the toilet. But instead of rising, Margaret's eyes rolled and her hands twitched slightly. A moment later, the twitching turned into clenching — arms, legs, teeth. And Margaret stopped breathing.

I was terrified; I screamed a soundless no.

Walker was lavishly buttering a baked potato, and didn't notice. But he caught what happened next because Margaret began to jerk violently. Frothy, pink saliva appeared on her lips. Walker rushed to her side of the table and knelt, holding her, cushioning her against his body as the contractions continued.

"What is it?" He was shouting, but there was no response.

Walker lifted Margaret's shoulders, trying to meet her eyes. But the eyes stared upward, and another spasm slammed her into his chest.

"Tell me what's wrong . . . Margaret, tell me . . . "

And then, as suddenly as they had begun, the seizures relaxed. Margaret's eyes closed; she commenced a rapid, noisy breathing. And a pool of urine started to form between her legs, growing finally to spill in a thin stream off the edge of the chair.

The coma lifted before Margaret reached the hospital. And by the time Sanjeev saw her, the only residual was some dried blood darkening the corners of her lips.

"Your condition has progressed," Sanjeev announced. "The seizure means you have full eclampsia. Ba-sic-al-ly it means we must deliver now. We cannot wait. I am sorry."

"And my baby?" Margaret's eyes cranked from Walker on one side of the bed to Sanjeev on the other.

"Naturally, we will do what we can, but I must tell you there's a strong risk the baby will not survive."

"How strong?" Margaret started a rhythmic pushing and pulling on the metal rail of the bed.

"I'm afraid that is not what has the greatest weight at this moment. The risk to you—to your life—is what concerns me. We have to deliver because the seizures could return at any time. And the next one . . ." She shrugged.

Sanjeev touched Margaret's hand—the one that was jerking the rail. "In this case, we will do a Cesarean. None of us ever wants to think of this . . . possibility. But it is always there. And now we must face and get through it."

"No!" The shout was loud enough to bring uniformed staff in from the hall. Margaret lashed them in the sharp, contemptuous voice I knew was Keg. "You want to kill her. Fuck that. I'm going home."

"You must not do this." Sanjeev was trying to push Margaret back while her patient struggled to sit up. "This could cost you your life."

Margaret ripped off the nursing tape on her hand, and pulled out the IV. Blood began to ooze from the vein.

Now Sanjeev appealed to Walker. "Stop her. She needs to stay right where she is." The doctor jabbed her pointed finger toward the bed. "If she leaves, I cannot be responsible for what may happen."

"Walker? My shirt and pants. They're in a plastic bag in the closet."

Walker fetched the clothes, but he was moving at glacial speed. "Let's think about this," he said.

"When do you do any thinking, except about your stupid book?"

Margaret jumped to the floor, and brushed past the slow-motion Walker on her way to the closet.

"I want to talk to Corine," Walker commanded. "Corine needs to come out now."

Sanjeev was looking around. "Who's Corine?"

Margaret yanked her black corduroys from the bag, pulling them over her urine-stained underpants. She shook out a balled-up flannel shirt, and rammed her arms through the sleeve holes.

"Corine, talk to me." Walker held Margaret's shoulders and forced her into eye contact.

For a moment her lids drooped, and then the lines at the corners of her mouth softened. She stopped moving.

"Dr. Sanjeev." It was somber-voiced Corine. "I am 26 weeks pregnant. You said, yourself, 28 weeks is the dividing line. Before that point, my baby doesn't have much of a chance."

"You want to wait two weeks?" Sanjeev's voice was rising into the glass-breaking registers.

"At least two. Hopefully more."

"I told you, this kind of seizure cannot be taken lightly. Your brain does not enjoy this. I am talking about cerebral edema. I am talking about a bleed. I am talking about death. Do you understand?"

"If you're trying to scare me, you're doing a great job. But I cannot lose this baby. Do *you* understand that? I have to hold on till she can make it."

Sanjeev shook her head and started for the door. But at that moment, she stubbed her toe on the wheel of the bed, and then bent to rub and inspect it.

"Oooof. I always do these things. I wreck myself." Sanjeev looked at Walker. "Are you going to let this happen? Do you have no fear for her?"

Margaret was walking out the door now. "Bye, Doctor," she said cheerily. "Don't worry. It will all come out right."

"I do not worry," Sanjeev shouted to Margaret's back. "I do the right thing and then I do not worry."

On the way home in the Porsche, Walker seemed to list toward the door. He drove with one hand draped over the wheel, the other mechanically rubbing his chest.

"You upset?" Margaret gave a brief caress to Walker's corduroy jacket.

"I'm scared. When I saw you seizing, I thought maybe I was going to lose you right then. And all I could think was, please, please, please . . . I don't even know who I was praying to."

"Were you afraid you'd have to go back?"

"Back to what?"

"All that nothing outside your living room when you were a kid?"

"That's not it." He took the turn onto Fell Street a bit too aggressively. "I love you. It's as simple as that."

Walker jockeyed the Porsche into a tight parking space in front of his flat. Afternoon sun lay jeweled on the polished hood. Neither one of them got out of the car.

Margaret pressed two fingers into the space between her eyes. "Walker?"

"Yeah?"

"I'm sorry."

A single tear spilled. Margaret rubbed it with her fist.

An hour later, she was in the bath and Walker was washing her. The faucet was on. Millie was prattling about the baby hearing the water and thinking she was in a submarine.

Now Walker handed her a soapy cloth to wash the places Millie was afraid to have him touch. He settled back on his haunches, frowned.

"Suddenly I'm worried the bath might be bad for you—'cause hot water raises your blood pressure."

"I'll get out if you want, but it feels good here. With you . . . being nice to me."

Walker kissed her forehead.

Millie's slightly wide-eyed look tightened; there were several slow blinks.

"Walker?" It was Margaret's adult voice. "It feels like I spent my whole life looking for this." She gestured back and forth between them. "And I don't want to lose it. But . . . I might. We might. Promise me this. Whatever happens, the baby comes first. Would you honor me—by promising that?"

He said nothing for a long moment. There was a faint splashing as Margaret's hand dropped back into the water. Finally, Walker gave a slow, whispery sigh and nodded.

Margaret's hand reemerged from the water—holding the washcloth. Which she draped coquettishly over her breasts.

"Ah love a man who makes promises," she said.

67

When Margaret was 28 weeks and four days pregnant, she had a dream. For months her dream life had seemed mostly benign. The death camp scenes were rare now. And images of the sister, when they arrived in her unconscious, appeared distant and ephemeral. So this dream caught me by surprise because it started in darkness, with only the sound of crying.

I could sense Margaret's anxiety. She was trying to locate the direction of the sound. It felt nearby, perhaps in the next room. Yet as Margaret turned in different directions, the crying seemed to shift as well. Now Margaret began to move, with a driven, reckless energy.

She called a name I didn't recognize. She seemed to be running, yet I sensed no footfalls. The darkness expanded before her.

Eventually I saw light. Distant at first, but growing to be a room with no apparent doorway. As Margaret drew closer, I could see a crib, and a mobile with stars and crescent moons dangling above it. In the crib a baby was crying. Arms waving. And above the child a man, back turned, reaching down to comfort it.

Margaret moved deeper into the room. I could feel her need

to do something. But the man was lifting the child, bringing it to his chest. He was swaying now, murmuring soft words I couldn't hear.

The baby kept crying. Margaret extended her arms, trying to take the child. The man turned toward us, and suddenly I could see he was Walker. We were in the bedroom of his flat. A frieze near the ceiling had steam engines and cabooses, and a revolving lampshade cast illumined elephants across the walls.

Walker jiggled the baby up and down. And though Margaret reached for the child, she seemed to touch nothing solid. I could feel her confusion. And a growing panic. She called Walker's name, but there was no response. Then she shouted, tried to pull the baby out of his arms.

Walker sang Brahms's Lullaby. He was pacing, kissing the child while he cradled her.

"Please," she said. "Let me."

And now the thought occurred to her that they might not be able to hear.

Walker was blowing on the child's neck. Making great farty sounds. The sobbing was starting to fade, and a moment later became laughter. Now he snapped open the pajamas and made more farty sounds on the baby's stomach. Laughter again. Wild, hysterical.

Now Margaret knew. They had gone on. Father and daughter, in that familiar room. Crying, laughing, living—without her.

She shouted again, but Walker was laying the baby back in the crib. He was uncurling her fingers, kissing them. Then putting his lips on her forehead.

In that moment, Margaret had entered the ghost life. Watching without touching. Powerless even to comfort her child. I felt in her the fear and loss I'd known during those first days in her rooms.

The dream ended. And as Margaret drifted away on a dark, unconscious tether, I was engulfed in my own losses. I remem-

bered the Ferris wheel shaking, and my last moment falling
onto the spokes and guy wires. I recalled shouting, with just
the memory of sound in the air. I recalled watching Margaret
sleep—unable to feel her warmth, her breath. I remembered
the days of silence. Of invisibility.

The thought occurred to me—perhaps for the first time—
that I was tired of it. Tired of watching her life. Though I
loved her, and I feared what might happen with the baby, I was
coming to a moment where I'd seen enough. Waited enough.
Perhaps, after I witnessed the birth, I would . . .

Margaret woke and asked for a glass of water. She was rubbing her temples. Walker was in the living room, lost in a read-
through of his editor's *Sunrise Effect* corrections. He didn't hear
her. She sat up, swung her legs over the side of the bed, and fell
back.

The seizure lasted maybe a minute. It started with a twitching in her cheeks and lips. Margaret's eyes stared, became protruded. Then her body began to contract. When Walker finally
came to check on Margaret, she'd been in a coma for close to
an hour.

At the hospital, Sanjeev did the usual things. A syringe of
magnesium sulfide to prevent more seizures. Hydralazine for
blood pressure, tongue blades, fetal monitoring. She scheduled
a C-section.

Margaret awoke shortly before going to the OR. The high,
breathy voice asked Walker where they were.

"I can't move my arm," Millie said.

"Which one?"

The right arm pointed to the left.

"There was a problem, a bleed. I'll tell Margaret later."

"Is it bad?"

"I'll talk to Margaret about it."

Silence.

"Can I draw?"

Walker's mouth tightened; he stared for a long moment at the woman in the bed. Finally he handed her a pen and held the back of an envelope steady so she could draw on it.

"I'm drawing something for you."

Millie did a stick girl in a triangle dress. The face was round and oversized, edged with pigtailed hair. Now she put in big eyes and a smile that rose above the two-dot nostrils.

"Who is that?" Walker asked.

"Me."

"She looks happy."

"Uh huh."

"Is she happy right now?"

"Uh huh."

"Even in the hospital?"

Margaret nodded. "You're with us."

A moment later, a Latino man in white pants and squeaky rubber shoes rolled a gurney into Margaret's room.

"We're going to the OR," he announced.

Walker kissed Millie's cheek.

As the orderly rolled her away, Millie waved. A fluttering, child's gesture.

"Bye, now," the little voice said.

The gurney turned and was gone. Walker sat in Margaret's room while techs and nurses galloped past the door. He never spoke to her again.

68

In October, Walker wrote the last chapter of his book.

I watch my baby reach for something on a string above her head. It dances away as she brushes it. Pale, autumn light slants through the glass to touch her face. She makes a small grunting sound—perhaps the beginning of some desire. Or distress. I touch her hand, but she is lost in other things.

I must tell you that I never expected to write this chapter. Because the story is mine. A story I would not have wished on myself.

My sweetheart died four months ago. While bringing our daughter safely to this world. And though Margaret's loss is personal to me, I realize that the story of her last year must be seen as nothing more or less than the *effect* of a long-awaited, all-too-brief sunrise.

Margaret was a *multiple*. Childhood sexual abuse had so traumatized her that she'd been forced to cope by dissociating the feelings into four distinct alter egos. During more than twenty years, the alters lived inside her as a squabbling family—controlling her behavior, bizarrely affecting her life.

I met her by quite literally running into her. With my car. She'd closed her eyes, stepped off the curb, and was doing an impromptu ballet in a busy intersection. It was, I'd later learn, a parasuicidal act.

Margaret was a woman without friends, whose only human contact came from trolling bars. The alters were running the show. One was lonely and angry—and trying to kill her. One—a flirtatious belle with a deep-South drawl—was finding and discarding men at warp speed. One was a nine-year-old who liked to draw and play on the swings. And one was a punk whose every other word was profane and whose main job was to drive people away.

Yet for all the chaos, Margaret had a mission. She believed herself to be the reincarnation of a girl who died in the Holocaust. And she yearned to be reunited with a dear sister from that life in 1945.

It wasn't destined to be easy. For years, Margaret grieved an abortion forced on her at age 13, thinking the lost child to be her sister. And she waited a long, unbearably empty time for the chance to have that child again.

Nine months ago, Margaret learned she was pregnant.

It was the day after an attempted suicide. But from that moment to our daughter's birth, she and the alters shared an oddly satisfying life with me. I won't tell you what it's like being with a multiple. It doesn't matter. What matters is I loved her, and the two of us got busy preparing for the child who lies before me now.

At 26 weeks, Margaret developed eclampsia, a potentially fatal complication of pregnancy. The only cure that early in the term is abortion. But Margaret's life was really about one thing—bringing that child into the world. She faced seizures, hemorrhage, and death, and she held on just long enough for the baby to have a chance.

Even before the child was lifted from her womb, Margaret was lost. I cannot tell you how brave she was.

I have to stop now—because our baby is awake again and needs me. But I want you to know one thing, the thing I've learned as I gathered these stories. There is a reason. There is purpose to life and death. Margaret died because she had done her work.

The baby wasn't really awake—that was a literary device. In fact, the doorbell was ringing. When he answered, it was Madrone and Julie, carrying several casseroles of a hot dinner. They all embraced. I stood in their midst, wanting to feel the press of their arms, the warmth of their bodies.

They talked at once, and I joined them. Describing my life of silence while Walker lifted the lids of dishes and commented on the aroma. After a few moments they migrated to the bedroom to look at the baby. She was sleeping, eyes moving in a dream I had no need to know.

They ate. And when the baby finally awakened, the three of them spent the evening passing her from lap to lap. Cradling and kissing her.

I had seen this moment before. Many times, in fact, since Margaret's death. The living take comfort from repeating the small tasks. From the simple and reliable pleasures. Julie was playing with the infant's toes; Madrone and Walker were heating a milk bottle in a pot of water.

I knew then I was beginning to leave. I no longer belonged there. They had their work, and I wasn't part of it. Some force, gentle at first, then gradually more insistent, began to pull me away. When Margaret was alive, I would have resisted it. But I was giving in. I felt a distance growing, and I let it happen.

69

My father used to say, every night as he turned off the set, "Half past 12:00, kiss my butt, time to go to bed." I think it just meant that he was done. Finished with another desolating day.

I am finished now. I have told you the story of how I learned what love is. It has been a long lesson—spent silent and untouched.

I'm glad it's over. And that I'm here. Did I do enough for one life? I don't know; you can decide that.

I feel tired now. And sad. I think it's for all the pain in the world. All the scars.

My whole life I spent imagining the joy of meeting someone. I imagined the first words, the first embrace. And the awkward, tender lowering of walls. I never did it. Not once.

I see you are about to speak. You have listened, and now the moment comes when you will separate the chaff from wheat, the life I lived from what I sought.

You have listened and you know what I will ask. In a while when we have finished, I'll ask if I can see her—Margaret. To begin again—without facade. To finally introduce myself.
About the author

About the Author

Dr. Matthew McKay draws from years of experience as a psychologist in clinics and private practice, which has included the treatment of the controversial dissociative identity disorder. He is a professor of psychology at the Wright Institute in Berkeley and author of more than thirty professional psychology and self-help books, which have sold a combined total of more than three million copies. He is co-founder of independent self-help publisher, New Harbinger Publications. He was the clinical director of Haight Ashbury Psychological Services in San Francisco for twenty-five years and is currently the director of the Berkeley CBT Clinic. Dr. McKay is an accomplished novelist and poet. His poetry has appeared in two volumes from Plum Branch Press and in more than sixty literary magazines. His novel, *Wawona Hotel*, was published by Boaz Publishing Company in 2008.